ACHAOS
MAGDALENA BRYNARD

krest
PUBLISHERS

KREST PUBLISHERS

ISBN: 978-0-6397-9709-0 (print)

ISBN: 978-0-6397-9710-6 (eBook)

First published by KREST Publishers 2023

www.krestpublishers.co.za

Durban, South Africa

To Hanno, my beloved husband.
Your belief in my dream is my biggest encouragement.
I could not have completed this journey without you.

For Elaine Adlen,
The strongest, bravest, and most devoted woman I ever had the
privilege to know.
You are treasured and deeply missed.

"Only from the heart can you touch the sky."
– Persian Proverb

PROLOGUE

The putrid smell of rotting flesh lingered in Mia's nostrils as she jerked awake. The darkness was overwhelming. Where was she? She reached out to search through her dark slumber, but there was no sound and nothing to touch, only the acrid smell that became stronger as she crawled forward on the damp ground. Her hands then connected with something.

It was hard to make out at first, but then she realised what it was—cold, wet flesh. She stumbled backwards. With awe, her mind started to spin as if struck by lightning, and then darkness swallowed her as the claws of reason dragged her back into a coma. She did not know how long it was until she became fully aware of her consciousness again; it could have been minutes or even days.

She heard a faint sound like a sack of flour being dragged across the floor. She tried to pry through her thoughts—somewhere hidden inside the mulch of her mind she had to know why she was here and who kept her locked in this dungeon … if that was even where she was.

She kept falling back into sleep only to be awakened by the same sound and the need for water. Where was the sound coming from? With determination and the need to know, she slowly crawled forward, following the smell of rotting flesh. The cold ground beneath her fingers squeezed fresh, wet mud underneath her fingernails. She was reminded of a cellar she once visited in

Greece with her father. Coming to the cold corpse, she drew all her strength together and reached out to touch the object of her fears.

Slowly, she started searching, pausing only to push back the nausea that wanted to overtake her. Steadying her body, she followed the arm until it came to a mangled hand. The last remaining finger latched itself to a small metal ring that led to a sword. A glimmer of hope reached her mind. A weapon. This could help her get out. Following the wall and the increasing sound, she came to a wooden latch. It was unlocked.

She unhooked the arm of the lock and slowly opened the door. Soft grey light filtered through the wooden floorboards above her head. Firmly gripping the sword in her right hand, she searched the wall. It was hard to make out her surroundings. The tunnel was low, and she had to walk in a crouch in order not to hit her head on the wooden beams of the floor above. She nearly stumbled over a large barrel containing soapy water.

The reflection that greeted her resembled a hurricane-ridden tree amid a turbulent summer. Her matted hair fell in long, drooping patches of dirt, and dark creases mapped her broken skin. Dipping her hands into the liquid, she realised how long it had been since she washed herself. Dried blood and dead flesh washed away from her arms. The truth of her situation still mixed with thoughts of what was to come.

She dried her arms and face on her dirty tunic before drenching her lips in the soapy water, flooding her parched body. She knew that she would regret this moment as soon as her body reacted to the saline solution. The barrel must have been used to wash off old blood as her tormentors exited the hole where they left her to die.

Moving forward, she could make out a small staircase leading to the frame of a door. She clumsily climbed the stairs that had clearly been trodden by many heavy feet. The light nearly overwhelmed her as she pushed the heavy wooden door aside, and she started to focus on the details as her eyes adjusted. A grating sound was coming from donkeys pushing and pulling the wheel of a mill, pushing up dust from the worn floorboards with each stomping hoof.

She looked around the room, searching for any way of escape. Three doors provided her with options—to her right were two doors possibly leading further inside the structure, and light filtered through cracks of the third door to her left. It was conceivable that this door would lead to an outer court where the animals were kept or exchanged.

Without hesitation, she ran for the door to her left, but it was locked. She pried it with the blade of her sword, but it only bent under the pressure. After the third attempt, she stepped back and breathed heavily with disappointment. Regaining her focus, she made her way to the first of the remaining two doors, and she slowly opened it. The contents of what seemed to be a store closet nearly came down on her head, but she elbowed the door shut before it all tumbled to the floor. The final door was her only option. She approached it with unease, and as she reached for the latch, a donkey stumbled, balking loudly. She watched as the animal struggled to stand up. Muffled voices shouted orders to one another from the other side of the first door she had tried, the one leading outside. The lock was turning; she had to hurry. She jerked the final door open and stumbled into the darkness before someone could see her.

As her eyes adjusted to the dim light, she saw a never-ending maze of alleys and small passages. There were so many avenues to choose from, but she decided to go directly ahead. The narrow passage widened, revealing various doors and chambers. Each door had a small window placed just above eye level. She slowly approached the first window, and peering inside, she saw a young woman curled up next to a heap of straw. She tried whispering to her, but there was no response.

As she moved down the passage, each window revealed a similar image, and it brought a chill down her spine. However, what she saw through the sixteenth window was beyond comprehension. A woman was hanging from the beam above her, her left arm stripped of its skin and lashes over her body cut to the bone. How she endured torture like this was hard to imagine.

"She did it last night." A voice from behind her made her spin around, sword at the ready. "She couldn't let him touch her again."

"Where are you?" she called out to the voice.

"Look to your right." She followed the voice until she came to the eighteenth door.

A petite young girl stared back at her. Perfectly dark circles surrounded tired and sullen eyes. Her translucent skin was covered in lesions and recently dressed wounds, and bruises painted her legs a faint hue of crimson. She was a skeleton of a once beautiful young girl. Mia tried to rip open the door but was unable to do so.

"It's no use," the girl replied. "It will not open. I've tried everything. He has the only key."

"Who is *he*?" Mia questioned.

"I do not know. He comes at night. Or what I think is night. It is hard to tell."

"How long have you been here?"

"It might be months, years even. They took me from my village when I was fourteen."

Tears streaked down the young girl's face as she recounted her journey. Her village was ransacked, all the men killed together with anyone else who opposed the evil emperor. All he wanted were his slaves to use and abuse to his pleasure—girls and young women. She didn't even know where her mother was, possibly locked up behind one of these doors too. All she ever saw were men and soldiers who threw her around like a toy, passing her from one to the other to rape, ravish, and taunt. Then she was washed, fed, and thrown back into her hole.

"You should get out of here," the girl pleaded with Mia. "Go before the soldiers find you."

"I will come back for you. I promise." A knot of sorrow choked her as words strained to echo clearly.

"I know you will try, but forget this place. My time will come soon, and then I will be free from his touch. Run and never look back."

With a last injection of purpose, Mia ran through the passage the girl told her to. The darkness and narrow corridors played tricks on her mind. The pungent smell of fresh blood threatened to throw her off balance, but she kept on following hundreds of small steps until she came into a clearing. The air was crisp and fresh. She breathed deeply, filling her lungs to full capacity. She looked around, hoping to have escaped the terror, but then hundreds of soldiers merged in the courtyard like ants on a mission of their queen.

A grand carriage arrived through the gate, pulling women behind it. Mia counted twenty women each tied to one another, their feet bleeding from the long walk. Beaten, bruised, and scared, they had no idea what awaited them. The image made her retch, and the thought of torture again enveloped her. Out of the carriage stepped two soldiers waiting with a chain for their victim to exit. With dignity, a woman emerged from the carriage, her golden braids twisted in neat arches around her royal crown. Mia immediately recognised the Prince of Athens' young wife, daughter-in-law of King Amyntas. The princess's fear-filled eyes met Mia's for a moment as she searched her surroundings for any help. Mia wanted to run to her and rip every chain from her wrists, but she knew she had to leave her behind.

From behind, a man kicked the princess onto the floor and twisted his broad shoulders as he exited from the carriage. He barked orders to the soldiers as he turned to look over his conquests. His dark hair fell in long dreadlocks around his scarred and tattered face, ruined by too many days in battle.

Romulus.

Like a stabbing pain, it all came back to Mia. They had abducted her in the forest while her horse was grazing. The flashes of torture assaulted her mind as she remembered being stripped, beaten, and covered in old sackcloth before being left for dead in the dungeon where she had awoken. She could feel Romulus' thick fingers touching and caressing her left arm, searching the covenant mark adorning her skin for its meaning. Emperor Romulus was a man filled with hatred and disregard for any form of authority. Abandoning all reason, Romulus took life as if it belonged to him and him alone. Her father had told her stories about their greatest enemy who had been exiled and banished from the courts of Persia.

"Hey!" a soldier yelled.

Mia jerked her head in his direction and knew that her hiding place behind the cart had been discovered.

"Mia!" Romulus gasped, astonished to see her. "Capture her! She is not to get out!" He spewed out orders to the soldiers around him.

Mia ran with all her strength for the open galley. The drawbridge was closing. The young gatekeeper and his three helpers were at a loss in the ensuing chaos, pulling hard at the drawbridge's chains to close the rampart, but his speed failed him. Soldiers ran after her.

Her escape would be difficult with all the soldiers blocking her way. Sheer determination pulled at her might. She jumped a large man from behind, surprising him with her stealth. Mia grabbed at his scabbard and jerked at the seams. The blade and its covering tore loose. She pulled the sword from its sheath and thrust the blade into his shoulder. The blade cut through muscle and bone as she severed his arm. He fell backwards, stunned and in pain. Deadly weapons became the extension of her arms.

Fighting with both hands, the blades worked in harmony, connecting with several swords and gliding in perfect unison. Metal clattered against metal. The gate was slowly closing, and less than three metres from its half-closed mouth, a tall soldier stepped in front of her.

His large hands closed around her wrists. She tried to pry free from his hold, swinging the blades wildly to connect with him. With a swift swing from his head, he hit her backwards. A flash of light deadened her momentarily, and she dropped both swords. Defenceless, she gave way under the pressure of his strong hold. Twisting her petite frame uncomfortably around him, she pulled his dagger from his leg strap and thrust it forward with all her might. Blood spewed from the clean gash on his right arm, and he instinctively let go of his grasp, allowing her to slip from his grip.

She ran for her life. Sliding her legs in front of her, she nearly connected with the teeth of the gate is it came down into a locked vice with its stone cradle. Romulus barged through soldiers until he reached the gate. Slitting the throat of the gatekeeper, he belched in anger, spittle flying in the air like a wild, raging animal.

"Mia, I will come for you! This time you will die!" he screamed.

The forest lay just west of her position. If she could reach the trees, they might lose sight of her. Mia sprinted at full force as she clamoured over boulders and small shrubs. Soldiers' voices echoed off the rock face to her right as they screamed orders to their archers. Green arms beckoned toward her, offering shelter from the screams and attacks of the enemy now aiming every piece of arsenal her way. Arrows whirled past her ear as she disappeared into the thicket. Every calculated move threw her off guard in the dark covering of the canopy. Her foot slipped into a small alcove in the forest floor, nearly breaking her ankle. She spun towards her right to regain her balance when a spear the width of her forearm screeched past her.

Leaves and debris from the summer rains assaulted her at every angle. Cuts started to form in the soles of her feet, leaving behind evidence that some injured animal made its flight through this never-ending green maze. Different sounds replaced the calls of fighting men—the faint whisper of a stream.

Her eyes swam in tears as the realisation of her predicament overwhelmed her. Sweeping her arm across her eyes, she could see the outline of the riverbank. The white squall washed over her ankles as she gently placed her burning feet into the icy waters, navigating her path across the river. Fear of a chase compelled her to keep going.

Mia finally collapsed, out of breath and out of adrenaline, in the relative safety of the trees. The soothing sound of leaves caressing one another in the wind lulled her into a deep trance before her world went dark.

1

The full moon spread its glow over the valley beyond as it stretched into deep gorges that rose to meet the Taygetos Massif in the south. Even at the peak of summer, a small silver lining crested the mountain in crisp white snow. Fir trees and black pine covered rows upon rows of jagged limestone from the crest of the mountain to the base where it met the Eurotas River, carrying a sweet summer breeze laced with scents of orange blossoms and mouth-watering whiffs of sautéed lamb on an open fire.

Dozens of bright bonfires littered the busy village square as people of all ages came together to celebrate under the starlit sky. A platform was placed in the middle of a circular clearing with servants graciously gliding around it, their long tunics swaying in the light summer breeze. Shadows played tricks on the faces of the children admiring their crown princess swaying along to the music on the platform.

Mia's azure silk tunic embroidered with golden thread stood in contrast to the white attire worn by the entire tribe in honour and tribute to their beloved princess. Clothed in colour and splendour, she was indeed the crown of the festival.

Mia turned towards the crowd, her radiant skin reflecting her beauty. Long golden braids fell from each side of her soft, slender face and rested beside the golden pins that held her tunic in place. Her lips pursed together in an attempt not to make a sound. Like a sudden string of instruments bursting to life, laughter broke the silence as the court jester finished his final act for the vivacious crowd.

Firelight exploded across the horizon, igniting the night sky in a thousand colourful flashes of light. The celebration could finally commence. This night was indeed worthy of celebration. Mia, crown princess of Achaos, was home. The tribe welcomed her back in starlight fantasy.

Six weeks had passed since a hunting party found Mia a week's ride from the village. She was severely dehydrated but lucid. After three months of capture, their princess was home and healed; her broken skin was replaced by soft rosy cheeks, and her strong jawline exuded confidence. How she had escaped from the clutches of their enemy, only a few trusted leaders knew.

To protect her village, her escape from Emperor Romulus' keep had been kept a secret. Beaten and broken, she was left for dead, but hope prevailed and gave her the courage to escape and challenge her tormenter another day.

Had the villagers known of the proximity to their enemy, it would turn their peaceful village to fear. The mere mention of his name drove fear into the hearts of men. The scouts could not even find the keep of their elusive enemy. For years, Romulus had been a mirage, ripped from the Persian Empire. The only evidence of his passing was burnt villages filled with tortured, mutilated bodies, a refuse dump of an inhuman monster, detested by all. The unknown location of the castle keep had been the only barricade to Romulus' fall.

Mia's husband, Estoban, stood a full head taller than his wife. With broad shoulders and a bright smile, the tribe not only revered the man beside their crown princess but loved him for his audacity and profound sense of adventure, winning the heart of every Achaean. Mia also knew that Estoban admired her strength more than her beauty, and this made her respect him even more. Since her return, Mia had learned how tough the last three months had been on him. Each night, disturbing dreams ripped him from the safety of his cabin only to find the bedside empty. Every day, the search for his beloved wife came back more negatively, until they finally called it off. Total abandonment of his beloved was no option for Estoban. He kept on praying, kept on believing that his wife would return.

"I hope you like the fireworks?" he whispered in her ear.

"Yes, they are delightful, aren't they?" Mia replied, still dazed by the sudden explosion of light.

"Not nearly as delightful as you, my love." Estoban kissed her neck gently in an emotional array of love, gently stroking the covenant mark on her left forearm, caressing the symbol that matched his own.

To symbolise the unity between husband and wife, each married couple shared a covenant seal tattooed on the inside of the left forearm. This covenant exchange was celebrated among the tribe. Glaucus Solon, supreme king and ruler of Achaos, introduced the covenant symbol in honour of their God and of the covenant He shared with his followers.

Glaucus often spoke of his time in the capital of Susa as a teenager. He was barely six years old when his mother abandoned him and his father Acamas to serve in the temple of Dionysis. Seeking a better future for his son, Acamas took Glaucus on a journey into the service of the Persian king.

Work opportunities in the army as a tentmaker were abundant. Glaucus learned about warfare and obtained great skills and artisanship from the tent makers in Susa, but the one thing he treasured above all was what he learned about the God of Abraham, named Yahweh. Many people travelled to Persia seeking a better life, except the exiles from Israel. He often listened to how these men and women prayed and travailed to their Lord for rescue.

Glaucus had a hard time understanding their prayers but found comfort in the presence of this unknown God. All he knew of the Greek Gods was that they were torturous and self-seeking. He remembered well how his mother chose a God above her own son.

When he was old enough to join his father on a supply trip to Pasargadae, Glaucus jumped at the opportunity. He would finally see the majestic city of renowned King Cyrus the Great. It was magnificent. Large atriums created openings all along the city walls, and perched high on top, ever-watching sentries kept an eye out for danger. Glaucus had never seen so many people bustling together in the cramped marketplace. Acamas urged him to stay at the fountain in the centre of the busy city square while he attended to his business.

It was quite a monstrosity that looked down at him. The centre of the fountain proudly portrayed a statue of a strong man with a spotted body and two horns. The deity was known to have two opposing energy forces. Spenta Mainyu was made of constructive energy, while Angra Mainyu was the source of darkness, destruction, sterility, and death. The inscription simply depicted "Ahura Mazda" in bold letters.

"Bow before the mighty Aveston!" a voice exclaimed behind Glaucus.

He spun around and came face to face with a young boy of about fifteen.

"Why would I do that?" he scoffed.

"You will bow because the celestial being deserves your reverence," the boy ordered.

"I don't believe in such rubbish," Glaucus defended.

The boy walked in slow circles around Glaucus as the crowd dispersed from them, leaving them out in the open.

"Insolent fool!" he screamed. "I serve the Angra Mainyu. If you do not bow to honour my God, I will call upon the powers of the deity and break your neck!"

Unsure what to do next, Glaucus froze. He was not about to bow down to a fabricated monstrosity to escape a fight. He pulled his fists up to his face, ready to accept a timely blow from the boy.

He stood two feet taller than Glaucus, and a shiny dagger hung from his waist belt. His short black dreadlocks were tied together in a bundle to keep them from irritating his eyes. He was wearing a kitchen apron over his short tunic. Glaucus didn't notice until now that blood smeared the top half of the apron, a clear sign that the boy had been carrying a bloody leg of lamb over his shoulder. The meat was thrown aside next to the fountain where he could still see the imprints on the ground from the boy's hands where he undoubtedly bowed down to the statue now looming over them.

"Do you yield?" the boy coaxed.

"Never!" Glaucus screamed in defiance.

Glaucus hardly knew what was coming his way. The first punch caught him on the side of his left temple, forcing him off balance. It felt like his ear was slashed from the side of his face, but Glaucus regained his balance only to be met by a roundhouse kick to his groin. He collapsed into a heap, barely able to focus on breathing. The kicks came in sudden succession, completely crushing his slender frame. The taste of copper filled his mouth as the boy's leather boot split open his lower lip, revealing broken teeth that would never quite heal.

Just before Glaucus lost consciousness, the beating ceased. He looked up to see several of the king's guard pulling the boy away from him. Glaucus could still see the hatred in his eyes. Acamas came running to his son, screaming out his name over and over until Glaucus fully opened his eyes to look back up at his father.

"Glaucus, we will meet again; I promise you that!" the boy screamed as he was dragged away by the king's guard.

The trip back to Susa was filled with pain. Every position on the back of the camel hurt Glaucus' body. He learned what it meant to serve a God that day. The crowd around the fight looked on as if it was a common occurrence. The guards told Glaucus the story of the boy. His name was Romulus Farhad, a Persian boy serving in the king's kitchen as a sentence for killing an Israeli boy for not honouring his God. Romulus had no regard for others unlike himself. He often tortured animals and young children to obtain strength from his God. The crowd would never interfere with Romulus and his business; they feared the very mention of his name.

After the traumatic event in Pasargadae, Glaucus accepted the refuge of the God of Israel and became a follower of Yahweh. He vowed never to return to his former beliefs. When he married his beautiful wife, Isemene, he made a vow to honour her and to serve her until his death. They etched a symbol on their left forearms with needle and ink—a covenant seal representative of their promise. Glaucus learned respect and honour through his service to the God Most High. He was unable to join the Israelites during their exile because of his Greek heritage, but Glaucus would honour the God Yahweh for the rest of his life and build an alliance with the living God.

With the memory fresh in her mind, Mia was swept off her feet by her husband and ushered into the circular clearing surrounded by the tribe. In a fanciful display, Estoban and Mia danced to the rhythm of the tambourine, displaying their covenant seal. Young and old celebrated this covenant as the crowd joined in dance and song.

Mia stared into Estoban's emerald eyes surrounded by soft golden locks. He was a beautiful man to look at with his narrow nose, high cheekbones, and exuberant smile. Every touch sent chills down her spine as he embraced her in his strong, lean, muscular arms. It was good to be home.

***

In the darkness, a figure felt his way around boulders and sharp trees until he saw some light. The steady drumbeat lured him onto a small, well-tread path, hardly recognisable in the dim light. Despite the glowing full moon, he still made his way by feel rather than look where he was going. Days had passed since his last meal, and hunger was crushing his strong body. He had to find shelter and possibly safety from the wild animals that lurked in the dark forests of the Taygetos.

His swollen eyes had started to heal, but his search remained treacherous as his sight had not fully returned. Overcome by thirst and fatigue, he finally collapsed near a large tree that offered safety under the alcove of its branches.

2

Morning came much too hastily for some of the villagers. A celebration was always followed by a dizzying morning of duties prematurely calling villagers out of their slumber. The celebrations lasted until the sky of blackest night turned into to a dazzling array of reds, oranges and blues as the sun pushed out over the horizon. Beyond the trees, sunlight glimmered off the wet rock face moistened by a light drizzle during the night. Autumn was fast approaching. Midnight drizzles marked the beginning of the changing seasons as broad green leaves started to turn a shade darker on their fringes.

Deep ravines in the limestone created small rivulets running all along the Taygetos, creating the perfect environment for cultivating fruit trees like the olive and the orange. Trees of all kinds sprouted in the village streets, imported from regions like Asia Minor and the south. The swampy, fertile region created the perfect location for a village hidden in its trees. Each house built from the wood in the area was shaped around several trees with various levels and swinging bridges—an intricate network connecting the villagers without being seen.

Mud veins ran through the village until it opened into a clearing in the centre of the forest where celebrations like the night before were a common occurrence. The northern mountains were treacherous, and travellers rather made their way around the mountains to approach Sparta and the Eurotas Valley from the south. The nearby village of Sparta provided protection in exchange for the abundant fresh produce of the Valley. Trouble hardly ever made its way into the peace-loving village of Achaos.

Mia rose early, unable to sleep through the short night. The celebrations were always exciting, and sleep never followed without some fight. Her father had been on a mission for the past month and would only return before the next spring harvest. Time was running out, and now that Romulus was found, she could no longer contain her frustrated excitement.

The pursuit would have to wait until next summer. The Eurotas River froze over during winter, making the divide nearly impossible to cross; the snow and freezing hailstorms could claim more lives than any battle ever would.

Mia studied the circular pattern laid in the floor at the centre of the king's chamber. From where she was seated in her father's oversized chair, she had a great view over the whole village. She loved to sit and read in this spot whenever her father was away; it made her feel closer to him. The room was large and stately. The curtains were drawn wide to let the last summer warmth in. Autumn was here, and the crisp air could be felt everywhere one went. Estoban looked at the room and marvelled to Mia how different it had looked six weeks ago. He had recounted the fateful day to her as if it had been only the day before.

***

Three scouts found Mia a mile from the village and brought her home. She was bruised and scarred but remained lucid, and dehydration and fatigue deepened the circles around her eyes, dampening the sparkle that he longed to see. She was laid in the king's chamber where the physicians could take care of her. Months of searching had finally brought Estoban's wife home.

The chamber was sparsely lit and the drapes drawn against the bright sunlight. Estoban had stood in the doorway and studied the physician as he wrapped every wound with tenderness. Mia groaned from time to time, and the physician bid Estoban to stay until he was finished. Anticipation to speak with his wife was driving him to jitters. The king stood beside Estoban, shaking his legs with constant worry. He longed to see to his daughter.

Jacobien stood in the corner of the room still as a statue. His long grey beard and bald scalp gave him the appearance of a warlock, but Estoban knew better. The elder was a wise man, and Estoban had seen him on numerous occasions in deep discussion with the king. He always wore the same brown tunic tucked snugly around his portly belly. He had a sharp nose and long face that seemed to grow as long as his beard. The thought made him laugh.

Mia spoke softly, and they all crept closer to her. She looked so much like her father. Mia had his strong jaw line and lean build but lacked the dark lustre of his skin. Glaucus' shoulders were broad, curving his back to a slender middle. His dark hair was silver along the hairline and reached down to his shoulders. His hands were strong, and he exuded the same confidence Estoban saw in his wife. Glaucus turned his head to Estoban and smiled reassuringly, his blue eyes sparkling with anticipation.

"She will be alright, son."

Estoban loved to be called son by his father-in-law. This love and respect was something every man desired.

The physician motioned to them that they were welcome to approach the princess. Estoban walked quickly to Mia's side, stroked her left arm, and whispered softly into her ear. Glaucus knelt beside his daughter, laying his hand on her forehead, the deep bruises still discolouring her face. He stepped back and nearly collided with Jacobien standing beside the bed. Glaucus offered his apologies, but Jacobien only scoffed and turned to leave the chamber when Glaucus grabbed him by the arm.

Glaucus Solon stood a full head taller than Jacobien, and his hands conveyed the strength of a young man. Jacobien turned towards Glaucus and spoke in a hushed tone in an attempt to mask their conversation from Estoban, but he still heard it.

"I will say it again, Glaucus. Your daughter might be detained due to her wounds, but I am very aware that this fantasy of hers is but a bad dream," he gushed. "If silly girls run into the forest alone and unguarded, what more could you expect?"

Glaucus raised his hand in defence of his daughter but brought it back sharply.

"If it was your daughter, would you not fight for her every breath?"

"If she was as stubborn as your daughter, I might have let her go to suffer the fate of an insolent youth," Jacobien protested.

"If I was you, I would watch your tongue, old man. You might be three times her senior, but you will not speak about the crown princess of Achaos in such a manner. Do you understand me?" Glaucus threatened. "In my absence, I declare my daughter the Polemarch of Achaos not because she is my daughter, but because the village would die for her and follow her into any battle no matter the cost. She is a wise woman, and you will see to it that your loyalties do not dwindle."

Jacobien stroked his long beard nervously. "Forgive me, my lord. I have spoken rashly."

Glaucus studied the man beside him. He respected Jacobien and relied on him for guidance whenever his emotions failed him.

"I need you to promise me something, Jacobien."

"Anything, my king," Jacobien said as he shuffled his weight around.

"Have my daughter's best interest at heart. Although she is more than capable to lead our people, she is still young and will certainly need the advice her elders are able to give. Provide that council to my daughter as you have done in the many years of my reign," Glaucus asked, stretching out his left arm ready to embrace the man in an oath of promise.

19

Jacobien stared into the crystal-clear eyes of his king, and in his heart, he knew that he would defend the man with his life, and in doing so he would most assuredly promise that same allegiance to his daughter.

"I vow to honour my king and any successor you so choose to stand in your place as Polemarch and future ruler of Achaos."

Jacobien embraced the king, arm against arm, and covenant seal against covenant seal.

"We pledge allegiance to one another this day, Jacobien. May Yahweh protect us and our vow."

"I agree," Jacobien bowed low before his king in complete submission.

Estoban looked in wonderment as the elder paid tribute to his father-in-law. The men spoke in muted tones as to not disturb the princess. Mia stirred, and he returned his attention to her.

***

Three other people had now entered the king's chamber, and Mia was seated at her father's drawing table playing with her hands. She was nervous, a stark contrast to last night at the banquet when she smiled and danced without a care in the world; today was a different story.

The elders stared at her with animosity, unsure what to make of her request. Justus sat patiently waiting for more news, his frail hands folded neatly in his lap. His hair stood in all directions, wild and in disarray. The elder struck Mia as odd. Although the man seemed old and tired, his eyes always sparkled with interest. He moved unexpectedly fast and spoke in a gentle rhythm, soothing to the ear. Jacobien stroked his beard, pondering the situation, his deep wrinkles crinkled into a frown. He paced back and forth.

"Do you believe he has reason to move from his current location?" the wise elder thundered, breaking the tense silence.

"I cannot be certain, Jacobien," Mia replied. "If they find the location of our village, a battle for our civilisation would be immediate."

"Mia, your father will not return until next spring. What do you propose we do until then?" Justus queried.

"Prepare the fighting men for any assault," Mia instructed. "As acting Polemarch of Achaos, I merely suggest that we are prepared. Romulus' army is large and strong. His reputation as a beast is not an exaggeration; I saw what he is capable of."

"My wife is telling the truth, Jacobien. He will do anything in his power to kill the woman who dared to escape from him," Estoban interjected, protecting his wife from the elders' onslaught.

Jacobien stared long and hard at Mia. His expression changed from sincerity to absurdity.

"I am aware of our situation, and I do not make the decision lightly. If he is to move from his current location, we will lose him again," Mia protested, waiting in suspense for his reply.

Jacobien stroked his long beard, pausing slightly.

"I promised your father that I would always side with you no matter what you decide. I believe you are right, my princess," Jacobien replied.

Mia breathed out slowly, processing the promised oath.

"Can his shelter be penetrated?" Jacobien prompted.

"It's not a simple shelter. It is a fortress of some kind."

Mia explained in her best effort to the two elders around her how Romulus' keep was surrounded by a high wall built out of stones from the nearby region. It resembled the dungeons of Athens with its steel bars and small tunnels. The fortification was strong and solid.

Mia believed that Romulus might leave his place of safety in an attempt not to be found by the Persian King. But in her heart, she knew that he would never surrender, merely fight to the death.

Mia described her journey in precise detail as they listened and notated the location and its surroundings. She had navigated by the stars and streams but found it hard to distinguish between day and night as the gorge engulfed any sunlight that tried to pierce beyond the large mountain peaks. Days were jumbled, but she was certain her direction had never failed her.

Romulus' keep was nestled amid two peaks in the Parnonas Massif just east of the Eurotas rift valley and the village of Achaos. A map was drawn and battle plans lain out. Twelve sealed envelopes were given to Estoban to distribute to his commanding officers. Preparations for all the fighting men in the village would commence on this very day.

Troubled, Mia stared after the elders as they left her father's cabin to prepare for any outcome that may befall them.

"Are you alright, my love?" Estoban tenderly took Mia into his arms.

"I believe that I am, but without my father and his wise council, I fear for my people." Mia stared into the middle-distance, shivering in Estoban's arms.

He pulled her towards him. Her tremor subdued as he gently stroked her cheek. "Your father made you the temporary Polemarch of Achaos. He didn't do it because you are his daughter. He did it because he believes in you. You are so much like your father, Mia. If only you could see what we see; then you too would believe."

Mia relaxed into his embrace and held onto his red tunic. Her life intertwined with this man, and she found comfort in the thought. But fear grew in her heart. She had been locked away and left for dead; the images that flooded her mind were running rampant in her heart, shredding away all hope of escape from the tyrant that breathed his sulphuric breath into her neck, whispering incantations over her bruised body.

3

Tall limestone cliffs protruded from the earth like slimy, ferocious teeth spawning deep trenches covered with black fir trees. Spiders and insects congregated in the dark, moist crevices of the Parnonas Massif. Hidden between two jagged cliffs caught in an endless battle stood a solitary fortress. Its walls were covered with thick green moss glistening in the firelight.

A deep, musty odour emanated from the green foliage. The fortress was surrounded by a semi-circular wall eight feet wide and protected by men draped in fur skins over leather armour. The men resembled the barbarians of the north more than the elite Persian soldiers of the east. Dark circles around their eyes tainted their olive skin, longing for sunlight and heat from the summer that couldn't quite penetrate the trees covering every inch of the mountainside.

Thick iron bars connected in a mesmerising web to create a six-ton gate covering the only breach within the fortified wall. An intricate pulley system had to be operated by four men at a time to raise the gate and return it to its cradle, and steel chains the width of a man's forearm held the gate in position. Numerous openings, cut away in the rock face, loomed over the inner courtyard crammed with merchants and hunter gatherers trading with battle-scorned soldiers around open fire pits.

Hidden inside were alleyways and small tunnels not only leading to bedchambers and great banquet halls but reaching down deep into the earth like an ever-increasing maze of death. Dungeons and torture chambers held hundreds of traitors, liars, and innocent women taken against their will.

The room was sparingly lit by candles dripping into pools of heated wax on the cold stone floor. A large bed draped with animal skins of all kinds dominated the room, with trinket boxes and treasure chests overlaid with costly jewels and gold strewn about the floor. Silk, fine linen, and sackcloth were draped over the armrest of a large wooden chair with its back to the room's only window. The opening was cut away in the rock, barely letting in enough sunlight to illuminate the room. Romulus was sitting with his head hung low, staring blankly at his palm.

Long, dark dreadlocks covered his tattered face darkened by years of abandonment and dirt, and his dry skin came away flaky. The cleft in his thin upper lip was moving profusely as he rocked side to side, speaking incantations to his God.

Romulus was tired, and his black eyes revealed no life. All light and hope had been stripped from him when his parents threw him away to be raised by the servants of their wealthy home. He remembered well how his mother danced for her father and his guests. Men gawked at her beautiful body and adorned her with gifts and wine hoping to have another look at his father's wife. Romulus hated even the thought of her. The harlot bewitched his father, and Romulus knew that no woman would ever have dominion over him, until now.

The mere thought of Mia made Romulus shudder. His eyes flashed open, and he stared at his left palm where he was tracing the strange symbol he'd seen on Mia's arm with his chunky index finger. Taking out the sacrificial dagger from its sheath on his thigh, Romulus started to trace the image with the tip of the red blade. The weapon was reserved for sacrifice, and Romulus treated the action as such.

Blood started to pool at the base of the chair, dripping onto the stone floor. The puddle expanded, staining the satin tunic draped

24

over the armrest. Every cut reminded him of their last meeting, the single moment that would torment him forever.

***

The floor had been covered with animal skins, creating a soft blanket beside the large fire atrium on the opposite wall, and the smell of rose oil wafted through his chamber. This night would be a night to remember. Romulus pushed the small woman into the room and kicked her resisting body to the floor. Mia scrambled to her feet, ready to rush the big man that kept her locked away in the cold darkness with nothing but a small tunic covering her fatigued body.

His large hands stopped her midstride, breaking her motion and throwing her back onto the floor and causing her to hit her head against a pile of firewood. Blood started to seep through her matted hair as darkness momentarily overtook her. Romulus shook her violently until she came to. Dazed and thirsty, Mia tried to push him away from her.

"Stop resisting, you wench!" Romulus screamed in her ear as he pushed her hard onto the floor, nearly crushing her ribcage with his rugged hands.

He ripped the last piece of her tunic off while holding her down with his left hand. That's when he saw it again. The fire building inside of him had to escape somehow—the mark had been tormenting him for the last four days. With a hard slap from his right hand, he drew blood again from her soft cheek. Pools of red liquid started to stain his favourite fox fur skin. Delighted in her pain, he pulled her upright, feet dangling in mid-air.

"What does it mean?" he whispered into her ear. "Why do you torment me with your secrets?"

With a sudden force, he threw her frail body against the opposite wall; her breath escaped in short rasps from her torn lips. He hated the very sight of her, yet he was inexplicably drawn to her. Her face mocked him in his dreams. He dreaded her secrets more than her survival. He hated Mia. She had to die, but not without delivering every detail of her markings. Warm drool oozed from the corners of his mouth as his appetite for her grew, fuelled by hatred and lust to overpower all that she was. She refused to turn away from his putrid breath and stared him in the eye. Each stare enraged him even more.

How dare she defy me and all my glory? Does Mia not realise who dwells inside of me? he thought to himself.

The Angra Mainyu would not stop until it unravelled her completely.

"What is inside of you, princess? You know it cannot withstand the Aveston!"

"You may take my body, Romulus, but you will never have my spirit!" Mia breathed out more than spoke. Blood red spittle converged on her broken skin.

With a new fury inside of him, Romulus spread her legs and started to undo the clasp of his garment when a sudden thud distracted him. The great wooden doors to his chamber exploded open. A burly young man entered the room and with his last breath quickly uttered the words Romulus had been waiting for.

"I beg your pardon, my emperor, but we have him," the young soldier announced.

A dark laugh emanated from inside of him, gurgling out like the scream of an unruly animal. He turned his face towards Mia and whispered soft incantations to her, his nose almost touching hers. The warmth of her breath encouraged him even more to squeeze tighter around her throat, the stench of his breath nearly driving her to convulsions.

"I'll get back to you, wench." With a last kick in her side, darkness closed in around her as her body went limp without the oxygen she so desperately needed.

Romulus' broad shoulders scraped the sides of the narrow passage. The doorway opened into his personal torture chamber.

Weapons of all shapes and sizes lined the back wall as he focused on the frail man tied to the chair. The bonds on his wrists cut deep, allowing blood to flow freely from the cut. His head drooped on his chest as the last remnants of his energy gave way to exhaustion.

"You have failed me, Nimrod. Look at me when I speak!" Romulus demanded.

The man remained still. With a quick movement of his hands, the attendant grabbed Nimrod's hair and jerked his face towards the emperor.

"I hear you have been supplying skins to the men in Sparta?"

"Yes," Nimrod whispered, staring blankly at the hefty man looming over him.

"You supply to me and me alone. Was that hard to understand? I am the one who protects you. My men have only to dislike you to kill you. But then again it won't matter; we will find another stupid hunter who can easily be bought to do the dirty work for us," Romulus taunted.

"I needed food, my lord. Your soldiers refuse to feed me for my services."

"No, they do not refuse you. It is I who refuses," Romulus sniggered.

Romulus could see the dread building in Nimrod's eyes. He should have known that making an alliance with the enemy meant certain death and destruction. The Aveston had come for its prize. Tears flowed down the traitor's cheeks, and soft sobs gave way to screams of anguish. Nimrod realised his fate, and there was no way out of it.

"Tears? Is that all I get?" Romulus turned his head sideways, feigning sympathy. "This will cost you your wife and your ravishing daughters."

"No!" Nimrod screamed in astonishment.

"You broke our deal, Nimrod. I should have known you weren't a true follower of Angra Mainyu."

"Is my life not enough of a sacrifice?" Nimrod pleaded.

Romulus giggled to himself, ignoring the man's pleas. "Your daughters will make a glorious addition to my dungeon."

Nimrod merely stared into Romulus' eyes. He tried to fight against his restraints but failed miserably; hunger and abuse had evidently taken their toll on his body. His once strong muscles were replaced by skin and bone, and he had no more fight left. Romulus imagined that his last thoughts would be of his wife and three daughters. Romulus had won, and his trophy prize was set for torture.

"Thank you, Nimrod. I am especially going to enjoy your youngest ... barely fourteen and ready to be mine." Devilish laughter echoed through the chamber, unnerving even the attendants well acquainted with the emperor and his exploits. Nimrod cried quietly as the attendants dragged him away to the dungeons to die a slow and agonising death.

Delightful thoughts of his conquest filled Romulus' heart. Nimrod had beautiful daughters, and the mere thought of their soft skin in his rough hands sent a chill of excitement through his entire body, desire churning in his veins. The tremble of Mia's body tensing under the pressure of his touch then quickened his step. Sprinting around the corner, he entered his chamber to find it empty. Mia was gone and the bloody fox fur skin removed.

"Where is she?" Romulus demanded.

"They took her body away, sire," the young chambermaid replied.

With a sudden turn of his wrist, Romulus delivered a blow to the young girl's shoulder. She cried out in pain as her collar bone fractured. She collapsed, dropping the tray of brazen meat at his feet. He kicked the leg of lamb aside and screamed out in frustration.

Guards ran around the corner, readying their swords for an assault. Romulus stared at the two men who then replaced their swords in their scabbards upon seeing that no attack had occurred. Romulus' long black dreadlocks were pulled back into a braid, revealing deep brown lesions on his shoulders—lashes given a long time ago by Darius the Great. The voice emanating from inside him did not resemble that of their emperor but rather that of an enraged bull.

"Where is the girl?" he hissed.

"They took her body away, my lord. She is dead," the guards replied in unison.

The confirmation of this news immobilised Romulus for a moment. Could he have killed her? Someone had to be responsible. The soldiers ducked as the emperor crouched and attacked them; however, they were too slow. Before they could react, Romulus had taken the sword from the man to his left. He severed the arm of the young man in an upward arc and beheaded the second when the blade came down. He then stabbed him in his heart and spewed out a prayer to his God as the life slipped from the soldier's eyes.

***

"Dead ... she was not dead," he mumbled under his breath, shaking the memory from his mind.

Romulus looked at his hand again; the mark cut to the bone. His hand started to shake as he flushed the final remnants of the memory out of his consciousness. Every day his scouts were out looking for Mia was a day too long. He hated the thought of every breath she drew. The Aveston was urging him on. Innocent blood was the only sacrifice Romulus could bring that kept the Aveston at bay.

He had to kill, had to destroy—it was his mantra and his every thought. Daylight brought only torment. The sharp crevices around his keep provided the much-needed darkness his heart required.

The 'dark side' did not only describe the mountains surrounding the keep, but it depicted the wholeness of Romulus and his lust for death, destruction, and decay. Mia would be found, and this time he would ensure that he personally completed her torture and the dismembering of her body.

4

Bright light awakened Belarus, and he suddenly scrammed away from the image coming near him. Frightened, he lashed out at the animal hovering over him in the blinding light.

"Be at ease. Everything will be alright," the boy assured him.

"Where am I?" he asked in a whisper.

"You are in Achaos. My name is Eugo," the boy replied.

The bright light subdued to a golden hue filtering through thin wooden slats covering the window as his eyes adjusted. He was covered with a thick animal skin, and lavish pillows enclosed his head.

"What is your name?" the boy urged.

"They call me Belarus," he whispered, still astonished.

"Well, Belarus, welcome." Eugo smiled and turned around to get something out of the dark wooden cupboard.

Belarus stared in amazement at the brave young boy. He could not have been more than fifteen years old. He was tall and quite aloof. He smiled at Belarus as he rummaged through the contents in the cupboard. He seemed excited and pulled a dark woven tunic from the bottom of the pile. He fumbled with it and nearly collapsed at Belarus' feet as he tripped over the corner of the garment.

"It might be a little short; you are much taller than my father. But it will do."

He handed Belarus the tunic and waited in anticipation for a reply.

"I have clothing, young Eugo. There is no need for your father's tunic."

"Are you kidding me? You look like you've been dragged through mud and smell like cow dung."

Belarus was stunned at the audacity of this young man.

"My mother threw your clothing out the moment we found you hiding under our house last night."

"I don't remember a house. I crawled in under a large overhang from a tree, but not a house!" he exclaimed.

"Don't worry, mighty Belarus. You will yet see all that Achaos has to offer. Please dress and join us for a warm meal." Eugo turned around swiftly and opened the door on the other side of the room.

Belarus was left alone in the bright light to examine his thoughts. He didn't know how long he had slept or where he really was. He hadn't noticed until now that he was naked under the fur skin. Every part of his body ached as he rose from the comfortable bed. He dressed and turned towards the mirror hanging on the opposite wall. A small shelf beneath the mirror held a basin of warm, steamy water and a fresh towel for his use.

The image that looked back at him was a ragged version of the man he knew. His cheeks were sunken into his skull, and dirt was still trapped in his curly beard. The broken skin above his eyebrow had been sewed neatly into a small arch that would leave no scar. He washed his face and quickly removed the garment and washed himself to eradicate the smell of 'cow dung' as Eugo put it. He smiled slightly at the young boy's remark and redressed in the dark blue tunic he had chosen for him. After Belarus rechecked himself in the mirror and was satisfied that he no longer looked like a frightened animal, he turned and opened the door.

The room was not much larger than the bedroom. A table laid with cutlery and plates was situated in the centre of the room, and the sweet aroma of rabbit stew welcomed him. His stomach rumbled at the new smell; it had been days since he last had a decent meal.

The room was empty except for the billowing fire beneath the iron pot. Belarus marvelled at the workmanship of the blacksmith. He could still remember how he made his first pot when he was barely five years old.

"It's a rabbit stew," said a woman's voice.

Belarus jerked around to stare at the petite lady in front of him. Her golden hair was pulled back into a neat braid that hugged her left shoulder. She was plainly dressed, but something familiar tugged at his memory.

"I remind you of someone, don't I?" she broke the uncomfortable silence.

"Yes," he replied, bashful.

"My name is Eve. I am Eugo's mother and very proud of him for dragging you all the way up here all by himself."

"Forgive me for staring, madam. You remind me of *my* mother." Tears formed in the corners of his eyes, and he wiped them away as he turned from her.

"A good memory, I hope," she said.

"Very good, madam." Belarus gave a slight nod in recognition of her and returned to marvel at the pot.

The front door burst open as Eugo barged into the room followed by a short burly man in his late fifties. Eugo stopped and the man bumped into him, pushing the boy forward until he collided with Belarus.

"Forgive me, son. Why stop in the middle of the door?" the man shrieked.

The man looked on as his son comically tumbled into Belarus. He lunged forward and steadied Eugo, still holding a bouquet of fresh flowers in his other hand.

"Gentlemen, please. Control yourselves or I might join the frenzy," Eve giggled at the lot of them.

"Your flowers, my love," the man said as he grabbed her around her waist and kissed his wife in her neck. Delighted, Eugo laughed at the display of love. Belarus was unsure if he was allowed to stare or if he should look away. This show of affection was unknown to him. Embarrassed, he simply turned towards the fire to hide his obvious discomfort.

"You must be the valiant Belarus my son speaks so highly of." The burly man shoved his arm out to embrace Belarus, but Belarus merely gave his hand and shook the man's in return.

"My name is Demetrius, and I would like to welcome you into our home. Please have a seat and enjoy a dish my wife is known for in the village." Demetrius took his place at the head of the table, and Eugo rushed to sit by Belarus' side.

No one dared ask a single question of where Belarus had come from or where he was going. They spoke about the festival and the exciting season that would follow the late summer rains. Autumn and winter were embraced instead of shunned in the village. Demetrius' eyes shone brightly, like his son's, as he told great tales of mighty men and battles won by heroes of a long-lost era. Eve and Eugo listened intently as he lured them into stories of danger, violence, and romance.

The man was short and heavy but had a friendly face. His broad smile resembled his son's. His face bore no scars of war, and his bushy eyebrows lifted repeatedly as his face twisted into expressions Belarus had long forgotten. He found himself mimicking the expressions as he was transported into a world of mystery sewn by Demetrius. Belarus decided that he could be trusted.

Eve cleared the table, and Eugo followed her into a small adjacent room to wash the dishes. Demetrius took a long drag from his pipe, billowing smoke into the small room. He studied Belarus with unease.

"What happened to you?" Demetrius nudged.

"It's not a long story. My village was plundered, and my family slaughtered. I failed to save them, and I have no idea how long I have been wandering the dark forests. I heard sounds of drums last night and followed them until I could go on no longer. The animals out there have attacked me more than once, and I knew I had to find shelter before I collapsed. And I assume, by the way your son explained, that I crawled in under your house?"

Belarus tried to compose himself but failed at the thought of his brutalised family. Tears rolled down his cheek and collected in a small pool on the table. Demetrius had no reply, but sympathy showed on his face. Belarus knew that he understood his pain and remained silent in order to not disparage the memory of his family. The remainder of the morning had gone by in a whirlpool of emotions. Demetrius assured him that he would be safe in Achaos and he would ensure that he was well looked after.

Belarus marvelled at the village. He would never have thought in the dim moonlight that such mystery awaited him. The village was built into the trees. Each little house was neatly carved into the large trees of the valley interconnected by rope bridges and many little paths hidden in the lush foliage of the forest floor. Dried mud paths were the only visible roads between the trees.

Moving farther into the village, the roads grew wider. Two horses would be able to run abreast along the neat paths leading to a meeting place in the centre of the village. He could imagine what the incredible circular pattern would look like from a high vantage point. Eugo assured him that even from the highest peak in the Taygetos, the village remained hidden by the trees, and the layout of the land obscured them from any lookout.

The young boy reminded him of himself, but Belarus knew that he no longer smiled the way Eugo did. His excitement had long been stripped away, and he was not sure if he was even capable of laughing like the excited fifteen-year-old leading him to meet the Polemarch of Achaos. Eugo knew all there was about the village and everyday life. Every turn held a new discovery for Eugo, yet he had lived in these forests his entire life.

Eugo's eyes smiled constantly, and his light brown curly hair nearly fell to his shoulders in messy tangles. His long face and dimpled cheeks resembled those of his mother, and even just the thought of Eve reminded Belarus of his own mother. He vaguely remembered her in his dreams and always wondered what it would have been like to have known her.

Belarus was ripped from his reverie as Eugo stopped him in front of a small building protruding from a rocky outcrop in the centre of the forest. The entire building was cut out of a limestone pinnacle to the right of a large clearing. Big wooden doors framed the entrance to the building. They stood wide open, inviting any passer-by. No guards were posted at the entrance, and Belarus assumed that no one was inside.

A short gasp exploded from his throat when he saw her. She was astonishingly beautiful. Long golden locks were tied together in a loose bun at the nape of her neck. She looked in his direction and smiled as she moved closer. In an array of emotion, she grabbed Eugo and hugged him hard. She loved this boy, and every motion of her hands displayed her affections for him.

She turned to face Belarus, and his heart nearly stopped. She was even more radiant up close. Her slender face with high cheekbones and strong jawline exuded royalty, and he was unable to breathe for a moment. She bowed low in front of him in honour, yet he felt as worthless as dung. He fell to his knees and stared intently to the ground.

"Rise, Belarus." She held out her hand to him, and he kissed it and rose to look down on her, feeling like a giant standing beside a midget.

"You don't have to do that, please," she said with a smile. "You are welcome in Achaos."

"Thank you, my lady," he replied nervously.

Eugo pushed him towards the open doors and urged him to follow the princess.

The chamber was lit by torches despite the sunlight shining through the open windows. He would not have imagined the splendour of the room if appraised from the outside. A light woven rug covered the stone floor, and a semi-circular table stood in the centre of the room with twelve wooden seats around its circumference.

The open end of the circle looked towards an elegantly carved wooden chair, like a throne but slightly smaller. The seated area was covered with thick blue velvet, and beside it, cut from the rock, was an open fireplace still filled with embers from the morning fire. The Polemarch urged him to take a seat and be at ease. A young woman entered and brought in a plate of exotic fruits and freshly squeezed orange juice. Belarus felt uneasy sitting on the royal chair opposite the group.

The princess sat amid three men. The man to her left was tall and handsome. His blond locks framed his strong face and suited him well. His smile was a little unsettling at first, but Belarus realised that it comforted him more than made him uneasy. The two elderly gentlemen to her right did not smile. Belarus guessed that they were far too busy to waste their time on new arrivals. They didn't seem to judge him though, and that gave Belarus a sense of acceptance by the leaders of Achaos.

"My name is Mia, and in the absence of my father, Glaucus Solon of Achaos, I am acting Polemarch of this village." She was regal and gentle, her smile never dissipating. Her blue eyes shone with excitement like Eugo's had done the entire morning.

Mia introduced the man to her left as Estoban, leader of the regiment and her husband. The men to her right were Jacobien and Justus, the two remaining elders in the village. Belarus learnt that her father had gone on a trip to Rome, escorting Amyntas I of Athens to the inauguration of the Mars Temple situated in the centre of the new district. The other ten elders escorted him on this momentous journey.

"Can you tell us what you remember of the last few nights?" Mia gently ushered him into his confession. Belarus was unsure where to start. As he began to tell his tale, all eyes were focused on him.

"Our village is situated in the northern regions of the Parnonas Massif. It's a small but close community. It was late morning when men on horses rode into our village screaming and breaking things. We couldn't understand their language, but it was clear that they were not there for anything peaceful. I was not going to let anyone destroy my new crops ready for the autumn harvests. My family depended on the finances that my grain would acquire in the surrounding villages.

"I stepped in front of the leader and demanded that there be a discussion. I tried to figure out what they were after, but nothing seemed to make sense. He only screamed at me, threatening me with a club of steel. A man to my left grabbed my sister by her hair and I immediately ran to her side, but before I could reach her, they had cut her throat and blood darkened her dress."

Belarus froze at the image of his beautiful sister bleeding unnaturally fast, her exuberant smile twisted in anguish. Mia just stared at him patiently, waiting for him to continue. Her expressions changed from confusion and anger to sympathy and understanding. She reached out and placed a delicate white handkerchief on his knee.

Swallowing his tears, he continued in a sporadic account of the worst day of his life.

"I caught her body in time before she dropped to the ground. As I reached towards her murderer, I felt a sharp sting at the back of my head. My hands came away red with blood. A kick to my stomach then rendered me breathless and totally incapacitated. I tried to get up but failed as everything went dark. The rest is a bit scrambled as I fell in and out of consciousness.

"I saw footsteps and things being dragged to the centre of the village. Something had fallen on my back, pinning me to the ground." Belarus took a deep breath, trying to unscramble what really happened. He sat on the edge of his seat tensed and out of breath.

"I smelled burning flesh and heard wailing and screaming coming to me from everywhere. Small rivulets of blood flowed in my direction, and I could see the men slicing into any body part they could find. What nearly stopped my heart was when I saw my five-year-old nephew crying in the arms of a mad man. He was thrown into the blazing fire. I retched and collapsed, out of breath."

The room went silent, and no one dared move.

"What happened next?" Jacobien asked.

"I woke up with sunlight in my face. I twisted from the rubble, and what I saw broke my heart. The village was burnt to the ground, and where my nephew had been thrown, a body pile still emanated smoke where they had been incinerated. My entire village was brutalised and dead."

"How did you find your way here?" Jacobien gently probed.

"I ran for my life. I was not able to save them, and I had to get away. I don't know how long I had been wandering, but it felt like a lifetime." Belarus finally collapsed back into the chair, clinging tightly to the white handkerchief now drenched with sweat.

Estoban stood from the table and made his way towards Belarus. He placed a strong hand on his shoulder, and the touch brought comfort to Belarus.

"You need not fear anything from us, Belarus. We will take care of you," he said.

Belarus just gave a slight nod as he was unable to reply.

"It would be my honour to have you stay with us, get to know our customs, and then when you are well able, you can make your journey to wherever you see fit," Estoban assured him.

Mia stared in amazement at the way her husband gently spoke to Belarus. His powdery blue eyes conveyed sincerity, and she knew that Belarus had experienced something closer to death than any horror one could imagine. Belarus was a strong man. His sunken cheeks and shoulder-length black hair emphasised his narrow nose and broad jawline. He seemed different in a way she was unable to pinpoint. He was confident yet broken and morose, but what more could one expect in the face of such tragedy.

"Belarus, you will stay with Eugo and his family until we have prepared a place for you," Mia offered.

"Thank you, my lady. I appreciate it more than you will ever know," Belarus answered.

After saying their goodbyes, Mia watched Belarus go and was filled with compassion. She turned to her husband and they both spoke at the same time, stumbling on their words.

"I think we will still see a broken man heal," Estoban insisted.

"I am certain that love will heal his broken heart," she mused. "Be careful to show him that what was lost can again be found."

"I will take him in my charge and teach him our ways. We might have won a great ally in Belarus." Estoban smiled as he led her out into the fading sunlight.

"I believe you are right," Mia replied earnestly.

5

Metal clanged as blades collided in an array of sparks. Belarus rushed at his opponent, pushing down hard on the shield, but Estoban deflected the blade easily. Belarus was a strong and valiant opponent. Estoban never imagined that the broken-down farmer of three weeks ago would shine and flourish in the ring.

"I am certain that the blade was always your favourite toy," he said, ducking the strong blow from his new friend.

"Never mistake a sickle for a sword, Estoban!" Belarus laughed.

Estoban threw his hands in the air and motioned for a break. All the fighting men rooted for their commander, who they feared had finally met his match. To avoid disappointment, Estoban agreed to a duel in the centre court just left of the barracks but regretted it now that he was out of breath and near fatigue. They had battled for nearly two hours, and his energy had started to wane. Belarus hardly broke a sweat. Estoban backed away and rested his arm on the wooden fence circling the small arena.

Belarus then ran in a zigzag motion towards Estoban, jumping high in an attempt to come down hard in a spiralling arc, but stopped short, making his turn incomplete and giving Estoban enough time to return the manoeuvre and catch him in his side, effectively killing the man in flight.

"Gotcha!" Estoban screamed in elation.

The blade brushed by Belarus' side, breaking the skin. Belarus pretended to collapse defeated, playing the role of valiant loser extremely well. A thin line of blood formed on his left side, dripping red liquid into the fresh mud. Thunderous clapping surrounded the ring as the crowd cheered for their general. Estoban reached out his hand and congratulated Belarus on a good fight worth fighting.

"I am impressed by your skill," Estoban laughed.

"I have a great teacher." Belarus smiled in return.

"But then again, it should have been me laying in the dirt, defeated, isn't it so?" Estoban challenged.

Belarus just smiled broadly, not saying anything. Estoban looked intently at him.

"Thank you for keeping my honour intact. I have to admit, I was tired, and when you purposefully let your arc swing low, I knew I had met an honourable soldier in the ring."

Estoban released his arm as soon as he felt Belarus relax and turned to the crowd surrounding the ring.

***

"Did you see him fly through the air?" Eugo asked.

"It was amazing! How did he do that?" Danelle wanted to know every detail of a move like that.

She had never seen anything like it. With his arms flailing in all directions, Eugo explained in slow motion how one's body would need to fold and twist to execute the exact manoeuvre Belarus made. Danelle marvelled at her best friend; Eugo had a way with words. Danelle had grown up with Eugo and could still remember the first day they went exploring in the village.

Every day had held a new adventure for them. She was barely seven years old and a new member of the tribe of Achaos when they met. The Spartans slaughtered her father for treason, and she and her mother had fled during the night and found refuge a few miles north in Achaos.

Eugo was her first friend, and she had been loyal to him since their first adventure hiking through the underbrush surrounding the meeting house. Her short legs averted rocks and bushes while brown curls dangled around her soft face as laughter erupted from her throat.

"I am going to fight like them one day, you'll see." Eugo jumped up, tracking his arm in the air as if he held a heavy sword in his hands. Danelle giggled to herself.

"I started to train with Estoban last week and he said I showed promise," he stated proudly.

"I bet you do," she smiled, arching her brows.

"I am of fighting age. Next month, it will be my sixteenth birthday, and then I can officially start training with the other soldiers," he declared.

"Tell me again of how you found Belarus," she urged.

"Well, I was coming from the celebration and was about to turn towards the rope bridge and slip into my room, when I heard a swish in the bushes beneath our house. I dismissed it for a rabbit and started to ascend the ladder. That is when I heard the voice. It was very gentle and not coming from the outside but from within me."

Danelle's eyes widened and she sat upright, ready to hear the rest of his brave story.

"I knew it was Yahweh leading me, like the prophets Glaucus taught us about. I knew then that I had to go back down and search for the sound until I found it. It took me nearly fifteen minutes until I saw the man. I didn't know if he was alive or not, but I quickly retrieved our satchel and pushed the hefty man into the sack and raised him to the next floor." Eugo stopped to relive that moment for himself.

Eugo spoke with such intensity that the other children around the ring started to listen intently too.

"He must have been heavy to hoist up by a single rope," Danelle marvelled.

"Yes, he was. But I guess sheer determination gave me strength to do it," Eugo replied.

"He is built like a Spartan." She pointed at the arena where the men gathered.

***

Eugo didn't notice until now how much taller Belarus was compared to all the other men. Spartans were known for their size and strength, and Greeks like himself were small by comparison. This gave him an even bigger smile knowing that he hoisted Belarus from the ground to his house all by himself.

"Think you will miss him when he moves to the barracks?" Danelle prodded.

"I guess I will. It has been so much fun showing Belarus around the village and teaching him our ways."

"I am certain he appreciated it as much as I did all those years ago." She winked at him.

"I hope so," Eugo said, shrugging off his blush.

"He seems to fit right in with the other soldiers," Danelle mumbled more than said.

"He is a strong man, Danelle. I believe he will be a great warrior for Achaos and help us in many battles to come." Eugo stared in wonderment as the soldiers prepared for another day in the training rings.

***

Belarus rested next to Estoban on a bench, awaiting their next turn in the ring. He looked at the intricate pattern tattooed on the inside of Estoban's left forearm.

"Why the marking? What does it mean?" he asked.

"Each symbol is unique. It is a combination of your name, that of your wife, and Yahweh, God Almighty." Estoban smiled.

"Why do you do it?"

"It's a covenant mark, a sign of honour and a pledge to love and respect your marriage union until the day you die. We only ever marry once. It is a decision we take great care in protecting. The covenant is a strong bond that cannot be broken. If you break that covenant, it is punishable by death."

"Have many fallen and broken such a covenant?"

"Never. To love all your life and to be united with one woman is the greatest gift of all."

"What happens if one of you dies? Can you ever marry again?" Belarus frowned deeply.

"Of course, but even after you lose a loved one that was once part of you, it's hard to move on, I suppose."

"My lord, it's your turn." A soldier motioned to Estoban.

Belarus followed his new friend into the ring and listened to each movement Estoban taught him. Their army was strong and was once trained by a special soldier from Sparta, just south of Achaos. Every battle they encountered had been won by Estoban's army due to their precision and group manoeuvres. Each movement would be synchronised and timed to perfection. If even one soldier retreated from formation, it would all collapse and the battle placed in great detriment.

Belarus then saw a green glimmer in his peripheral vision. The momentary distraction caught him off guard. Unable to keep his focus, Estoban tripped him and threw him flat on his back. The edges of his eyes started to blur as the force of the fall brought tears to his eyes. Princess Mia was walking past, closely followed by a young woman dressed in green silk. The women giggled in amazement.

His heart bunched up in his throat. His ego had shattered, and he blushed as Estoban helped him up. His face flushed deep red, more out of embarrassment than lack of breath.

"Distractions like those brought low the heroes of old," Estoban nudged playfully.

"I am sorry. It will not happen again," Belarus explained, trying to focus on the next move.

He had never seen such beauty in his entire life. Belarus remembered well how pretty his sister was, but this maiden was far more glamorous. Her green silk tunic flowed around her ankles, revealing silky smooth skin. Her short black hair curled softly around her sharp face and fell in circles around her shoulders. Her gaze was set on him; she still looked over her shoulder. Dazzling brown eyes winked and made his knees weak. He let out a soft sigh as he pulled his eyes from the vision.

"She is a virtuous woman, Belarus."

He tried to focus on the next move from Estoban, but he merely stared after the women. Daring a quick glance, not wanting to miss another shattering blow, he lost his senses and found himself wanting a love like the one between Estoban and the princess.

Every day Belarus saw them together would pull his stomach in a knot. He never realised how much he longed for the embrace from a woman he loved. Estoban and Mia had only to glance at each other and one could see the love he had for his wife and the respect she held in honour of her husband. It was a bond Belarus had never seen before.

"I was just looking," a bashful Belarus replied, standing with his legs apart and ready for any strike from his mentor.

***

Belarus puzzled Estoban. This man was not only a stranger to him, but his heart seemed crushed and lonely. Belarus had grown so much in the last three weeks and showed great interest in the army, eager to join the forces, yet his demeanour was still uneasy. Estoban knew that love would be the conquering factor.

"If you long to pursue her, you have my permission," Estoban teased.

"I don't know what you mean?" Belarus looked surprised.

"I have seen the way you look at her. Her name is Ariana; she is the niece of one of our village elders, Justus. Our ways are simple, but I believe you have the heart of a warrior. I trust you, Belarus. You will have my full support and that of my wife." Nudging him in the ribs, Estoban broke out into a laugh and jogged briskly to his wife, grabbing her from behind in full surprise.

***

Belarus experienced a challenge unlike any other. His mind was in a fight against his heart. How could a woman pull every ounce of desire from him and throw him into turmoil so easily? He was trying to focus on his purpose, his call, but his eyes kept drifting to the young maiden patiently waiting for her friend. There was a longing in her eyes as she looked in his direction. She was indeed a beautiful creature, perfectly sculpted by the Gods, if such a thing was even possible.

His mind clouded as it searched for meaning. He turned his back towards her hoping that the longing would disappear, but it remained in his heart, constantly growing with anticipation of another chance meeting with Ariana.

***

The room was dark and smelled of thick smoke from the previous night's fire. General Valah awoke to the echo of the sound entering his chamber; an unnatural scream reverberated through the confines of the keep. Valah ripped off the skins covering his naked body and dressed in less than a minute. His routine was easily executed in the dark, as years of hard training and ambushes had made him the man he was today.

General Valah answered to one man alone. Emperor Romulus had been his inspiration, and he vowed to follow him the rest of his life. He had not anticipated his sudden rise through the ranks but was thankful to his Gods for offering him this position of honour. The sound had come from deep within the keep, and Valah knew that the animal that evaded his guards would be found. He was certain that it was a wolf in search of easy prey and the smell of blood had attracted it to the dungeons within the keep. This wasn't an uncommon occurrence.

Valah rushed past several heads poking outside their bars looking in the direction of the sound. Prisoners retreated when they saw him run past, making sure not to make a sound to provoke the man. Valah specially requested that his chamber be placed on the outer ring of the dungeon in order for him to quickly make his way inside the heart of the keep or outside to the courtyard where most attacks would come from.

He stopped suddenly when he heard the sound again. He tried to still his breathing but failed as his heart pounded louder and louder in his ears. He had difficulty tracking the sound seemingly coming from the centre of the keep. A young boy bumped into him and nearly threw him off balance. He recognised the boy in the dim light as Romulus' private blacksmith. The gaunt boy could not have been more than eighteen, but his skills and craftsmanship were well known.

"Where are you going at this time of night, boy?" Valah questioned in a whisper.

"I am preparing this for my emperor." The boy showed him the new sword that had just been formed in the fire. "My lord needs it urgently; I must pass."

Valah allowed him to pass by in the narrow tunnel leading towards a stairwell that would take him to the highest level and chamber of his emperor. The sound echoed again, but Valah realised it had not come from down in the dungeons. It echoed from above.

With a new urgency, he ran towards the end of the passage and took the stone steps two at a time. The animal was running towards the emperor's chamber. It had to be stopped before it disturbed his master's slumber.

***

Romulus' chamber was lit by a single candelabrum sporting eight red candles. He wore a full-length red robe that pooled at his ankles. Black eyes surrounded by deep crevices stared into the candlelight. Romulus was mumbling incantations in a rhythmic motion as he swayed his body left and right. His dreadlocks were unkempt, and he had not bathed since last night. Mia's escape was tormenting him every moment of every day. A deep hatred started to brew in his heart. He despised her for ripping out his black heart and destroying his appetite for other women in his possession. He had killed three girls the night before. They were unable to enjoy his power and shied away from him every moment he touched their skin. Spittle flew from his mouth as he screamed in anguish, unable to bear the raw intensity of lust. How they were able to resist a man like himself he could not understand. He offered them life and they refused him.

The sound of his door opening barely distracted him from his fury, but the sound of metal on stone prompted him to turn around. The boy knelt low, keeping his head level to his shoulders. The golden blade shimmered in the dim light. Romulus retrieved the sword from the boy and studied it with great intensity. The boy remained hunched over, awaiting his next order. The weight of the sword was great compared to its actual size, but the handle fit perfectly in Romulus' hand. He swerved the sword in several arcs, testing the balance and motion of the blade.

"Sir! I implore you, don't do it!" a man then yelled at Romulus.

He suddenly looked up to see his first general with arms raised and his weapon unsheathed. He realised then that Valah suspected him of attempting to murder the young boy kneeling before him.

"Valah, do you believe that I am capable of beheading my own?" he challenged.

"No. Forgive me, my lord." Valah replaced his sword in its sheath and bowed in reverence before his emperor.

Romulus marvelled at the audacity of his general and wanted to reprimand him, but his sudden submission convinced him otherwise.

"Both of you rise," he said. "Hamid, leave us."

The boy bowed and exited the chamber without making another sound.

"This is the best blade I have ever had, Valah. It would be a valuable asset on our next mission."

"We do not set out until spring, my lord. The haste to complete the sword is in vain."

"We will set out at sunrise. Prepare an elite force of sixty men," Romulus ordered.

"But the coming winter months would slay more men than any battle, my lord," Valah urged.

"I did not ask, Valah. It will be done."

"Yes, my liege." Valah started to turn around when Romulus grabbed his arm and pulled him close. He spoke directly into Valah's ear in order for him not to miss a single word he was about to say.

"Go and rid this keep of all the girls except the Athenian princess." His warm, stale breath seemed to incapacitate Valah for a moment.

"My lord, it would be a rash decision. They aren't animals," he protested.

"You will do as I say, or you will be the first one I test my new blade on," Romulus sneered.

***

Valah bowed deep and fled the chamber of his emperor. He knew Romulus had a lust for young women, like he himself enjoyed, but to kill them all without reason would be slaughter. Valah was overwrought with his own thoughts. Had his emperor gone insane?

He had to admit that Romulus had not been the same since Mia's escape. He had withdrawn himself from his banquets, and more girls died at his hand than ever before. Valah had doubt in his heart concerning the man he vowed to follow his entire life. A three-week assault, amid the coming season, seemed rash and unplanned.

Valah retreated to his chamber and bowed down in front of the carved images of the Aveston and sought guidance.

6

"Seven horses were spotted at the eastern perimeter, sir," the young soldier reported to Estoban.

"Were they heavily armed?" Estoban inquired.

"No, sir. They looked like some of our own."

"Are we expecting a convoy to return at this time?"

"We are expecting a scouting party around next week, but they are only three in number, sir."

"Keep a sharp lookout and prepare for anything. A whole army might be following their very trail."

"Yes, sir," the soldier replied as he sharply saluted his general and left the meeting house.

Estoban walked in circles around the single seat facing the curved table. The last three months had passed without a single disturbance in the village. The arrival of Belarus caused quite a stir among the soldiers, but he seemed to settle quickly into the barracks among the men. Estoban still wondered about Belarus and his story.

Nothing seemed out of the ordinary except his acquired skill in the ring. Belarus claimed to have never been near any battle until the day of the attack on his village, but the familiarity with which he handled a weapon unnerved even Estoban. The way he moved about the ring could only have been learnt from a young age. He was swift and certain of every move. He calculated the next strike from his opponent with perfect precision.

The thought scratched at the edge of his reason. How could a farmer be so natural with a blade that should seem so clumsy in his hands? Estoban dismissed the thought as the young soldier rushed into the room again.

"It's Nathanial and his men, sir. They brought with them another four banished for their religion," he said excitedly and rushed outside to meet the men dismounting from their horses.

Estoban adjusted his eyes to the bright light when his three youngest scouts bowed and saluted their general. It had been five months since their departure, and it was a delight to have them all back unharmed. Nathanial spoke with authority, and Estoban could see the growth in his leadership. He had gone on the planned mission after Mia urged him to stay. Nathanial had just married his beloved Meriba but decided that he would not remain in the village the allotted year of celebration and complete his mission as planned.

Achaeans took pride in their appearance, and not one of them was dishevelled or unkempt. Khalil, the second scout in the group, had dressed all four newcomers with a warm tunic overlaid with lavish embroidery, a piece of clothing which stood in great contrast to their own tattered and torn clothing still hugging their emaciated bodies. Hunger and abuse still showed despite the smiles exposing some broken and lost teeth.

"Nathanial, you are free to see your wife. She has been missing her beloved." Estoban gave a crooked smile as he saw Nathanial's eyes brighten at the release of his duty.

He bowed deep and waved goodbye to his crew and ran at full speed towards his house. William, the group's third scout, recounted their journey quickly but in great detail as the bystanders listened in excitement—it had been a perilous journey filled with adventure.

Estoban could remember his first conquest into the unknown. He was barely twenty-three, and the four-month trip to the eastern borders of the known world was the most exciting mission he had ever embarked on. Estoban welcomed the four strangers to their village and sent them, together with Khalil, to the barracks to prepare a place for them to stay.

Nathanial, William, and Khalil had been sent to the southern regions of the Egyptian Empire to scout new lands and peoples. William remained with Estoban to talk in private about their mission and its accomplishments.

They travelled by boat via Crete to a small town in the northern regions of Cyrene. They were welcomed into the Greek city but found no peace among the idols and teachings of Socrates. A day later, they found Lamar and Homer tied together in a pit nearly dead from thirst.

They had been banished by the disciples of Socrates because of a moral disagreement and left to die. Upon hearing of Yahweh, they recognised freedom and asked if they could join the three soldiers on their journey. Nathanial had accepted them quickly and traded some weapons for horses to carry them. They found hardly anyone not subjugated under the Pharaoh.

Six weeks of travelling through the arid southern desert made their journey slow as hunger and thirst overwhelmed them, but determination carried them further. They found a young boy, Rebo, by a river crying out of shame as he had run away from home. He had killed his older brother in a play fight and was ashamed to return and decided to drown rather than live a life of regret. William told him of Yahweh and how He rescues the broken.

Rebo had remained silent the rest of the journey, but with each day he grew closer and even started to smile at their jokes. Karabo impressed them the most. The young African man stood nearly a full head taller than all of them. He was lean, muscular, and a good fighter.

He was found when Nathanial and his crew lost their way during a violent desert storm. The landscape was bleak, dry, and dead. They hadn't found water for days and feared death would overtake them at any moment. The cry had come in the middle of the night.

With their last strength, Nathanial and William had run to the scream and saw the blades of the Pharaoh's men come down on a man. As if an unknown force pushed them, they ran to the man's rescue, beheading the soldiers in silent motion. They stopped the execution mid-stride. Karabo did not even stir; his face was at peace, and they realised that he was praying.

Upon further inquisition, they had learnt that Karabo was on a six-month journey to manhood. He spent his days learning about Yahweh and life. Karabo was a wise man, and they knew that he would be a great teacher and blessing to the tribe of Achaos. He instantly accepted their camaraderie and showed them the way to the great city of Memphis—the capital of Egypt and the way home.

Each scouting trip brought home men and women banished for their beliefs. Glaucus Solon taught them that every life was worth saving, and if the banished members were believers, they were welcome to gain security in the village. Estoban and his parents were banished when he was still a baby. Had it not been for Glaucus, Estoban might never have lived within his purpose and in Yahweh.

"We shall hold a great banquet in your honour tonight, William," Estoban stated.

"Thank you, sir, it would be a great honour indeed." William just smiled, satisfied with a mission of success. They had brought home more valiant men to join the tribe.

Estoban saluted the young scout and dismissed him to return to his family. Achaos was growing, and Mia would be delighted to celebrate the victory.

***

It took Belarus nearly an hour to walk through the overgrown forest, but he welcomed the distraction. The blue sky above reminded him of the day he had his first apprentice blacksmith session. His father was burly, but his hands were gentle and small by comparison.

Darius Khalili knew how to wield a sword better than anyone. He was a blacksmith by trade, and the intricate skill of shaping a blade gave him the necessary insight into its movements, weaknesses, and strengths. He was not a fighting man, but his wisdom in working with metal was essential to his service to the king.

The blacksmith station in Achaos was fairly large and set deep into the forest quite some distance from the village. Billowing smoke might be seen for several miles, and the strategic placement away from the village would not give away their hidden location.

Belarus heard Eugo laugh before he saw him. The young boy was carrying a bucket of water and spilled as he walked. He was unable to contain his laughter as his friend tripped over the underbrush. Belarus never saw Danelle without Eugo. The short girl was his best friend, and Belarus could see why she found him so irresistible.

Eugo had a way of making you feel like the only person alive and that every waking moment was about you. He always made Belarus smile, no matter what mood he was in.

"Belarus!" Eugo shouted when he saw him coming towards the workstation.

"Eugo." Belarus bowed flamboyantly, making the boy burst out in laughter again.

"It must be my lucky day to work at the station. I get to see my favourite warrior." Eugo put down the bucket and clasped his hands together.

"I would hardly call myself a warrior, Eugo."

"Don't be absurd! You are amazing in the ring. I have never seen anyone fight the way you do." He turned in a circle pretending to knock away a blow.

The station was very busy, and many men tended to the firepit at once. The familiar clanging of hammers on hot metal echoed into the forest. Belarus retrieved his sword and handed it to Eugo. Eugo studied the blade for a while.

"This should be no problem. It will only take a few minutes to straighten the blade." Eugo's smile widened into a big grin; he was quite pleased with himself.

Belarus rested on a fallen tree stump near the entrance of the station. Danelle sat next to him, staring in wonderment at the big man beside her, her dark eyes sparkling in the sunlight. Belarus was certain that he could have crushed her with his little finger. He just smiled at her, uncertain what to say. She looked at him as if he was some kind of mystical creature. He just stared straight ahead and tried to ignore the admiration in her eyes.

The silence was deafening yet not uncomfortable. This might be what it would feel like to be a king. The thought unnerved Belarus, and he quickly got up and walked to the firepit in the centre of the workstation.

"All done, my lord!" Eugo bowed deep, holding the sword in both hands for Belarus to pick up.

"Don't do that," Belarus scoffed.

Eugo stood quickly and tried to look relaxed. Every muscle in his body tensed and Belarus knew why.

"I'm sorry, Eugo. I didn't mean to be hard on you. It's just not a phrase I am accustomed to. It doesn't suit me." Belarus tousled Eugo's hair and smiled.

The boy grinned and quickly returned to his station for his next blade.

Belarus marvelled at the workmanship of the sword and realised that his father might not have done a better job. The boy was indeed crafty. A glimmer of gold caught Belarus' attention as he turned to leave. Eugo held a foot-long dagger in his hands and was about to shove it into the fire when Belarus stopped him.

"Who does this blade belong to?" he questioned.

"It belongs to Princess Mia." Eugo simply stared at Belarus as he handed him the dagger. Persian inscriptions were carved into the gold-encrusted blade. Belarus cradled the weapon in his hands like a familiar counterpart. He reluctantly gave it back to Eugo.

"It's a beautiful weapon," he whispered.

"You handle it as if you know it well." Danelle spoke softly from behind Belarus.

"I'm used to daggers. I used to shear my own sheep with a blade like that, only much simpler than this one." Belarus smiled uncomfortably.

"Will you join us for the banquet tonight?" Eugo asked.

"I most certainly will." Belarus was delighted that he changed the subject. "I will see you at sunset."

"I will keep a lookout for you." Eugo smiled.

Belarus looked back at the two teenagers staring after him. He waved and they excitedly waved back. The last three months had gone by smoothly, and Belarus settled in easily into the barracks. He was happy, and the sure sense of emotion made him laugh loudly to himself.

A large part of that happiness had also been his blossoming romance with Ariana. Ever since the first day he saw her, he had known that his heart would never be joined to another. He had to admit that the sudden affirmation from Estoban weeks ago was a surprise. Belarus never carried his heart on his sleeve, but his affections for the girl had clearly been evident. Butterflies tingled in his stomach just thinking about her. Their courtship was yet young, but the passion in their relationship was undeniable. Every afternoon they had taken a stroll through the orange grove thick with ripe fruit, and as the bud had pushed forward for a new season of growth, so too did their love grow into a beautiful flower offering fruits of hope and promise.

Today was indeed a good day. He couldn't wait to see Ariana that night. Love was in the air, and he enjoyed the surge of freedom it brought.

***

The valley clearing was bathed in golden light as the sunset painted red and orange streaks across the sky. Nightfall would bring a dazzling array of starlight and a bright quarter moon. The whole village attended the banquet save for a few soldiers at their lookout posts. The tribe of Achaos was a close-knit family.

Although they consisted of Greeks, Medes, Persians, and even Egyptians, there was a brotherhood Belarus had never before seen among a people. It gave him immense joy to be welcomed into a family like this one. He had believed that all was lost and that he himself would perish from his grief, but Estoban and Mia took him in and gave him safe passage to become one of their own. He knew now that with Ariana by his side, he was indeed the luckiest man alive.

Suddenly the centre of the crowd dispersed as if in a sequenced dance. Nathaniel stepped into the centre followed by a vibrant redhead. Her long locks frizzed in small zigzags. She wore a long green tunic with gold trimmings on the hem. She seemed fragile out in the open, her eyes darting in all directions. When the flute started to play a solitary tune, she started to sway left and right, building in speed and strength.

She started to dance, and all her fragility disappeared. She moved gracefully yet entirely purposefully, and Belarus immediately recognised the covenant dance she was performing for her husband. Estoban had told him about the dance that displayed the sign of union between a husband and wife.

Ariana squeezed his arm tighter as Nathaniel and Meriba danced in a display of love. The covenant marking on the left forearm was displayed in each turn, and Belarus could see the intricate pattern unique to Nathanial and his beautiful wife Meriba.

"Next week it will be our turn to dance." Ariana nudged his left side.

Belarus blushed at the thought and gently kissed the back of her hand. "I love you, my princess."

Ariana giggled and hugged herself tighter under the protection of his arm. The music reached a crescendo, and the whole tribe started to dance as the celebrations began. Mouth-watering delicacies and fine wine flowed from the abundant valley; the people of Achaos knew how to celebrate. Life was indeed worth living.

Belarus scrutinised the new man that arrived this morning. Karabo was taller than him, and was slender and regal. His wisdom could be seen even from this distance. Belarus reminded himself that he had to meet this man before the celebrations waned into the night.

Belarus left Ariana talking to her friends, showing off the new golden band around her ring finger—gold intertwined with bronze to create a twisting shape that held together the ruby that shone in the firelight. Belarus had made the ring himself and carefully chose the stone to suit her fiery personality. He loved to look at her from a distance. Her red tunic bundled in a twisted knot around her slim middle and dropped to form a red pool of lace around her sandaled feet. Golden pins held her tunic in place, each shimmering with radiant rubies matching the band on her finger.

Ariana shone like a lady in waiting should. A mere week from today and she would become his wife. His hands trembled at the thought, and he closed his fingers around the blade that hung from his scabbard to still the trembling. He retreated into the tree line away from the crowd and jubilant singing. He needed to be alone.

The stars shone brightly. Belarus found comfort in the enigmatic covering of night as each constellation offered meaning and purpose. He pondered his own in the quiet darkness. Then he saw her—she had followed him.

"I didn't hear you," he said, startled.

"I don't mean to impose, Belarus," Mia answered and turned to leave.

"No, please stay." He motioned for her to take a seat next to him on the fallen tree trunk.

Belarus hardly knew what to say to his crown princess. Just to be near her put him on edge. She was the Polemarch of Achaos, and she concerned herself with his wellbeing. This was uncommon; never would he have tried to discuss his heart with his ruler. He was a man of submission and understood authority and rank.

She sat quietly, admiring the starry spectacle overhead. The moon had not yet risen over the horizon, and thousands of lights illuminated the dark night sky with no trace of cloud cover in any direction as far as they could see.

"You love her, don't you?" Belarus broke the silence.

"Ariana?" Mia questioned.

"Yes."

"She is like a sister to me, and I would hate to see her heart broken by any man." Mia still stared at the sky, unwilling to give an accusing stare at Belarus.

"I will not fail you, my lady," he protested.

Mia turned towards him, and her eyes only conveyed love, not the accusation he thought she was burdening him with.

"I believe you are the right man for her, Belarus. I trust my husband's judgement about you. Estoban sees a great man, and Ariana can only display joy and love when your name is spoken."

Her compassion made him slightly uncomfortable. Belarus quickly changed the subject, very aware of the way Mia was looking at him.

"Your tribe is very peculiar." He stared straight, looking at nothing.

"What do you mean?" she asked.

"You all seem at peace." Belarus was uncertain how to place the right words in the right order. "There is havoc around us in the world, and I don't understand how any of you just live as if nothing can penetrate these barely protected forests."

"We have our identity. We know who we are and where we came from. There is nothing to fear when you know who your protector is," Mia replied solemnly.

Belarus just stared at her, trying to make sense of the world he found himself in.

"My father once told me a truth that I keep hidden in my utmost being," she continued. "During his stay in Susa as a young man, he learned about the Jews and all the other deities of the Persians, the Babylonians, and of course the Greeks. 'It's all a chase after the wind' he told me.

"It's all for nothing, just a bunch of dead idols that can do nothing for you. They cannot speak, they cannot think or act, so why would you put your trust and your hope in a piece of wood?"

Belarus pondered the question, looking out into the forest for a semblance of understanding.

"I learned about Abraham, Isaac, and Jacob from my father. These men spoke with God, and things in their lives changed. My hope is in such a God, one of truth, love, and mercy. Not some edict placed there by a man who looked to fill the void in his heart. He is our protector. God is tangible, Belarus. He is waiting for you to come to Him. He won't put restraints and rules on you like the pagans do." She gently nudged him in his left side and looked at him while he scoffed the thoughts away.

"He delivered my father, you know. My father was in bondage, and he didn't even know it. He set my father free to live a life of purpose. He showed him the way and led him here, to this abundant valley, hidden and secret. God allowed all Achaeans to live in freedom."

"How does it work then?" Belarus asked.

"You need to believe." She gently placed her hand on his heart. "You must open your heart to Him. Allow Him to come inside, heal you, and embrace you."

She looked with sympathy at this new foreign recruit her husband welcomed in.

"Let time and our ways of celebrating life speak for themselves. You'll see, someday."

She gave him a warm smile and turned to walk away. Her long curls swayed in the light breeze as specks of gold shimmered off her head in the starlight. Bronze, blonde, and gold hair intertwined to form a golden hue in every curl. Her royal tunic swirled around her bare ankles as she seemed to float away. A deep longing stirred inside of him. *What if it's true?* he pondered. With a quick jerk of his head towards the barracks, he dismissed the thought as easily as it emerged.

"Deception, that's all I say," he mumbled to himself as he refocused on his thoughts.

***

Estoban saw his wife comfort Belarus and knew that if anyone was to show Belarus the ways of the tribe, it would be Mia. She was gentle and kind but possessed a certain fire that ignited passion in one's heart. Whenever she spoke, life seemed to flow from her, allowing everything else to make sense in the world. She was heroic, and everyone in the tribe admired her for her constant positivity and sense of pride to be a follower of the great Yahweh.

"It must be hard for a man as strong as he?" Estoban said as he gently placed his arms around Mia as she slowly approached him.

"Give him time, my love." Mia gently stroked his smooth chin and turned his face towards her. "You are going to show him. Every moment of every day is a miracle. Belarus will see that."

"He lost everything. He is our responsibility now." He sought her blue eyes, looking for the comfort of his wife.

"But he will regain so much more. You will see. His life is not in *our* hands, Estoban. Yahweh will heal his heart; we only need to steer him in the right direction."

She gently kissed him with soft lips, allowing every anxious thought to disappear from his mind. Estoban took her small hand into his and led his wife back to the banquet to celebrate life and love.

***

Blood splatter covered the canvas roof of the small tent. Valah stood motionless as he stared at the small girl cradled in the corner of the room. She was barely seventeen and would become his concubine for the remainder of the journey.

Five weeks ago, he had reluctantly followed Romulus on a two-week plunder session into the northern regions of Macedonia. The people of the region had never heard of the Angra Mainyu, and due to their disbelief, they were slaughtered. It was a theme Valah knew very well. He might not have agreed with Romulus' methods, but until now he was certain that all people had to bow before the Aveston.

The frail little girl stared at him with wide eyes. Valah knew that if he put her outside, the other soldiers would not only fight over her but probably rape her successively and certainly kill her before the sun rose over the valley.

Valah moved closer to the girl, meaning not to harm her. With speed and surprise, she lunged at him, grabbing him by the shoulder in a strong vice. He tried to pull her off by her hair, but she didn't budge. Her screams echoed in the tiny tent, and Valah knew that no-one would come to her rescue; instead, they would listen and be enflamed with blood lust.

Valah pulled her far enough away from him to see determination in her eyes. She spit in his face, and he jerked back, exposing his neck. She dug deep into his shoulder muscle and bit down hard, pulling at his flesh. He screamed in anguish but failed to pull her off.

A soldier rushed into the tent at the scream of his commander and saw the wench clinging to him. With a smooth twist of his arm, he unsheathed his dagger and plunged it deep into her torso, piercing Valah's chest at the same time. She released her grip and fell backwards, allowing the dagger to stick out further. She looked down at her abdomen and back to Valah. She said something he was unable to understand before the soldier cut her throat, exposing her spine through the gaping wound. Blood splurged all over Valah's Persian prayer rug he never travelled without.

"Are you alright, sire?" the soldier asked, quickly seeing to his wounds.

"Call the physician," Valah whispered.

The soldier turned to leave immediately, creating a fuss as he went. Valah looked at the girl lying in her own blood. Her entrails started to bulge through the hole in her stomach. She looked like a porcelain object mutilated by a five-year-old boy. Her limbs were twisted under her back as it arched towards the roof. Her head lay askew with her dark eyes still glaring at him.

What did she say? he thought to himself. The torment of another soul would haunt him more than the loss of function in his shoulder. Its usefulness might never recover after the deep gash she made with her teeth. Valah collapsed as tears of remorse flowed freely, forming a clean line in the blood that covered his face.

7

The morning was overflowing with a flurry of activity. Tambourines and drums were already filling the village with excitement preceding the day's events. The trees were adorned with sweet white blossoms from the valley arranged in spectacular arches, starting from the centre of the village and spiralling outwards toward the groves of orange trees in the distance. Every tribe member had a part to play in creating the celebration.

Today, two individuals would be bound together in a vow of promise. Glaucus Solon, supreme leader of Achaos, had taught them the importance of the covenant.

"I had come to know Yahweh. The God of Israel is real and alive and gives His gifts freely to whoever would choose Him," Glaucus would exclaim in utter wonderment. "Love, mercy, and grace abound in his nature."

Mia had known about Yahweh her entire life and lived her life knowing that God was walking with her, but today something stirred in her spirit.

She loved Ariana like a sister, and she celebrated the covenant that she was about to close with mighty Belarus. The joy that was supposed to accompany this celebration was slightly muffled by an anxiety she was not accustomed to. At dawn, Mia was already kneeling by the window, silently praying to God for deliverance.

Estoban saw her kneeling in prayer and admired his wife for her commitment and loyalty to their Father in heaven. He had sought wisdom and guidance from God the day he was about to ask for his wife's hand in marriage. It had been a terrifying day, but Glaucus welcomed him into the family and never even contested the match. Glaucus had come to know Estoban as a strong leader worthy of Mia's hand.

The sun shone brightly into their cabin, illuminating the golden curls falling around Mia's waist and creating a golden glow around her. She was a vision, and Estoban remembered how he used to gaze in awe at their leader's daughter when he was only fourteen years old. It had been quite a journey to win her favour. She was raised to become a queen, and getting an audience with her was no easy feat.

Estoban had served in the king's guard since he was of fighting age and learned from the best marksmen in the village. He had even spent a year and six months training in Sparta. When he returned, Mia had blossomed into a beautiful young woman.

She was eighteen years old and ready to be courted. Estoban was afraid to even dream about such a match. He had remained focused on the ranks and quickly advanced to become a young general in the king's guard.

Four years had passed since he returned from Sparta, and at twenty-five, he was ready to settle down. Achaos was filled with beautiful women, but none could stir his heart like their crown princess. He could never possibly forget the day he knew that no other woman ever would.

Estoban was allowing his horse to graze a mile out of the village when he was nearly trampled by one of the king's horses. The animal had come loose and was raging wildly in the valley. He calmed the horse and tied him along with his own to graze in the field while he went looking for the rider that should have accompanied it.

He saw golden hair lying in a tangled mess on top of a small heap on the verge of the clearing. He approached slowly with his sword drawn, ready for an ambush. As he approached, the scent of sweet orange blossom soap welcomed him, and he knew that the little heap was indeed Mia of Achaos.

He rushed to her side and gently searched for her face in the mass of hair. Mia had cut her left cheek where it must have collided with a branch. Estoban looked towards the tree and saw the branch responsible for knocking her from her horse. It hung on the tree, barely held by a small piece of bark. She stirred in his arms and suddenly punched his chest and face as consciousness returned. She stopped short when she recognised him.

"Estoban, what are you doing here?" she demanded.

"My lady, I was just grazing my horse."

"You never saw me, okay?" She forced him to let go, grabbing her dress high and exposing her muscular calves. She was built like a warrior, and every portion of her was perfect. Estoban stared at her, unable to utter a word.

"Did you hear what I said?" she demanded again.

"Yes, forgive me. I understand." Estoban blushed.

She ran to her horse and untied him with such speed he hardly saw her undoing the knot that held the two animals together. She mounted her horse and started to gallop farther away into the clearing. She looked back at him, smiling broadly. Estoban was numb, unable to move. She was running off into the next section of forest, and he knew then that he had to pursue her.

He ran to his dark-coloured horse and set out in pursuit. He followed her trail until he saw her horse tied to a tree beside a massive expanse of clear water he had not seen before. He dismounted and tied his horse to hers, then rounded the foot of a small granite cliff protruding from the water's edge. Its sharp contours created footholds only crazy people would climb. He couldn't see Mia, only fragments of her garment strewn about the small beach bordering the crystal-clear pool.

Suddenly the clear surface broke in a large splash. The water settled, and a small circle of bubbles started to boil as she surfaced the water from beneath. She laughed and screamed in elation as she lulled in the water, gliding on her back. The dive must have been more that sixteen feet. He would not even dare to jump from that height.

When she saw him, she squirmed and tried to hide herself in the water, but the clear sky lightened the surface, revealing the bottom of the lake with pristine clarity. She was perfect.

Estoban swirled around suddenly as he had never seen a naked woman before. He was so ashamed to have stared at her perfection; she was indeed beautiful beyond comparison. He heard her get out of the pool, and he sheepishly handed her the garments with his back still turned towards her.

"You can turn around now," she said.

Her hair was stuck to her face in dark blonde streaks streaming with water. She looked at him. His heart was about to burst when she spoke again.

"Why were you following me, Estoban?" she asked gently.

"I'm sorry. I was worried, that's all," he said bashfully; he was unable to look her in the eyes.

"Thank you," she said as she placed her hand on his arm.

He looked directly at her, and what he saw unnerved him. Mia froze, and her eyes connected with his. His breathing quickened, hastening his heartbeat. In her eyes he saw a sense of knowing, a realisation that she too saw in him what he had seen in her all along. Both perplexed in wonder, they drew away from their touch and simply smiled at one another.

They walked to their horses together, not saying a single word. Mia kept looking at his hands, and he felt comfort instead of unease. To be well kept was an important virtue, and he could sense that she approved. For a warrior, Estoban was not excessively big, but what he lacked in size he made up for in skill. She smiled as he helped her mount her horse with her tunic dragging behind her in the mud. He stared longingly as she disappeared into the thicket, his heart filled with a new sense of purpose.

That day was the first of many secret adventures into the unknown. Estoban would be her protector, and together they would one day change the world.

Returning from the memory, Estoban kneeled beside his wife and embraced her. Today was the wedding of her best friend, and she seemed somewhat pessimistic.

"Are you alright, Mia?" he nudged.

"Yes. Everything will be alright in the end," she smiled.

Mia stood up and gently hugged Estoban where he was still kneeling. The warmth of her embrace soothed him and lured him back into his reverie.

***

Mia shook off the restraint she was feeling and decided that it was merely the excitement that was wearing her down. Planning the big day was more stressful than leading an army and much more exhausting. She dressed in a bright yellow tunic trimmed with gold and sapphire. Her hair lay in loose curls around her face. She placed a small golden crown on her head and pinned a few strands of hair from her face.

She laid out a matching tunic for Estoban accompanied by the royal golden sceptre. Today he would take the place of her father in the ceremony, a place of high esteem and great honour to usher in the new couple.

***

Belarus stood motionless as the entire village focused on him. He was incredibly nervous and knew not why he felt so unsure of himself. He was a strong, valiant man, and he believed that he would be a great husband to Ariana.

But to stand here all alone in the clearing with hundreds of eyes looking at him was unnerving. He tugged at his white tunic, feeling somewhat uncomfortable as the drums started to beat a steady rhythm announcing the start of the ceremony.

Eugo and Danelle both stared at Belarus and waved excitedly as he looked in their direction. Belarus saw the pair smiling in delight and returned the greeting with a nod of acknowledgement.

His eye caught a glimpse of yellow and gold sieving through the trees to his left. A small entourage led by Princess Mia and Estoban robed in yellow splendour turned the corner and made its way towards Belarus. His chest tightened as he awaited the crowd. Mia waved at the villagers, and they cheered in delight. Estoban remained focused on his task at hand and walked fearlessly next to his wife.

Mia and the Achaean elders stood to Belarus' right and simply nodded in greeting as Estoban walked past Belarus to stand behind him, awaiting the arrival of his bride. The structure under which Estoban stood was made from slender branches twisted into an arch and decorated with white blossoms that gave off a sweet fragrance.

To its left stood two chairs also fashioned out of branches and decorated with the same white flowers to create two unique seats for the second portion of the ceremony.

The drum beat faded as it was replaced by a flute playing a solitary tune. Belarus relaxed his shoulders and looked in wonder as a white stallion came walking through the tree line. He was unable to breathe when he saw Ariana in white splendour riding the stallion with grace.

Her short hair was taken up in several curls that bounced around her face. A flower garland was placed on her head, spreading a white glow around her. Her white tunic was trimmed

71

with brilliant gemstone glistening in the sunlight. The only jewellery she wore was a necklace that hung to her waist sporting the symbol of their union crafted in silver.

Ten feet from Belarus, the horse slowed to a stop, and a young soldier helped Ariana dismount. Her long tunic fell in layers around her sandaled feet. As she approached, Belarus could see the train of her garment stretching out to create a fan of material that sparkled. When she stopped in front of Belarus, he could see the tears well in her eyes, and only then did he realise that he had been holding his breath.

"You are a vision," he breathed out slowly.

Ariana burst out giggling and jumped into his arms. The village cheered in elation as the two embraced. Estoban cleared his throat and motioned for the couple to turn towards him.

"Today marks the first day of the rest of your lives. You are the Father's immortal beloved, and He showers his grace upon you today. Yahweh is Lord, and His love endures forever," Estoban declared to the crowd.

"Amen!" they shouted in unison.

Estoban spoke gently to the couple and led them into the understanding and importance of marriage. The crowd stood in agreement with Ariana and Belarus at every new discovery. When he finished speaking, Estoban asked them both to kneel before him, holding out their hands.

He laid the golden sceptre in their hands and simply stated, "Today, you have become one in mind and spirit. This sceptre is a symbol of unity and respect. This journey cannot be completed alone; you are intertwined in your destiny. Be at peace and experience the love of God in your union and be blessed."

Belarus rose and held out his hand to Ariana. They turned towards each other to complete their vows in Achaean tradition. As Belarus spoke the words, a single tear formed in the corner of his eye. It rolled off his cheek, splashing on her hand. She seemed enamoured by his gentle spirit and looked at him lovingly in response to the emotions that softened his demeanour.

"I set you as a seal upon my heart, as a seal upon my arm, for love is as strong as death and jealousy demanding as the grave. For many waters cannot quench this love." Ariana repeated the words after her husband.

The whole village clapped and danced as the words were spoken. Flower confetti was thrown into the air as the elders made their way towards the couple. They enclosed them with a circle of trust.

Ariana looked deep into Belarus' eyes as the elders reached out their hands to speak a blessing over them. Belarus saw Ariana close her eyes as they blessed them, but he was unable to keep his eyes off the beautiful creature standing in front of him. He was filled with a deep satisfaction he only dreamt of, and to experience it was unbelievable.

Mia beckoned the couple to come and take a seat on the wooden chairs. Taking their right arms together, Ariana and Belarus sat side by side facing in different directions. Two artists kneeled beside them. The young man asked Belarus to place his left arm on the armrest with his palm facing upwards.

The man cleaned the inside of his arm with an antiseptic derived from plants grown in the region. He then inserted a thin metal needle containing indelible ink into the top layer of Belarus' skin. Belarus was familiar with this art form. He had seen many tribal leaders from the east wear ink face masks as a way of identification. He had even seen several markings on people in Egypt when he travelled with his father.

The gentle curves of the symbol came together to create a perfect circular emblem etched into his skin. Belarus looked at the piece of art that would now become a permanent part of him. It was indeed a spectacular design.

He looked to his right just as the girl finished the covenant marking on Ariana's arm. She looked at the symbol for a long time before she looked at Belarus. She was indeed ravishing. She silently repeated the words of their vow, and he finally understood the meaning of them.

I set you as a seal upon my heart, as a seal upon my arm.

Belarus laughed as the revelation became a reality. Estoban and Eugo had tried to explain the phenomenon of the seal to him, but he didn't grasp it until now. It was so simple yet entirely significant. They had a bond; they were one in mind and spirit and would later consummate to become one in body. Yahweh was in covenant with His people, and that promise was holy, just like the agreement between husband and wife is holy unto God. Nothing can separate that bond, and nothing should.

To be separated after this seemed like a death sentence to Belarus. He finally understood how much God must love him, to make a pact with him. A mere mortal human can indeed be in a covenant with an everlasting, all knowing God. The thought was profound and yet it simplified the love of a saviour. There was indeed more than hatred and betrayal in this world.

Celebration screamed into the night as the sun set over the valley. Every man, woman, and child danced and celebrated love. Belarus laughed with the men and observed his wife across the clearing chuckling with the other women. She smiled at him, and her radiance outshone the entire crowd.

The music then stopped, and people started to disperse in all directions, leaving Belarus and Ariana in the clearing. Surprised, he looked around not fully understanding the breakup. Flutes started to play a familiar tune as Ariana began to sway left and right. Belarus realised that it was their turn to show off their new covenant mark in the traditional dance.

For three days he prepared with Estoban, yet he feared that he might forget every step. He focused on the rhythm and beat but lost all motion as his wife came near. Mia must have seen him freeze and started to tap her feet along to the music, showing him a slight move that jerked his memory back. He beamed and performed the dance to perfection.

The whole village was involved in making the day memorable. Belarus realised how much the tribe depended on one another and how much they devoted themselves to each other in respect and harmony.

The celebrations had now settled down to only a handful of guests. Belarus nipped Ariana, raising his eyebrows playfully. They bowed in grandiose fashion, leaving the party behind. Belarus helped Ariana mount the white stallion Estoban had given him for a wedding present and made his way towards the eastern perimeter of the village.

Dwindling through the trees and homes, the besotted couple made their way to a quaint house spread between three trees. It was a simple yet elegant abode. Belarus followed Ariana up the steps to the landing and opened the door for her, ushering his bride into their new home.

The room was sparsely decorated, but the fireplace and candlelight made it look like the most beautiful palace they had ever seen. Estoban and Mia had built them their own house, and Mia had decorated it herself, for she knew her friend better than anyone. No one had ever lived in the house before and neither had the bed been used.

The linen was woven from fine silk, and animal skins had been laced together to create a warm sheet to cover them in the winter months. Belarus picked her up and carried her into the bedroom. Orange blossoms were strewn about the floor, creating a floral fantasy they could only dream of. This was the best day of their lives, and they knew that the best was yet to come.

Belarus walked to the window and closed the drapes, blocking out the moonlight shining through the opening. He pulled Ariana closer and kissed her gently on her forehead before reaching out and touching her cheek, admiring her beauty.

"Your hands are rough, like that of a battle-worn soldier." She caressed his hands in hers.

"Working the fields made them rough, my love," he giggled.

"You can rest now, my beloved. You can rest." She hugged him close, sensing his reservations.

Belarus relaxed into her embrace, gently stroking the small of her back. Ariana looked up into his eyes which glowed like fire, ready to consume her. She reached her small hands and embraced his strong neck. He kissed her deeply and melted into her arms. He was unsure how to explain what he felt. He felt alive and on fire, consumed all at once.

Belarus slowly unclasped the pin that held her tunic in place. Her garment fell from her shoulders, revealing perfect skin. He had never seen such beauty. Her body was indeed a wonderland; no other woman could ever compare to this sweet, innocent, alluring woman. He stepped back and admired her. She giggled and jumped towards him.

She's a feisty one! he thought proudly to himself. He could hardly believe his luck.

Ariana then unpinned his own tunic and smiled as he slowly allowed the cloth to fall to the ground. Belarus knew she had never seen a naked man before, and the sight clearly intrigued her more than she expected. Belarus had strong muscles perfectly sculpted all over his body. Every curve and sinew gently laced together to complete the man she came to love.

He allowed her gaze to sweep over his body, quickening his heartbeat. His breath escaped his lips in short gasps as she traced his muscles with her fingertips. He stepped towards his wife and lifted her onto the bed. The soft animal skins hugged her body, welcoming him to take her. Their lovemaking exploded with passion and delight as they sealed their covenant and became one in body and spirit.

8

A rusty smell stirred him awake. Belarus reached for his night table but instead stumbled onto a cold floor, and he followed the pattern of it with his fingers. It was not the warm covering of wood, but rather uneven stones puzzled together. Getting up, he hit his head on a low ceiling. Belarus was confused and felt his way around. He was stuck in a tunnel of stone, and claustrophobia started to set in.

His breathing tensed, and he had to force it to settle down. He moved forward on his hands and knees, feeling his way through the confined space. He finally came to a wooden door, and he felt around the perimeter for a latch which he found at the top of the door. He struggled to loosen the bronze lock, for he was shaking heavily. All he wanted to do was to be free of the constricting pain threatening to crush his heart. It gave way in a moment, and Belarus tumbled forward into the bright light.

He lay on his back, sucking in big gulps of air, until he finally stood to have a look around. His eyes adjusted to the light, and he was surprised to find himself in the open clearing in Achaos. He spun around to see the tunnel he came out of, but there was nothing but the clearing surrounded by the familiar homes and the meeting house to his left. He turned to go home but then came face-to-face with a little boy. He recognised the familiar face in an instant. Medium straight black hair and powdery blue eyes stared at him. Belarus knew that he was that boy at five years old.

"Why?" the little version of him asked.

Belarus did not understand the question. He saw the boy reach behind him and pull out a foot-long dagger with Persian inscriptions carved into its blade which was encrusted with gold. With tremendous speed, the boy took the dagger and stabbed himself in the heart. Blood splurged out onto the grass. Belarus reached to catch the little falling boy, screaming out, "Bijan! No!"

Belarus leapt upright, unable to breathe. He vomited out air like a cat regurgitating a ball of fur. Gasping in rapid succession, he looked around him in search of the boy, but he was safe in his own bedroom covered by the fur skin Mia had woven together to keep the newlyweds, now one week into their marriage, warm. Belarus fell back into the pillows as he relaxed his tender muscles that struggled with his dream. Ariana was not lying beside him. He spotted a flower trail leading into the living room next door. He smiled at his romantic wife and eagerly jumped from the soft bed and ran to the door with anticipation.

He opened the door, but again confusion set in. The room adjacent to his bedroom was dark and cold. It was a stone chamber Belarus remembered from a long time ago. He heard sniffling coming from a corner. He took the torch that was placed in its holder from the wall in his bedroom and walked farther into the dark room. He saw a small figure with her head down crying and rocking from one side to the other, pulling at an open wound on her left forearm.

"Are you okay?" he asked.

The girl raised her head and pointed fingers at him. It was Mia shaking in the corner, the sides of her mouth foaming and her skin an unnatural shade of grey. She started to scream at him. Belarus was hardly able to understand what she said, but he recognised cuss words streaming out of her mouth in accusation.

Her face started to contort and pull at various angles, and her eyes darkened to red. Her smooth skin then gave way to a day-old beard; a man was staring back at him, his pallor laced with dark veins covering his neck and bare chest. The man laughed at Belarus and still pointed fingers at him like Mia had done. Belarus shrank back, stumbling over the threshold. He hit his head on the stone and blacked out immediately.

Belarus awoke in fright. A scream erupted from his throat as he jerked upright, confused and distressed. His straight black hair stuck to his neck, tangled with sweat. He grabbed his left arm and looked down to inspect his new covenant seal. Belarus stroked the curling lines with his fingers, retracing the pattern and easing his breath into its natural rhythm. Ariana reached from behind and placed her left hand on his arm. She then retraced his seal with gentle fingers while caressing his chest with her right hand. He took her hand and kissed it.

"Be at peace, my love," her words swam over him like a wave of quiet, calming his shattered nerves and luring him closer to her. He turned around to deeply embrace his wife. Ariana placed her hands on his rough face, stroking his beard. Her dark eyes with their familiar golden flecks met his powdery blue ones in the dusk of the morning.

"You are safe here; nothing can harm you. In the love of God and under His wing, you have peace."

The tenderness with which she whispered these words of comfort to him brought him low. These words had never been spoken to his heart, and he was overwhelmed. Emotions mixed with fear, passion, and raw delight flooded his senses as he allowed himself to be entirely released into her embrace. At first he stiffened to Ariana's touch but then felt himself relax under the pressure of her body.

***

Tossing and turning, Mia threw the skins from her; her body was soaked in its own sweat. Mia gently lifted off the thin silk cover, worried that she might have awakened Estoban. He lay still, snoring softly in the dim light. The moon had gone down and shrouded the village in a mystical afterglow.

Mia guessed it must have still been very early in the morning when she made her way to the window. She drew back the thick drapes and stared out to the clearing just to her left. There was no other movement besides the few guards that made their rounds through the village. Mia dressed and covered herself with a coat woven from mohair her father had sent from China on one of his journeys. She loved to receive gifts from her father, but tonight she wished that he was here. She needed his guidance and wisdom.

Estoban stirred. Mia covered his back with the animal skin blanket she had thrown on the floor. A week had passed since her best friend's betrothal, and everyone in the village had returned to their normal activities. All the scouts had returned, including the trading party all the way from the eastern borders of Babylonia. Achaeans had long ago learned to trade their precious produce of oranges, olives, and special oils for spices, a valuable commodity in Achaos.

The season had finally started to turn. Winter was fast approaching, and Mia knew it would be a matter of time before the first snow started to cover the trees. The village was already preparing for the long, frigid winter. The Eurotas River would freeze soon, and passage from Achaos would become impossible. Her father would only be able to return after the spring blossoms appeared.

Mia started to pace back and forth in front of the window. She did not know what was wrong, but something terrible stirred in her spirit. She was unable to pinpoint what was keeping her from her sleep. Mia wasn't used to sleepless nights, and ever since the wedding she had a strange feeling keeping her alert. Her father would have known what to say to relax her; he knew her better than anyone, even Estoban. Mia was not unlike her father.

"You are bold and courageous, my princess," Glaucus would tell her.

"No, you are precious and feminine," her mother Isemene would add, contesting with her father.

She always marvelled at how they wanted to outdo the other complimenting their daughter. Mia loved her mother and missed her terribly when she awoke at night. She had barely been twenty-two when she married Estoban. Her mother tragically died two years later of haemorrhagic fever. Mia fell to her knees and looked outside the window. She did the only thing she knew that would give her peace—she prayed.

***

Estoban jerked awake. He had a sense that something terrible was happening somewhere and that something evil was coming. He reached out for his wife but found the space empty beside him. He sat upright and searched the room for Mia. He found her kneeling beside the window praying and humming a soft melody. He knew then that she felt it too.

He got dressed in a warm tunic and knelt beside her. He slipped her hand into his, not wanting to break her concentration. Yahweh would know what to do. He closed his eyes and started to intercede for their tribe and for his wife.

9

Mia didn't expect another party arriving but was elated to hear news of her father. The men brought a large oak chest with them filled with incredible gifts. Precious oils and spices were placed in the chest, apparently all the way from Macedonia. There were maps and geographical charts for Estoban and many scrolls for the library all the way from Rome.

Mia desperately wanted to see Rome for herself. She kept saying to Estoban that whenever her father returned from his next journey, they would set out for Rome, but that time never came. There had always been more pressing matters at hand.

"This is for you, my lady." The scout handed her a small parcel tied with colourful strips of linen.

As she carefully untied it, a letter fell from the package, and she picked it up. It read: *To my beloved daughter.* Mia carefully opened the letter and walked to the window to read it. The parchment smelled of canola oil, and she wondered where her father had found the paper. It was quite thin and almost transparent; it was rather spectacular.

> *Herione,*
> *Many nights have passed since my departure, and I wish you could have made this journey with me. I am glad that you urged me to still go on this adventure even though I did not want to leave your side after your return from capture. I am delighted to*

hear about your complete recovery and believe that God has a great plan for your life.

I arrived in Rome three days ago. How I wish you could see all the new buildings for yourself. I am sending a parchment with an artist's impression of the Servian Wall, the new defensive barrier being constructed around the city of Rome. It is to be thirty-two feet in height, twelve feet wide at its base, and seven miles long. The wall is named after Rome's sixth king, Servius Tullius. The wall will take months to complete, but I found it tremendously interesting and even considered replicating a similar boundary around Achaos.

I am also including, along with sketches of the construction, a special drawing in full colour of the Porta Esquilina, the first entrance gate to be completed. Amyntas and I entered the city through it. It is spectacular! I hope that you like it. Walking the streets with our guide is tremendously exciting. I have learned so much already.

I look forward to my return and wish you all the best for the coming winter. I wanted to send you a small token to remind you of me during the cold nights. It is called cotton, and the tunic has an added pair of trousers like the Babylonians are accustomed to wearing. It is a wonderful night dress, and I am certain it will keep you warm.

I love you, my precious princess. Send my greetings to our people and my beloved son-in-law.

Keep well my love.

Yours always,

Father

A single tear rolled down her cheek. Mia knew how much her father loved her, and reading her full name in the letterhead made her cry. She was eager to see the new night dress he spoke of. She withdrew a soft white tunic woven with long sleeves from the package. The trousers looked strange and unfamiliar to her, but she decided that they would make quite a funny-looking outfit. She giggled to herself as she tried to figure them out.

The door then suddenly burst open, and Belarus stumbled in followed by a frightened Ariana. He was bleeding from his side, and his face had lost most of its colour.

"What happened?" Mia gasped.

Belarus tried to speak but failed miserably. Ariana was lost for words and could hardly keep away the tears.

"Send out a full search party, and do not return without finding the person responsible," Estoban ordered to his first commander.

"No, they are long gone," Belarus interjected in a husky voice.

"Wait." Estoban held his right hand in the air. His commander waited, organised and ready to go.

"What do you mean they have gone?" Mia urged while trying to have a look at the wound.

"Mia, I don't think it's serious. I just have difficulty breathing," Belarus protested.

The wound was small but bled a lot. The cut was made with precision and was clearly not intended to bring too much harm.

"They told me that they were coming for you, princess," he said.

"For Mia?" Estoban asked. "Who? And why would they?"

"I was unable to sleep last night and decided to walk through the forest like I usually do when I am unsettled. I was attacked by three men in dark cloaks. I couldn't see their faces clearly as the moon had already set for the night. They threatened me and wanted to know who I was. I said nothing, but they saw the marking on my arm and knew I was an Achaean. I tried to get loose when they stabbed me. They told me that Mia escaped from someone, I am not certain who, and that he was coming for her with all he had. They told me to deliver the message and left as quickly as they had arrived. I am certain they were scouting for the village," Belarus said, sounding puzzled.

The rest of the room fell deathly quiet. Belarus evidently didn't know what was going on as he looked from one to the other. Mia was pale and sat back in her chair, and Estoban just reached for her hand and held tight trying to comfort her.

Finally, Ariana told Belarus of Mia's escape from Romulus and the torture she had gone through. It was nearly six months ago, and no-one had been able to find their hidden village to claim revenge until now. Belarus was silent.

"Do you know when they will be here?" Estoban asked Belarus.

"They said three weeks."

"Then we had better be ready. Anticipate the attack and make sure they do not find the exact location of the village," Estoban stated to his commander.

The young man turned immediately, ready to prepare the fighting men for a battle to come. The physician arrived, still dishevelled from his run to the meeting place. He ushered Belarus outside so that he could look at the wound. Belarus was reluctant to leave but accompanied the old man, quickly followed by Ariana.

"Everyone, leave us," Estoban instructed.

Mia sat motionless, holding tightly onto her new present. Her knuckles turned white from the pressure. This was the day she had been dreading for months but knew would eventually come.

"He found me, Estoban," she said in a flat voice.

"Romulus will not touch a hair on your head. I promise. I will kill him before he lays a hand on you again."

"We must respond before he does. His scouts will take time to reach his fortress, but he will be ready to set out with his entire army when they do," she said slowly.

Determination started to grow inside of her. Mia knew that this monster would simply take everything they had and rape and torture all the girls of their tribe without a care in the world.

"I need some time." She stood and walked out the door, leaving Estoban in the room mulling over the threat.

***

Only a day had passed, but it felt like an eternity. Mia finally understood what kept her awake at night. The Lord's Spirit was warning her, as she expected that He would. As soon as she started to pray about the situation, it all became clear.

Mia knew beyond a shadow of a doubt that Yahweh wouldn't just keep quiet and allow His chosen people to perish. His guidance was all that she needed to come to a conclusion on the matter. Against her own will, she had to allow the men to go and fight for their tribe.

Every time Estoban had to go out, she dreaded the outcome but always believed that God had a plan. He again reminded her that this battle was no different. *It is for my Glory,* He told her. Yahweh worked in mysterious ways, and she knew well that His way was not like their way of thinking. God would provide a way, and He would be glorified.

Billowing clouds moved together with fierce lightning, which shrouded the meeting house in darkness. Rivulets rolled from the limestone building as the heavy rains came pouring down in anger. The only light coming from the structure was the glow of firelight from inside.

Five hours delivered no verdict, and Mia was starting to feel agitated with her elders. Jacobien had been as stubborn as she knew he would be. She was reminded of his comments when she returned from her capture. Even then he had been reluctant to prepare the warriors for the onslaught that she expected would follow her escape.

The tribe had been ready, and the men stationed around the clock, but his attack did not follow. Mia could never have imagined that it would take a man like Romulus six months to find her. She had hoped that her father would have returned before the winter snowfall, but his journey had taken longer than expected. Mia paced in front of the table, musing over the challenge that faced her tribe.

"What if it is just another deception?" Jacobien asked.

"Jacobien, how can you say that? This is not some fantasy created by a man stuck in a dark corner, pressed down by defeat," Estoban protested.

"When Princess Mia returned from her capture, our guards were posted day and night for an assault that never came. What makes you think this is any different?" Jacobien inquired.

"Belarus is my friend. I believe his word to be true," Estoban said.

"You hardly know the man, Estoban. Do not be so naïve," Justus mumbled.

The comment stabbed Estoban to the core, and Mia felt it too. How could the elders who have known him as a valiant man doubt his judgement? Estoban was sent out countless times to fight and scout regions unknown to them, and he always returned with a good report. Estoban walked to the window to allow his anger to subdue, and the room was quiet again. Mia could not manage another five-hour debate and made a decision for them.

"Estoban is right, Justus. Belarus will gain absolutely nothing from lying to us. He lost all he had and made a covenant with your brother's daughter. You know the man. He will not betray the trust of his wife," she contested.

Justus bowed his head and thought to himself. When he looked back at Mia, his green eyes shone brightly as if he had received a revelation of sorts. "You are right. I do trust him."

"Am I the only one with reason?" Jacobien threw his hands in the air.

"No, Jacobien. You are the only one who is *afraid*," responded Mia.

The pair stared at each other. Mia was certain that the tense atmosphere could be felt throughout the entire village. Jacobien broke contact and sat back in his chair, breathing heavily. He was an old man, and his body refused sudden action. He had to know very well that Mia was right. They could no longer sit by and wait for the king to return. They had to take action or face the possibility of destruction, not only from their enemy, but from within the council of elders.

"I will submit to my Polemarch," Jacobien sighed.

Mia breathed out slowly and sat down next to the man. She picked up his hand in hers and felt his dry skin move under her palm. Jacobien was pale and hardly sported any hair, and his baldness only emphasised his deep wrinkles. He was still a strong man, but she feared he had lost the convictions he once held as a young warrior.

"Jacobien, I know you are a wise man, and my father would still in his position rather than take your word over anyone else's. I would do the same, but this is not just a random threat from an enemy. Romulus is not your mediocre villain. Our survival depends on our incursion. We must move before they do," Mia said gently.

"We shall delay no longer. Estoban, what do you propose our strategy should be?" Jacobien asked as he walked to the corner of the room and retrieved the scrolls he brought with him.

Jacobien opened the geographical charts and laid them out on the table. They all huddled together as Estoban described his plan with expertise and precision. Mia marvelled at her husband. He was a great warrior, and his strategies resulted in success every time. After another two hours, they all agreed in a unanimous vote that the soldiers would set out by week's end.

"Summon the village. Tonight, we prepare for war!" Jacobien shouted.

"May Yahweh guide you and lead you through this time, my fair maiden." Justus bowed before Mia and gave her an assuring hug before he left the chamber to call for the assembly.

The remaining three discussed further practical applications to assure success on the battlefield.

Bright sunlight kissed her cheek as Mia stepped out onto the makeshift podium and steadied herself for the announcement. The last time she stood like this before the entire village was after her recovery. That was a happy moment, unlike today. Every member of the tribe was summoned and knew that this announcement would change their fate.

Mia was dressed in a simple brown tunic with her hair pinned into a bunch. *To camouflage in the woods is to survive,* her father had taught her. Today they had to be alert, looking out for one another. She was looking at the tribe and sensed the atmosphere change from excitement to disappointment. They all knew what her outfit symbolised, and some even bowed their heads in defeat.

"I know that you are all disappointed and rather expected to hear great news from Rome. Glaucus Solon of Achaos sends his greetings to all and looks forward to his return. They've had a successful journey and enjoyed many celebratory nights with Amyntas I of Athens. But today I bring grave news. It is with sadness and grief that I summon all the fighting to account." Mia stood tall, expecting the crowd to stir in response.

The crowd gasped, seemingly waiting for her to announce that it was all a joke. Estoban and the elders looked out at the people but remained silent.

"Romulus the Great has threatened our village not only with battle but with annihilation. He wishes to see all who serve Yahweh destroyed. It is this same selfish man from whom I had narrowly escaped with my life not more than six months ago. My father met him as a youth, and he had barely evaded death then. Romulus is not a man of courage or integrity. Wherever he goes, blood and death follow in his wake. Belarus himself was the sole survivor in one of his raids. We cannot allow this man who has defected from his own people to destroy ours." She looked at Belarus and returned his nod of agreement.

The people murmured.

***

Ariana held Belarus' hand as he started to shake. She knew him as a strong man but had difficulty understanding why certain events made him shy away from his courage. He ascribed it to Romulus. The man not only abducted her best friend but had destroyed all her husband held dear. If it were she, she would have pinned him down and killed him without a sense of remorse.

***

"As acting Polemarch of Achaos, the elders and I have decided that every man of fighting ability will set out by week's end to battle. Our scouts have given us the exact location of the keep, and our army will set out immediately to confront our enemy before they reach our borders." Mia swallowed hard before she made her next statement. "It is with reluctance that I announce that all the young men between fifteen and eighteen who have started their training will be commissioned to go out along with the others."

The people screamed in protest, and Mia understood that this was not an easy burden to bear. She had many friends who had but one son, and they would now face death long before their time.

Justus stamped his cane on the platform, calling for order. "Let the Polemarch finish."

Screams quietened down into a hushed murmur. Mia had lost all focus and wanted to cry along with the mothers and wives. She held her head high and continued.

90

"I know that this is hard for everyone, but we need all the hands we can get. Romulus was once upon a time a great Persian general, and his men will kill anything that moves. We are confident that our strategies of war are far superior to those of the Persians; success will follow. A handful of our best scouts and older men will stay behind to protect the village. Yahweh will protect you, but I implore you, prepare for a difficult battle." Mia bowed her head and stepped back for Estoban to take centre stage.

"Men, report to your stations. Your battalion leader will be ready with further instructions. All the young men not yet assigned to a regiment, meet Belarus by the main practice ring to receive your orders." Estoban saluted the crowd, and all the men raised their arms in agreement, ready for the battle that awaited them.

10

Romulus stared blankly at the palm of his hand. The circular pattern etched into his skin had started to bleed at the edges. The cut had to be treated with an antibacterial ointment made by his alchemist. Romulus despised the man more than most but regarded him with a sense of awe and wonderment.

Rosenduz lacked the capacity to battle but never disappointed Romulus with special trickery; he had saved Romulus' life on many occasions, and the fact that the magic resurrected a certain power in the man was not lost on Romulus. He regarded him closely and never allowed the man to leave the keep without proper escort.

Rosenduz retrieved most of his herbs and other properties for medicinal purposes from the forests around the keep and rarely made his way to the great city of Athens to acquire special items for his potions. His frail body seemed a hundred years old, but Romulus knew better. The man was barely ten years his senior and already looked like an old man. For sixty-five, he was sickly and weak.

His eyes, however, conveyed quite the opposite. Dark pupils were rimmed with gold like the eyes of an eagle. He adorned his pale skin with almond oil that kept the flexibility in the tissue firm. His teeth were all missing, the result of a pleasant torture session for practising black magic in the king's court.

Cambyses II had dismissed Rosenduz just like he dismissed Romulus when he took the place of his father, Cyrus the Great, on the throne. They were but filth in the eyes of the new king, aiming to destroy and take the rightful place of the king away from him. Romulus was trouble, and Cambyses foresaw that. Rosenduz was quick to run after Romulus when he defected from the armies of mighty Persia, a triumphant moment that Romulus had not forgotten.

***

Rosenduz moved quickly, not wanting to increase his emperor's temper. He was a head shorter than Romulus, but he was smarter. Rosenduz knew the Aveston that plagued his master. It was a spirit longing for more blood than was able to quench it. Romulus had grown in power and strength, but Rosenduz believed he lacked conviction.

Ever since the escape of Mia, the crown princess of Achaos, Romulus had become consumed with hatred like Rosenduz had never seen, and Rosenduz believed this would be the key to his undoing. Romulus grunted as Rosenduz applied the salve to his palm. The blood started to coagulate when the pungent mixture met raw flesh. Rosenduz quickly covered the wound with bay leaves and a woven glove made from fox hair to keep the leaves in place.

"Three days, my lord, and your hand will be healed." Rosenduz bowed low, letting his grey hair fall over his face.

"Remove your hair from your face so I can look into your eyes," Romulus ordered.

Rosenduz raised his head and combed his thin hair back, revealing deep scars that resembled the cat-o-nine tails that slashed his cheeks and forehead into several deep cuts. He recalled the time he attempted to place a curse on Romulus. The emperor had personally reprimanded him and now enjoyed seeing the benevolent alchemist squirm under his authority. Since then, the old man kept to himself, revealing his secrets to no one but Romulus.

"We are to set out to a great battle. Be prepared and have your medicines ready for the fallen," Romulus said, still looking in the man's eyes. He raised his treated hand and nodded in thanks.

"Yes, my liege. I will be ready." Rosenduz smiled.

***

Valah paced the hallway in front of the emperor's chamber. They returned this morning to the keep, and a great banquet awaited the men tonight in honour of their conquests of the northern territory of Africa and the spoils that they brought back with them.

Their three-week rampage stretched into a two-month rally. *The gold of Egypt is worth losing men*, Romulus had told him. Hundreds of men had lost their lives in the wake of Romulus' greed; mighty men from every regiment fell and bled in the deserts of Africa. Valah failed to understand why.

The Aveston was hungry for power, but to lose men in battles that bore no significance was still a mystery to him. Valah might have sworn an allegiance to Romulus, but he would much rather serve in the royal guard of Cambyses II, king of mighty Persia. If only his beliefs did not deter him from service. The thought quickly left him as the door to the chamber opened. A man Valah knew well exited the room. The old, skinny man inspected him with uncertainty, his red cape drawn over his small head.

"Valah," he sniggered.

"Rosenduz." Valah could not make eye contact for longer than a fragment of time with the scheming alchemist. He failed to see why Romulus had kept the man alive and in service. Countless times, Rosenduz was caught trying to foil the plans of his emperor. Romulus knew of but one incident and only maimed the man instead of killing the deserter.

Valah gazed at the man's feet. Rosenduz wore no shoes, and his toes bore large calluses. His fingers looked the same, and Valah wondered if his whole body was covered. Valah waited patiently for the man to walk away before he entered the chamber, fearing that he might spy on the discussion to be held.

Rosenduz sucked mucus from his throat and spat it to the side. The vile act disgusted Valah. The man was dirty, and cleanliness was of high regard to Valah. Rosenduz seemed to float away as if he was carried by unseen hands. Shaking off the image, Valah knocked and entered his emperor's chamber.

Romulus waited patiently for Valah to kneel before he spoke.

"Has Rosenduz retreated to his chamber?" Romulus whispered.

"I believe he has, my lord." Valah remained on his knees until Romulus ushered him to be at ease.

"I would like to commend you on your excellent service, Valah. I am well pleased by the weight of gold, fine silks, and ornaments we retrieved from our enemies. I expected the Egyptian Empire to be more robust. I cannot imagine how an entire empire with such weak convictions ruled the ancient world. Had they done but one thing right, I would not have had this thorn in my side," he scoffed.

"What do you mean, sire?" Valah probed.

"The destruction of the Jewish nation, Valah; they should have been annihilated then when they were under slavery to Pharaoh," Romulus exclaimed with vigour.

Valah swallowed hard as he tried to imagine the genocide of an entire race. *Would something like that ever happen?* He sat pondering the thought when Romulus nudged him. He jerked his head around to look at his emperor. Romulus held something in his hand.

Valah stepped closer to inspect the object but knew what it was before he came close enough to see it in full. Blood tainted the red dagger and stained the white cloth in which it lay. The dagger was only to be used during sacrifice, and Valah wondered whose fate befell in the act of worship.

"The scouts brought my sacrificial dagger to me. The blood on its blade is that of our enemy. A warrior of Achaos attacked at night. We have found the village," Romulus exclaimed, eyes shining brightly.

Valah stared at the dagger for a moment. It made perfect sense. His emperor had waited his entire life to bring Glaucus Solon, King of Achaos to account. Their rough encounter so many years ago had driven Romulus insane. The thought of discovering the secret location of one's lifelong enemy was indeed a moment to celebrate.

Without hesitation, Valah turned to the door and quickly gave orders to bring their finest sack of wine. Tonight, they would recline and laugh about their conquests, and in the morning they would prepare for war.

Romulus and Valah sat opposite one another enjoying the late afternoon sun. Fragrant candles were lit, and the wine flowed freely. The two men spoke mainly about the battle to come and never discussed the spoil that would be retrieved. Valah knew that Romulus would have his princess and he shall have any woman he so chooses. Mia was a beautiful woman, and he was assured that the maidens of her tribe would be as radiant as she.

"We will set out at daybreak," Romulus ordered Valah.

"Daybreak?" Valah was not expecting Romulus to set out immediately. "Sir, with all due respect, my men are tired and worn out. I do not think it wise to set out immediately."

"They will have the evening to rest, but by morning all the horses will be ready to depart," Romulus restated.

"Sir, I beg you. Two days at the least. Your men are valiant, but they need to recover. A few good nights' sleep back in the comfort of their own homes will do them good."

"No, Valah. Do you think Glaucus would let the threat go with a flick of his wrist?"

Valah gazed at the sunset and hoped it would not be his last. Romulus rose to his feet and walked towards Valah. He threw his glass of wine on the floor. The crashing glass made Valah freeze. The man he feared more than death was standing right behind him.

***

Romulus studied Valah for a moment. The man was strong and built like an ox and was by far a better warrior than Romulus himself. What puzzled Romulus was Valah's need for cleanliness. Standing behind him, he could smell the sweet scent of orange blossom.

They had been back for three hours, and the man was bathed, shaved, and even sported a cropped haircut. Most of the men didn't bathe for the entire journey, but Valah was different. Romulus didn't even prefer his women as clean as he was. What an interesting thought. Romulus bent down and whispered into Valah's ear, threatening him with a tight grip on his shoulders.

"Glaucus would have set out by week's end. He would not rest until the last threat to his daughter's life was eradicated. Family is a weakness, Valah. Never allow a miscreant like a daughter to spoil your lust for war."

Romulus released his grip and felt Valah breathe, slowly contemplating his precarious position. Valah remained seated and pretended to look at the sunset, enjoying his wine. Romulus knew that it was a pretence. He walked to the window and closed the thick drapes, engulfing them in candlelight.

"Sir, I have one question and then I will do as you please," Valah motioned.

"Yes?"

"I agree that if it was I, my horse would reach our perimeter by week's end. Sir, for fifteen years we could not find them, and every journey we set out on took us right past their perimeter and we never knew. I am not certain of their incapability. Are you? Your army is tired and not to mention the loss of a substantial regiment. What confidence do you have that we will win?"

Romulus studied him for a moment. His first commander was a brave man. To question Romulus' motives and authority directly after a threat upon his life was indeed a bold move. Romulus took the sacrificial dagger from the side table and handed it to Valah.

"You see the blood on that blade?" he asked.

"Yes I do, my lord," Valah said plainly, not wanting to hold onto the weapon.

"That assures me that they are not expecting anyone. The threat will have them in chaos. For a group of people tucked away in a valley, they are not skilled in warfare. How can an army rise from the valley floor and defeat the mighty Persians? We have proved that we are the stronger and wiser warriors. The Aveston reassured me that every drop of blood spilled will be that of our enemy. I am confident and believe we will have victory over the followers of Yahweh. If you are not with us, you are welcome to stay behind and rot in the dungeons below." Romulus eyeballed Valah.

Valah simply nodded and poured his emperor another glass of wine. "Tomorrow, we will ride to battle."

11

Light flooded through the open windows facing to the south. The autumn sun was fading in its strength, yet its warmth spread around the room. The well-lit house, with the sun glaring inside, was now dark and sombre as if the walls had absorbed all the joy that entered the room.

Ariana watched Belarus as he prepared his knapsack for the journey. Glaucus Solon instituted the year of celebration to all men who recently married, which meant they were able to abstain from war for a whole year to enjoy the wedding union and grow with their wives. Belarus loved his wife, but he refused to stay for the year of celebration.

"What good is a new marriage if we are not able to stay together for more than a few weeks?" Ariana pressed.

War and conquest were never a month's affair; they always stretched beyond expectation and tight schedules never realised under the circumstances, but Belarus didn't want to remind his new bride of this fact.

"I will be back in a matter of days, my love." He tried to console her with a smile.

"I still don't understand why you cannot stay and make use of the year of celebration?" Ariana swallowed her tears of frustration and started to pace around the room.

Belarus looked at his beautiful wife pacing like a child spinning in a tantrum. How could he explain to her the workings of a man's heart? He needed to go. Estoban relied on him, and the mere thought of staying behind while the other men fought for glory was too much for him to bear. Estoban had trained him well. Three months prepared him for this battle, and he was not about to let the men he came to trust fight alone.

He walked to her and made her halt by the door. Belarus took her hands in his and looked into her brown eyes, their sparkle spent. Full lips pressed into an unwarranted grin, and her dark eyebrows were arched higher than normal. Belarus loved this woman; even her angry faces were attractive. He started to tickle her and knew very well that she loved to tease him.

"Belarus, this is not the time," she scoffed.

"Come on, give me a little smile." He pouted sadly, continuing to taunt and tickle her.

"I am being very serious." Ariana tried to keep her frown but found it hard not to laugh.

Her sharp features bunched together in a controlled temper. Belarus was on the verge of letting it go when she fumed. Laughter broke the silence, and she ran into the corner trying to breathe in between laughing fits. He rushed at her and tickled her onto the floor. He sat with his legs spread on top of her, pinning her body to the ground. Holding her hands together, he tickled her thighs. She was unable to move, and he knew exactly where her most ticklish spots were.

"Stop it, I beg you!" she screamed loudly. Her laughter became a cough, for her breath evaded her.

Belarus let go of her hands and let her breathe for a moment. When she regained her focus, he bent over her, hovering just about an inch above her. His eyes searched her face. Tears streaked down her cheek. He gently wiped away the moisture and kissed her full lips, his stomach ablaze with love and desire all mixed into one.

"I love you, my princess. I am sorry to leave you, but please, I beg of you, remember how much I've loved you. Ever since the first day I saw your face, long legs, and cute, curvy body, I knew."

She shoved him a little in surprise to his comment about her body. He knew she secretly enjoyed the fact that he enjoyed her so much. His powdery blue eyes conveyed nothing but the truth. He struggled to find the right words, so she simply placed her finger on his lips and ended the conversation for him.

"You will come back to me no matter how or when or where. You will fight like the valiant man that you are. I love you, Belarus. I am yours and you are mine forever. I will fight for you until the day I die. I set you as a seal upon my heart, as a seal upon my arm." She held onto his left arm, and he realised that she was placing hers next to his.

He blushed and remembered the day he made the vow to love her. Her brown curls were bunched together looking like a lion's mane. She tried to comb them back into order, but Belarus just shuffled them back in disarray. They looked at each other for a long time. They were in love, and the passion between husband and wife was almost tangible. She silently walked to the bed and started to fold his garments in small rolls, ready for him to place them in his knapsack. They moved as one, preparing Belarus for the day ahead.

***

Mia laid out a plain tunic along with Estoban's waist girdle, leather sandals, and short cloak for warmth. The armour was plain, but Mia knew the importance of each piece. They provided little warmth, but the placement covered all major body parts.

Mia lifted the bronze chest plate and rubbed off some polish still left in the small crevices of the carvings. She admired the men who made each and every breastplate with precision and expertise. The carvings were done by hand, and each inscription represented the armour of Yahweh, as it is written in the scrolls: *Take unto you the whole armour of God that you may be able to withstand in the evil day.*

Centred on the breastplate was a circle, its edges interwoven by small vines of ivy. The name of Yahweh was gently gilded in gold, shimmering in the sunlight. The circle was surrounded by six inscriptions written in ancient Greek. In a circular pattern, the following words were etched into the bronze with bold letters: Faith, Peace, Salvation, Truth, Righteousness, and Spirit—the word of God. The breastplate was fastened by small metal clips attached to strong leather straps. Achaeans were known for their stylish tunics and intricate armour and wore it with pride.

***

Estoban came out of the small bathing room to see Mia staring in wonderment at his breastplate, her fingers stroking each word as she silently prayed. Her husband was about to go into a brutal battle with no assurance that he would return, yet she awaited him, ready to assist with his armour.

She neatly laid out his clothing beside his knapsack and weapons on the bed. He admired her for her strength; most women would cry and plead for their husbands to keep to the back of the battle. As leader of the regiment, Estoban had the privilege to do just that.

He knew that Mia understood the risk of fighting in the front-line, and not once did she ever try to persuade him to be fighting in any other place than he was comfortable with. Estoban walked towards her, and she quickly placed his breastplate next to his tunic. She remained silent and only smiled at him. He could see the admiration in her eyes, and he was thankful to be sharing his life with a woman who revered and respected him.

Estoban placed the towel on the side table and stood still as Mia approached him. She caressed his chest and placed her head on his shoulder. He put his arms around her and squeezed lightly. She hugged him with all her strength, and Estoban felt her tense. He smoothed her hair and held onto her for what seemed like an eternity.

The smell of orange blossoms filled his nostrils as he breathed in the scent of her hair. She was dressed in his favourite green tunic; embroidered along the seams with fine silver thread was the name of her beloved. She gazed into his eyes, and his heart wanted to explode. Estoban loved his wife and could hardly wait for his return to be united with her again.

Mia released Estoban from her embrace and handed him his undergarment followed by his tunic. Lacing up his leather sandals, she gently kissed his feet, his knees, and his hands. This show of affection was one of many reasons why Estoban admired her.

She was a royal princess, and yet she bowed down like a servant to assist him. Her humility made him feel like a valiant warrior. Estoban tied thin strips of material around his hands and wrists followed by metal coverings to protect his forearms. The metal covered his covenant mark and all major arteries that were so easily damaged in a fight.

Estoban's wrist coverings were engraved with ivy leaves, their vines curling along the metal edges. Estoban held the breastplate in place as Mia quickly closed the clasps under his arms and back. A single bronze plate polished to perfection was tied to his back. Mia clipped his small cloak in place on his left shoulder, allowing his right hand freedom. Estoban fastened his belt holding his scabbard in place.

Mia held out his sword to him but didn't let go until she studied the blade for any imperfections. She had designed the sword for him, and it was forged not more than three days ago. Etched into the blade were words written in gold—the spirit of Yahweh. Estoban studied her and smiled.

"I love you, Mia. I will return soon," he reassured her.

Mia released the sword into Estoban's hands. He then sheathed the sword and dagger, picked up his shield, and studied the work he had done on it. Most of the markings remained, and it showed its scars to the world. Many battles had been won and lost with this shield by his side. It was a gift from Glaucus Solon, and Estoban regarded it as a special addition to his armour.

**

Mia studied Estoban. He was a brave man that would fight to the death for his men. She regarded this noble quality and felt a sense of awe as she watched him. He was fast and very skilled. Mia didn't fear for his life; it was in the hands of God, and her creator would be made known through the valiant efforts of the men of Achaos.

"I love you, Estoban." Mia bowed and kissed the palm of his right hand. "Let this hand not shed innocent blood but defend the righteous and the needy."

"It will be done, my beloved." He placed his hand on her cheek and bid her to stand. Her blue eyes shone wildly as he embraced his wife in a passionate kiss.

**

The village stirred. The streets were vacant, but the men were preparing for battle and the atmosphere felt alive. Battle was not only imminent but tangible. Tensions in the barracks were surprisingly serene. Young warriors received their armour and bragged to one another about their shields, each carrying a personalised message to the enemy. Laughter echoed through the halls.

Belarus smiled at the enthusiasm he saw around him. He knew that this was where he belonged and looked forward to the battle. Estoban was a valiant leader, and it was his privilege to fight beside a man such as him. The task ahead carried its own burden, but Belarus believed that his reward would be more than satisfactory.

Belarus could just about see his covenant mark sticking out under the wrist guards, and he smiled. He loved his wife, and he would carry her image with him to his death. The brightness of the light blinded him as he came out of the building. The barracks were busy in a flurry of activity.

Horses were saddled and straddled with protective armour unlike anything he had ever seen. Belarus marvelled at the intricate joints around each protective plate. The ingenuity of Achaos still surprised him from time to time. He longed to have spent more time learning about their ways and battle plans, but time was not in his favour.

The call to arms came sooner than he expected. Belarus turned the corner to see Karabo saddle his horse. The tall black man intrigued Belarus. He had enjoyed many conversations with the man from the south and had found his knowledge invaluable.

Karabo looked right at Belarus, making him slightly uncomfortable. It felt as though he could see right through him and unravel his fears, wants, and dreams. Belarus shrugged off the thought and gave a slight nod. The man then returned his greeting and refocused on saddling his pale horse.

"Belarus!" He heard his name being shouted over and over before spotting Eugo.

"Belarus, look how handsome I am!" Eugo posed in front of Belarus with his sword held high, pretending to fend off a blow from an enemy.

"You would make a great statue for the courts of Achaos," Belarus laughed.

"That's not funny," Eugo smirked.

Belarus grabbed him by the neck and ruffled his curly hair. His dimples sank even deeper into his cheek as he laughed at his friend. Belarus studied Eugo's shield and commended him for the craftsmanship. Eugo beamed and hugged him tight.

"I will follow you, my liege, and by nightfall we shall have a feast of victory!" Eugo sprinted towards his friends and left Belarus standing in the middle of chaos and preparing mentally for the fight ahead.

***

Nathanial's face disappeared in the fiery curls of his wife. His morning stew was filled with his favourite spice, and the smell of pepper still clung to her hair. Despite his need to fight, today felt somewhat peculiar, as if a strong force yielded calamity.

"Are you alright?" Meriba asked.

"Yes, my love, the jitters that's all." Nathanial gave her a crooked smile.

Meriba hugged him again, and his heart settled. There was nothing to fear. He fought the soldiers of mighty Pharaoh and discovered new lands and peoples; why would a single battle be any different? Nathanial whispered a prayer together with his wife.

"May Yahweh protect you and His will be done," she ended the prayer.

***

Karabo waited patiently for Nathanial to say his farewell to his wife. Estoban walked up to Karabo and looked in the same direction he was.

"They are a beautiful couple," Estoban said.

"Yes, sir, they are a great inspiration and example of the love Yahweh has for us," Karabo stated.

"Karabo, it was an honour to meet you, but I cannot expect you to fight with us," Estoban interjected. "You are a foreigner among us, and it wouldn't be right to expect you to fight on our behalf. You are our guest and I bid you farewell. Go home and be at peace."

"My liege, I will fight next to my kinsman until my debt is repaid. I will fight, and it would be my honour." Karabo bowed low, submitting his life to the tribe of Achaos.

"May Yahweh protect you," Estoban said as he shook the man's hand. Karabo was strong and valiant. It would be a great asset to have a mighty warrior like this man by their side.

"In the end, God will receive the honour and the praise; glory to His name," Karabo motioned.

"Glory to His name." Estoban echoed his cry.

***

Nathanial and Meriba walked hand in hand down the narrow street towards the barracks, readying for the final procession. Karabo marched to their left, and William accompanied by his betrothed, Emelia, walked to their right.

Flower petals filled the air as confetti came down on the couple. It reminded Nathanial of his wedding day. Meriba with her wildly frizzy red hair was the most beautiful bride he had ever seen. White and red petals flew about her face as she slowly walked towards the clearing waiting to become his wife. Nathanial again hugged Meriba and kissed her passionately. She whispered something in his ear that made him blush. The others nudged him, pressing the message from him, but Nathanial could only smile and reply, "It is not for the virgin ear to hear, but alas, your moments of passion will arise from the ashes of your dreams soon enough."

Meriba and Emelia stood hand in hand as their heroes mounted their well-groomed brown horses and waved them goodbye as they joined the procession, falling into their battalions. They were good friends, and Nathanial knew that Meriba would be the one to encourage Emelia when they were away. His wife was a bold counsellor and carried burdens easily. Meriba was the one woman he knew would wait and fight till the day they met again.

The singers marched in front while playing their instruments. The joyous noise could be heard through the entire village. They were followed by Estoban and Belarus each riding a white stallion, bred for battle. Each regiment carried colourful flags. The men held their heads high.

The latest recruits remained protected in the middle flank. Eugo waved at Danelle and his mother as he passed by his house. Eve remained sad to see her son and her husband depart but knew well that they were not just fighting to win but for the promise of freedom.

She smiled at herself and returned the wave to her ecstatic son. Demetrius waved her a kiss as he pulled Eugo back in line. *'O, how she loved them.'* Eve pulled tight the necklace Demetrius gave them on their wedding night. She carried the symbol of their union not only on her forearm but also around her neck, close to the beating of her heart.

Flower petals were thrown from the homes high up in the trees as the men passed through the village. The crowd cheered and acknowledged their warriors as they were enveloped in floral confetti. This celebration was one of good fortune and a blessing to the men who might not return to their loved ones. Not a single tear was wasted in mourning, but instead they were tears of joy.

A total of 534 men rode out on horseback followed by another 481 on foot. The great celebration was an honourable tribute to all the fighting men, including the new young recruits. Fear was absent from their eyes; they were proud to carry the armour of legend following a leader of renown.

Estoban enjoyed many such processions before battle and remembered well his first. He was so excited and could hardly contain his joy. His father marched by his side, and never once did he allow an enemy to overpower him. Estoban admired his father and wished he could once again march alongside him. Claudius fell by Estoban's side when he was but twenty-two.

Today Estoban would honour that legacy by staying true to his father and never allowing Belarus out of his sight. His life was far more precious than spilled blood. He made a vow to Glaucus, King of Achaos, that he would fight to the death to save his people, keeping evil from running rampant in the village.

Silence closed in around Ariana. The village quietened down as the last men and horses disappeared from their sight. Only a few scouts remained along with the elders. She imagined the worst, and despite the preparation and celebrations, she still feared for her husband's life.

Belarus was not skilled like the others, and she knew him well enough to know that he would not back down from a fight. Tears streaked down her face as she looked to the village, bereft of its men, for tonight would be a lonely night.

12

Mia lay awake listening to the wind screeching between the trees, almost like it was complaining about the oncoming winter. She imagined the soft singing of the men marching towards her tormentor's keep, but she knew that it would be impossible to hear.

It had been two days, and Mia knew that it would be one more before any battle would ensue. Hope lingered in her mind, but the reality of spilled blood still plagued her sleep. Ariana lay still beside her. Mia was her only comfort, and, as was custom in time of battle, homes along the perimeter were evacuated and the tribe members stayed close to the clearing, securing unity in case a trap was laid and the village infiltrated.

Mia stroked Ariana's soft, pale cheek and prayed silently for the men trudging to the fight.

***

Belarus sat quietly at his post overlooking the valley far down below. He couldn't remember the last time the night air was so crisp and the sky so clear. Wrestling inside of him, fear overpowered hope. *What is Ariana doing? Is she safe? Will I see her again?* The thoughts all contended for his attention while his eyes examined the forest surrounding him, looking for any sign of scouts or intruders.

The camp stirred as sunlight approached. Today they would march down to the valley below, and Belarus would face his fate. Whether victory on the field or in the heart was foreseeable, he did not know. All he ever lived for and trusted would this day be put to the test, coming face to face with his adversary. The demons that plagued him in the night would no longer be put aside but challenged through the blood and courage of the men standing next to him. Achaos was now his home, and he would defend it to the very end.

A twig snapped behind him. Turning, he slipped his dagger from its sheath, pointing the weapon towards his attacker.

"Don't! It's me, Eugo!" the boy yelled.

"Never ever sneak up behind someone on a lookout," Belarus reprimanded him.

"I am sorry." Eugo stood still, not quite knowing what to do next.

Belarus felt his unease and relaxed his shoulders, placing the dagger back in its scabbard.

"There are so many things you have yet to learn, young Eugo," he shrugged.

"I didn't mean to sneak up on you." Eugo sat beside him, handing him a mug of steaming liquid. "Coffee for the tired warrior."

Belarus still couldn't stomach the brown liquid the villagers seem to love. He never thought that a roasted bean could taste of anything, but the bitter, strong liquid did have a strange effect of rejuvenation, and he appreciated the offer from Eugo. They sat silently sipping the hot drink. Its warmth filled Belarus' body, and he strangely delighted the feeling even though it came with such a terrible taste.

"Did you sleep?" he asked Eugo.

"Not at all; I kept lying awake wondering what it would feel like to lose a limb or to be stabbed." Eugo stared ahead wide-eyed, smelling his coffee.

"Well, I cannot say what it feels like to lose a limb, but to be stabbed is not a pleasant thing. The warm blood oozing from the wound is quite strange. I think it is more the thought than the feeling. Your adrenaline is pumping so hard you cannot feel a thing, only the blood." Belarus looked at Eugo, waiting for a response, but Eugo's eyes remained focused on the horizon as if he was looking for something.

"What are you looking for, Eugo?" he nudged.

"I don't see them today." Eugo seemed stressed.

"Who?" Belarus asked.

"The armies of God."

Belarus had no idea what he meant but respected his thoughts, so he let him be. The trumpet then sounded, signalling their departure. Eugo jerked upright, messing coffee on his tunic.

"Are you afraid, Eugo?" Belarus attempted a last question. He remembered well how terrified he was before his first rough encounter. It might not have been a full battle, but it remained terrifying.

"No. God is with me, and I fear not for my life. It is in God's hands. But I do fear for *you*. You do not yet know Him, and that saddens my heart." Eugo stood tall, and Belarus could see the courage in his eyes.

He didn't understand Eugo's remark and brushed off the fear that swelled inside his heart.

"May Yahweh protect you, Belarus." Eugo stretched out his arm, waiting to embrace him.

"May Yahweh protect you, Eugo." Belarus grabbed the boy and hugged him tight.

***

The cleft in his upper lip twisted with each breath. Dry skin started to flake as the wind tugged at his face. The black stallion stirred beneath him, its long hair blowing in the wind. Romulus' braided dreadlocks kept pushing his helmet from his head. Screaming in frustration, he ripped the helmet off and flung it at his servant.

"Bigger! Make it bigger and hurry! The light is approaching!" he ordered.

The Persian army blended into the tree line. Archers and foot soldiers surrounded the eastern perimeter of the clearing. Valah had secured the area, and his scouts returned with great news. The army of Achaos approached the clearing, and with singing nonetheless.

They were certainly brave or stupid enough to be heard a mile away. Romulus had never faced an army so bold or so arrogant in his entire life. He heard the singing faintly before it disappeared in the strong winds.

The horses stirred violently around him, snorting loudly. Romulus prayed aloud for all his men to hear, calling in the name of his mighty Aveston. The men bowed their heads and prayed silently as their general repeated the same incantations over and over. Valah sat next to Romulus, steadying his horse.

***

The harder his emperor prayed, the more his horse trembled. It was filled with fear, and Valah was no stranger to that. The previous night, in a dream, he was transported into a world he had never seen before.

A man with large horns and a spotted body screamed in anguish. Valah was uncertain if it was due to pain or elation. Spittle flew from his mouth and foam started to form in its corners. Valah felt a strong pressure pulling him down onto his knees. Hot breath from the man's mouth scorched his neck, and shivers ran down his spine.

He was terrified and wanted to run, but his limbs failed him miserably. Tears spilled from his eyes—blood red. A sharp pain ripped through his body as the man ripped his neck from his shoulders, flinging Valah into consciousness.

When he awoke, his tent was dark and malodorous, as if someone had unleashed sulphuric acid into his room. It was the same aroma that now reeked off Romulus. Valah held his breath and stilled his horse as the incantations stopped abruptly. As soon as the prayers were complete, the smell evaporated as if it was never there.

A light flickered in the tree line right opposite him, and gold shimmered in the rising sun, blinding him momentarily. The valley was blood red as if the battle had long been fought and lost. The sight of the red waters unnerved Valah. He wondered if anyone else saw the blood glimmering on the valley floor.

"Yahweh!" He heard the scream from behind them.

Valah was unable to turn his horse around as arrows flew right beside his head, leaving a thin trail of air swishing beside his ears. He had no other way to go but forward, propelling himself over his own archers and foot soldiers. Rows of cavalry shot forward, trampling men underfoot. Valah looked to see Romulus spur his horse towards the open clearing.

The man was indeed madder than Valah had anticipated. He followed suit, squashing men that were screaming for escape. His dark horse jumped high over the spikes meant for their enemies. He rounded the black stallion of his emperor, looking for more arrows heading in their direction.

The woods were quiet except for the fallen men flailing in the tree line. Suddenly a ball of fire flew from their own defences, lighting a fire circle neatly drenched in tar around the perimeter. Horses ran in random directions trying to flee the fire that attacked them.

Valah watched in amazement as his men were set alight, their skin burning. They ripped their armour from their bodies trying to rid themselves of the fire, but they only unarmed themselves for the arrows that penetrated their exposed bodies.

A wall of soldiers surrounded Valah and his emperor, shields held high in defence blocking off the arrows that still penetrated the weaknesses in their armour. Perfectly aimed arrows cut through the opening in between the breastplates and shoulder guards, penetrating deep into the heart.

Men fell from their horses with their own animals crushing them underfoot. Not a single horse was injured, and Valah failed to comprehend what was happening to them. An entire legion fell within a moment.

A hundred men must have been either crushed by horses or shot and burned. The only sound around Valah was that of burning trees and grass; the brightness of the flames burned his eyes. No more arrows or spears penetrated the fiery defence. He couldn't explain how his men were surprised and killed so quickly.

It was as if the entire battle plan turned in on itself and killed its own. Valah looked towards Romulus who patiently waited out the flames, ready to kill anything in his path. His black eyes glowed like two embers in the firelight, and the deep folds in his skin emphasised his large nose and thin lips.

The image was not unfamiliar to Valah, but he didn't expect the man in his dreams would be the spitting image of his emperor. All that Romulus lacked were horns and spots on his body, although his many scars might as well have been demonic spots.

***

Smoke filled the valley below. Estoban ran towards the outcrop of limestone offering a great vantage point the enemy had missed. This was the same outcropping his wife would dive from towards the water below. He smiled at the thought.

Two waves of strategic fighters surrounded the Persian army and bellowed frightful screams from behind, creating chaos and confusion. The men responded just as Estoban had thought they would. Romulus failed to protect his back. The careful grave Romulus had dug up in the valley for days was not a secret to the Achaean forces.

Estoban anticipated the battle plan, which he had to admit was a good one. Elias returned with good news as the second attack was about to begin. Estoban was confident that his scout was the best he had ever seen. He was proud to be an Achaean and diligently followed his orders.

"I estimate they have lost over 139 men—mostly those on foot—and at least a dozen horsemen," Elias reported.

"Have they taken the bait?" Estoban wanted to know.

"Yes, sir. They are making their way towards the lake's edge." Elias saluted his general and disappeared as quietly as he arrived.

Estoban waved at the men wallowing in the lake, their armour tied down with rocks to remain hidden in the shallows. He and Belarus watched as the men made their way deeper into the water armed with thin reeds. Belarus had expressed his doubts about this plan but ultimately chose not to question Estoban.

"Why do you do it?" Belarus asked, lying next to Estoban on the thin slab of rock.

"Diversion," Estoban said. "I learned quickly to divide my enemy and in so doing purge them when they least expect it."

"And you think it will work again?" he asked.

Estoban studied the man beside him. Belarus had many questions, and Estoban wished he could teach him more tricks, but there was no more time. He simply nodded and waited for the first men to breach the tree line. Twenty-five men dove down into the water, dirtied by mud and moss. Thin reeds protruding from the water were the only thing Estoban and Belarus could see. Belarus had been certain that some would give away their position with bubbles, but not a single reed stirred for an entire fifteen minutes.

Belarus was about to leave to take his place on the western flank on the lake when the first soldiers appeared. The Persian men were frazzled and many burnt. The lavish fur skins they wore around their shoulders were scorched, and some flesh was singed together with fur, unable to loosen. One after another, the men dismounted from their horses.

A man bowed down to drink when, suddenly, a hand came out of the water, grabbed the man by his head, and slit his throat and pulled him into the water without anyone noticing. Belarus crawled farther towards the edge in disbelief. Estoban turned to him and looked at him trouble-free, smiling mischievously. Belarus bowed his head, confirming that Estoban's plan had indeed worked.

More men approached the water, some kneeling and others walking deeper. A few horses came closer to drink. A pale stallion was suddenly revolting in protest as a blade cut through its leg. The horse collapsed into the water, and a young man jumped from the lake. He was drenched in mud and blood. The Persians realised what was happening, but many were too late to respond. Belarus looked at Estoban, waiting for him to give the signal, but Estoban held back.

An Achaean soldier named Julius ran ahead, scattering the horses in all directions. He unsheathed his sword and collided with the blade of a Persian. Blood sprayed over Julius' face as the soldier's arm came loose from its cradle. The archers moved closer to the edge and waited for the signal.

"Wait for my mark!" Estoban yelled. "Wait!"

Belarus looked like he was itching to give the signal before Estoban could. Most of Estoban's men had fallen by the sword, taking down at least three times as many of the enemy along with them. He likely assumed Estoban was waiting for the prize, but Romulus remained out of sight, probably still making his way towards the lake.

"Now!" Estoban screamed.

At his command, dozens of arrows flew across the sky, penetrating arms and legs. Some shot right through the neck, taking along with them skin and tissue.

Persians fell on top of each other, barely escaping the onslaught. Estoban nudged Belarus, entranced by the sight. It was time. Three arrows flew past his ears. Retreating Persians shot arrows in all directions trying to run and hide. Two Achaean archers fell right beside them as they ran for their horses.

Belarus was about to help them up, but Estoban jerked him on his breastplate just in time for a spear to pass them by. Dozens of Achaeans fled into the thicket to take their place beside Estoban for the final onslaught. Belarus would finally have his part to play in the orchestra of violence.

***

Romulus kicked hard in the side of his stallion, bidding him to go faster. The ring of fire had dissipated, leaving a small opening to the south for an escape. Horsemen filed out one by one, fleeing the raging heat that threatened to engulf them.

The forest was thick, and Romulus expected soldiers to bombard them along the route. He was unfamiliar with the territory beyond the clearing, and the unknown made him alert. His eyes adjusted to the darkness under the trees. The sun had barely risen above the horizon, and illuminating beams of sunlight filtered through the canopy. His nostrils were still filled with smoke, and breathing was near impossible.

Valah rasped and coughed next to him. His mighty general had failed him to the point of treachery. Romulus was about to pull his dagger from its sheath and impale the man beside him when the soldiers retreated with sudden speed. Romulus could see a clearing through the underbrush filled with arrows and fleeing men. He despised the savages who had no guts to face their foes.

He dismounted his horse and knocked his way through the flailing men running from the clearing.

Romulus hid behind a large tree. He looked about the lake's edge to see friend and foe slaughtered, wallowing in their own blood and guts. His eyes searched the surroundings until he finally saw the glimmers. Running down the side of the limestone cliff, he saw men in grandiose armour raging down the slope to meet the Persians in their confusion.

Romulus regrouped his men, relaying a quick strategic plan to catch his adversary off guard. A lowly 300 men remained. Valah leaned in close to his emperor, and Romulus grabbed him by the hem of his garment.

"You had better not fail me again, Valah! Win the battle or it will be your last!" he screamed.

***

Spittle flew into Valah's face. He felt no remorse towards his emperor and would gladly slide his dagger through his neck when the battle was over. Before Valah had time to relay the message, 200 riders attacked from their eastern flank with another 200 from the east.

The Persians were surrounded, facing a strong frontal attack. Blades connected and horses snorted wildly, with steam evaporating from their hot bodies. The sun was barely visible through the canopy but allowed for enough light to illuminate the armour of Achaos. Its splendour was ravishing, and Valah wondered what a breastplate would be worth on the black market. He reminded himself to take as much as he was able to carry.

Slivers of bronze and gold threatened to blind him as metal clanged. Blood spilled onto his horse's mane, colouring the pale horse a dark crimson. A young boy ran towards him holding his sword high. Valah was unable to cut down the fifteen-year-old and was shunned from his horse. He fell backwards, out of breath, and crawled towards a fallen stump and lingered.

***

Belarus heard the sword fighting long before he reached the bottom of the hill.

"It is time, valiant warrior!" Estoban yelled above the racket, holding his sword high.

Filled with adrenaline, Belarus followed Estoban right into the middle of the fighting men. He dismounted his horse in a single jump and landed squarely on his feet. Estoban stood right behind him, offering shelter to his back. The men of Achaos stood back-to -back protecting each other—if one's partner was slain, one would immediately protect the back of another.

Belarus realised the success of the battle lay in the protection of one's mate. Belarus swung his sword low, severing the front legs of a brown horse. The animal tumbled forward, falling on its rider and crushing him beneath its weight. Like the covenant dance where he moved with his wife, Belarus moved in unison with Estoban, slaying three to four men at a time.

***

The scene before Estoban moved in slow motion; he was able to study every move coming from his opponent. Men dressed in grotesque animal skins and long trousers emerged from every- where. They were strong and filled with lust for death.

He could see the hatred in their eyes whenever they saw the name of Yahweh on his breastplate. Belarus moved in unison with him, ducking and jabbing at just the right time, as they practiced in the ring. Beside him fought a valiant man who was worthy to be called brother.

Estoban looked behind him to give a quick nod to Belarus but found him nowhere in sight. *Did he fall?* The thought stabbed like a searing blade through his mind. Looking down, he then saw Belarus trapped beneath a large black horse with furry legs. The horse was holding him down by his chest but did not give way to crush his ribs. Estoban then saw the man riding the giant animal.

Dark, long dreadlocks fell around a dirty and deeply scarred face. His grin reminded Estoban of death itself. Without thinking, he ran towards the rider and its horse, dropping his sword at their feet.

"Leave him be! Take me!" Estoban screamed.

***

Belarus jerked his head towards Estoban's voice and motioned for him to fight, but it was too late. A thick club hit Estoban from behind, sprawling him on the blood-splattered foliage. The horse finally relented, and Belarus was able to breathe once more. He looked around the area.

The men of Achaos were caught off guard, some dropping their weapons in surrender while others fought even harder. His heart ached as he saw men and boys being cut down—arms severed and heads imploding. The battle was turning, and he was still alive.

Belarus jumped up and ran towards Estoban, jerking his dagger from its sheath. Belarus took down nine more men before he was hit with the broad side of a blade, engulfing him in darkness.

13

Waves of white fluff blanketed the small village, engulfing the cabin in darkness. Snow pummelled down on the wooden roof of the building situated near the centre of the village as they awaited news from the battlefield. A sombre tune played as five bodies gathered heat in front of the open fire. Justus stroked the flute as if it was a long-forgotten companion. Ariana loved her uncle and found solace in his wisdom. She sat by his feet like she used to when she was a little girl.

Sultry stew brewed in the cast iron pot hanging over the fireplace, filling the cabin with its strong aroma. Ariana didn't realise how hungry she was until she smelled the sweet rabbit stew. Eve was preparing her husband's favourite and enjoyed the company of friends when her husband was away in battle.

Eve was a strong and brave woman, and Ariana envied her for her peaceful countenance. Ariana was not nearly as brave. She longed for her husband and dreaded the outcome of the battle. Mia had kept her positive over the last six days, but the thought of her beloved sitting in the cold outside made her shiver.

Ariana looked around the room to see the people she loved the most. Her uncle sat in a large wooden chair Demetrius had made and played his flute while Eve stirred the stew, swaying in rhythm with the tune. Mia stared at the fire deep in thought, and Ariana wondered what might be going through her mind.

Evelyn paced around the room mumbling, which put everyone slightly on edge. Ariana did not know the woman very well but respected the old lady. Her hair was dark grey and never tidy— her curls were wild like those of her granddaughter, Meriba. Evelyn was nearly eighty-seven, but her age was not showing in her body. She had very few wrinkles except for the crow's feet along her bright green eyes. She smiled a lot, and Ariana always hoped that she would be as exciting as she was in her old age.

***

Mia stirred uncomfortably in the noise around her; she was suffocating under the pressure. She missed her father and longed for the embrace of her husband. Everyone around her expected something she was unable to give them, for she was as lost as they were. Mia gathered the thick fur coat her father had given her and stepped outside for some fresh air.

"I will come with you," Ariana offered.

"Thank you, but I need to be alone and think things through." She bid Ariana to relax and keep warm and promised to return before dinner was served.

Darkness closed in around her, and Mia retreated momentarily from the cold wind. She couldn't go back inside and smile at their jokes. Her heart was troubled, and she didn't know what to do. Yahweh was her only comfort, and she prayed every moment she had to herself.

She walked aimlessly around the village streets. Only a few windows were brightly lit, and no one was celebrating. Life was sucked from their homes and replaced with tension and fear, all expecting the worst. The heads of their homes were missing, and without their leadership, Mia feared for her people. Romulus bending over her whispering incantations plagued her every moment. This adversary was not like the others they had skirmishes with before. He was ruthless, cold, and bitter.

Shivers ran down her spine as the images of her torture again ravished her mind. She had to find some way to relieve herself of their grip.

White snow started to converge at her feet. Winter was early this year. She was about to return to Eve's home when she saw two figures approaching. It was late at night, and Mia didn't expect anyone to be outside in the cold. She couldn't make out who it was in the dark until they were two feet away.

A battered Eugo stumbled towards her followed by Estoban's best scout, Elias. They were both covered with blood and deep gashes to their face and body. Eugo collapsed in her arms and was unable to hold back his tears. She cradled the boy, expecting more men to follow in their footsteps.

"There are no others, my lady," Elias uttered, following her gaze into the open street where they came from.

Mia was unable to breathe. It felt as though life was ripped from her lungs and death would come to claim her. Elias bent down next to his princess and touched her arm. She jerked upright, filling her lungs with air as she screamed into the night. Windows lit up all around her, and faces peered from them expecting an attack. A few women came out to stare at them.

"Everything is okay. Go back to sleep; all is well." She consoled them.

Some returned as quickly as they had come out, but others remained transfixed. Mia helped Eugo stand up and pulled her fur coat around him. He started to protest but she insisted. Elias walked with a strong limp, and Mia knew that these men had just barely escaped with their lives.

***

The door to the cabin burst open, frightening Ariana. Mia entered without her coat, and tears streaked down her face. She

124

was followed by two people. Ariana immediately expected an attack and jumped behind the large couch to protect herself.

A battered Eugo entered the room engulfed in Mia's fur coat. A second man entered, but he was unknown to her. She cowered behind the stool, suspecting foul play. Eve suddenly ran to her son's side and pulled away the fur from his face. Eugo looked bewildered, and tears started to form in his eyes.

Eve gently placed her hands on his broken cheeks and embraced her only son. Tears of joy spilled down her face. Her boy was safe. The commotion in the room settled. Mia handed the other man a warm blanket and a glass of water. He gulped down the liquid in one breath.

"More please ..." His voice was hoarse from thirst.

"What news, Elias?" Justus interjected.

"I am sorry to say that no one else survived," the man named Elias said in a plain tone of voice.

At his remark, Eve collapsed at Eugo's feet and started to sob uncontrollably. Eugo tried to comfort his mother, but nothing seemed to help. Evelyn had quietened down completely and only stared at the fire, pondering the fate of her beloved granddaughter. Meriba was now a widow. Evelyn lost her husband at an incredibly early age, leaving her behind with her only son who was to follow in his father's footsteps.

She had hoped that Meriba would not suffer the same fate her whole family had, but her hopes were now completely shattered. She turned to leave, but Ariana bid her to stay the night and not venture out in the early snowfall.

***

Justus waited as patiently as he could for the two men to clean themselves and have a warm bowl of stew. The tribe was badly hurting, and the news would surely overwhelm some women to the point of suicide. He needed Mia to understand the impact the nation would have if she did not offer the widows a way of reconciliation or even revenge.

Justus marvelled at Mia. She was stronger than he expected. She waited as patiently as he did, and not a single tear dared to escape her eyes. She seemed distant, but Justus understood her demeanour very well. The annihilation of a tribe is a terrible thing to bear. He didn't believe until now that Glaucus had indeed chosen his successor very well.

"Everything went as planned, with two waves of assault nearly breaking the enemy flank. They had lost more than half their men, and Estoban was certain that they would retreat to fight another day," Elias told Justus and the others.

"I was near the eastern flank when the full attack happened. Romulus and his men did not back down but kept on coming like raging animals. They were outnumbered three to one. Estoban and Belarus drove their stallion to the centre of the fight and killed many Persians."

Ariana paid more attention when she heard Belarus' name. Her husband was valiant, and she knew that he would fight with all his might.

"Please continue," Justus urged.

"I still don't know what happened, but Belarus was suddenly caught under the foot of Romulus' horse. Estoban ran to his aid but surrendered his life in exchange for Belarus." Elias looked at Mia when he spoke, and he could evidently see the pain in her eyes.

"The men were confused at what to do. Some surrendered and others fought harder. They hit Belarus on the back of his head with a large club and he collapsed." Mia gasped but held her breath until Elias finished.

"Belarus must have killed more than ten men before he fell. He fought valiantly. The battle turned; our men were slaughtered." Elias looked down in shame. He could hardly believe he had to bring such terrible news.

126

"How did you find Eugo?" Mia asked.

"Demetrius protected him throughout the entire battle. They were no more than three feet away from me. A large man came down hard on his back with a large axe, and he fell on top of Eugo. I was able to sever the Persian's arm and pull Eugo out from under his father's body."

"He told me to go with Elias. To flee, survive, and prosper. Mother, he held my face in his hands when he breathed out his last. He did not suffer much," Eugo interjected, hugging his mother again.

"It's true, Eve." Elias confirmed Eugo's story.

"And how did you escape?" Eve wanted to know.

"We crawled to the outcrop and hid in the bushes for two days until we were certain that everyone had returned home. What seemed like only eighty men retreated, beaten and bruised. Even their horses were broken," Elias continued.

"What about Romulus?" Mia wanted to know.

"Everyone was covered in blood and mud; it was hard to make out who was who, but I saw the red cloak of the emperor as they fled into the forest."

"Are you certain no one followed you here?" Justus prodded.

"Yes, sir. They took no bodies and no plunder. They then disappeared quickly, leaving behind even their own injured. Most men breathed their last when we left the field. We are the only survivors." Elias finally collapsed from the fatigue of delivering the ill-begotten news.

Silence ruled in the cabin—the only sound was heavy breathing and wood kindling in the fire.

"We will call an assembly in the morning announcing the news to the people. The women have a right to claim their dead," Mia whispered.

They all agreed and remained quiet until sleep claimed their thoughts.

14

Contorted bodies covered the forest floor. The earth had indeed had its fill of blood seeping deep among the roots, and the trees around Mia were coloured deep purple from blood splatter. Arms severed from bodies mingled with the hoofs of horses and fur skins drenched with intestines and skin. It was hard to differentiate between Persians and Achaeans. The armour of Yahweh was the only identifiable object detectable in the mangled mess.

The smell of death hung in the air; five days of decomposed body parts reeked in the fresh morning breeze. Cries broke the silence swallowing the morning. Wailing and moaning escaped like the sounds of ravaged animals from the pit of death. Around Mia, women were running to their husbands' sides hoping that a remnant of life was still in them, but no breath or vapour coursed from the dead.

There were far too many bodies to make out who belonged to whom. She searched the area and ran towards the middle of the clearing. She fell over a hand only attached to a forearm reaching to the skies as if awaiting a helping hand to stand up. The tattered skin showed a covenant marking of one of their own. The body was missing from its arm, and Mia cried for the mother who might not find the rest of her son.

She stood from the bundles beneath her and cleaned off the blood that started to drench her tunic. Her leather sandals were red with liquid and mud mulched together. She spun around, unwilling to look at the severed head of a young boy, and attempted to crawl over the bodies into the clearing up ahead.

Mia stopped mid-stride, holding back the nausea that threatened to overtake her. She retched into the grass to her left and collapsed in a heap. Ariana ran to her side, helping her to stand.

"Are you alright?" she asked.

"No, Ariana," Mia searched the sky for any sign of comfort, "something sinister stirs."

***

Ariana let Mia slide towards the dirt but failed to see anything worse than standing among the dead.

Her heart was aching for her friend, but she still held on to hope. Her beloved Belarus was not here. Ariana was determined to look beneath every fallen horse and enemy until she found what she was looking for. Her heart might have been lying to her, but she felt as if her husband was still alive. Ariana stroked Mia's hair and whispered into her ear.

"It is not the end. They will be found, and we will be united with them once again."

Ariana left Mia huddled in the centre of the battlefield. She followed the line of bodies until it thinned out and led to a lake in the distance. She ran along the fallen men until she came to another clearing hugging the small lake.

The carnage by the lake stunned her. A single body pile of more than a hundred men waded in the edges of the pristine lake once again cleansed from the blood that must have coloured it dark red. Ariana started to frantically pull bodies from the pile.

Sweat beaded on her forehead; she wiped the moisture, leaving behind a dark trail of mulch. Breathing heavily, she pulled men from the pile, turning them over in hope that she would find her beloved. She collapsed in the dirt, out of breath, looking at the small dent she had made in the pile when she saw the glimmer along the road up ahead.

She studied the shiny object and gathered all her strength to climb up the path leading to an outcrop of limestone protruding from the lake. The sun started to brighten as noon approached.

The trail up ahead seemed to have carried unusually heavy traffic. Ariana crouched low, searching in the mud and tall grass for the shiny object. As the trees swayed in the breeze, a beam of light settled on a breastplate strewn aside. She crawled to the piece of armour and studied the inside for any names carved into the metal.

She wiped off the mud with her bloody tunic. Hope stirred in her heart as she read the name: ESTOBAN OF ACHAOS. She looked around the area until she found a matching breastplate; the name of her beloved Belarus was carved deeply into the back of it. Tears overwhelmed her and she finally sat down and cried.

***

Mia spotted Ariana cowering down in the path leading to the outcrop she used to dive from. The memory of her meeting with Estoban clashed in her heart with the vision before her. She made her way along the steep path to comfort Ariana. As Mia knelt beside Ariana, she saw her holding something tightly in her arms. The woman looking at her was not in mourning but filled with excitement. Mia hardly understood her demeanour and was about to reprimand her when she handed her a breastplate. Mia studied the armour and followed the carvings with her forefinger.

"Turn it over, Mia," Ariana told her.

Mia slowly turned over the piece of bronze and the name jumped out at her; she had found the only remaining property of the man she loved.

"I told you it is not the end," Ariana smiled, showing off Belarus' breastplate as well. "They were taken. We can still follow the trail and find them."

"We cannot follow them, Ariana," Mia said, gently placing her hand on the woman's shoulder.

"Why not? They are alive, and who knows what awaits them!" she protested.

"I know what awaits them, Ariana." Mia simply stared at her.

Realisation suddenly appeared on Ariana's face as to what Mia meant. She was held captive for days, tortured, and raped. Ariana was the only person who knew precisely what happened to Mia in the cradle of Romulus' keep.

Hope disappeared from the young woman's expression. Mia realised that by telling the truth, she had ripped open the heart of a maiden long before its time. A single tear fell from Ariana's cheek. Mia hugged her tight and took her face in her hands.

"It is not the end. We will pursue, but we need to prepare first and secure the tribe's survival. We cannot run and expect to conquer evil if we do it right now. You do understand that I will not let my husband be tortured and murdered without attempting to rescue him?" Mia studied Ariana as she processed the information.

Ariana shook her head in confirmation. "We will go home, bury our fallen, and prepare for war."

The two women knelt together for a long time until the sun was disappearing behind the cliffs. Mia knew it was time to gather the women and to go home.

She slowly walked to the water's edge, bowing down gracefully and murmuring to herself. Gentle tears streamed down her face, dripping silver fragments into the lake that disturbed its perfect reflection. Mia's heart ached for her companion.

He was out there, and she was now the tribe's last hope. Beautiful, innocent flowers of virtue were crushed this day as lovers, fathers, brothers, and friends were ripped from this world.

Filled with turmoil and anger, Mia came to a decision to use her strength and wisdom to face her enemy.

She would lead an army against her opponent before he had a mind to pursue.

15

Heavy breathing lulled Estoban back to consciousness. A searing pain ripped through his arms as he tried to loosen his grip; ropes cut through the skin on his wrists and threatened to break his thumbs when he moved. Darkness surrounded him; he was blind to a world he once recognised.

His ears adjusted to a steady rhythm he didn't notice before. Estoban felt around him, trying to figure out where he was. Buried alive was his first thought, but the sound ensured him that he was not laid low under a pile of earth and instead moving. He rasped and coughed slightly, not wanting to give away that he was still alive.

"Estoban." He heard his name being called.

Estoban stilled, listening for the voice calling to him, but he only heard the constant tapping rhythm. He felt around the wooden object. It was barely large enough to move in. The sides were solid but sounded hollow. His feet touched the bottom, leaving no room to move them, and his head was pushed low by the top of the box, pressing it at an awkward angle.

"Estoban." He heard his name again.

"Yes?" he replied softly.

"I am so glad you are alive." He immediately recognised the voice.

"Belarus, are you alright?" Estoban asked urgently.

"I will be once I get out of this box."

Belarus sounded even more cramped than Estoban felt. He chuckled at the thought, imagining Belarus with his huge body trapped in a box the size of his own.

"What happened?" Estoban asked.

"All I remember is that they hit you on the head with a club before I got out from beneath the horse's grip. I must have taken down a few men before they hit me on the side of my head," Belarus recounted.

***

Estoban didn't respond for a long time, and Belarus wondered what he was thinking.

"Are there any others alive?" Estoban eventually asked.

"I don't know. I hope that some have escaped the bloodbath." The thought still lingered in his mind. Belarus couldn't believe where he was, and he felt responsible.

"It's not your fault, Belarus," Estoban comforted as if he could read his thoughts.

Belarus was overcome with grief and started to sob quietly. They didn't speak for a long time, and he fell in and out of consciousness a few times. He noticed the change in terrain—the cart carrying the boxes was shaking heavily. His body moved up and down, chafing his bare skin on the rough wooden plank. Belarus was stripped of his armour, his tunic, and even his undergarment, humiliating him even more. As the thoughts swam through his head, his box tumbled sideways, knocking him around.

The cart stopped abruptly, and men screamed accusingly at one another. The wheel had broken, and the boxes were now lying upside down. Blood pressured his head as his full body weight crushed down on his neck. The pain was nearly unbearable.

Belarus was about to faint when he felt the box tilt over, shoving him on his stomach. A hard knocking sound came from behind his head, and a faint ray of light seeped through the opening. The hammering increased and more light followed.

Heavy hands pulled his hefty body from the floor. The light blinded him, and he had a challenging time finding his balance. A man hit him over the head with a thin leather object. The edge of the whip curled around his throat, closing in around him, and released its claw, leaving behind a thin trail of blood seeping from his chin. He looked around, trying to recognise the terrain.

Thick, overgrown trees converged into one mangled mess. The cart was broken beyond recognition, and the horse pulling it was lying upside down with its legs twisted along with the metal limb connecting the cart to the leather straps around its belly. The animal groaned in pain, but the men just left it to suffer its own fate.

The soldiers were dressed warmly in thick fur skins and long trousers. Their feet were covered with closed sandals made of fine leather. They seemed comfortable enough. A tall, fierce-looking warrior pulled hard at Belarus' chains, forcing him to move forward.

He finally saw Estoban as they retied his hands to the front of his body, connecting his bleeding wrists to a chain leading to the horse in front of him. Estoban's naked body was covered in blood smears with deep gashes on his legs. He held his head high like a prince being led to a banquet in his honour. Belarus marvelled at the man. Estoban was far braver than he anticipated.

Pushing Belarus down on his knees, the warrior untied his hands and held a blade to his neck in case Belarus should attempt an escape. They retied his hands like Estoban's, mounted their horses, and continued on their way, leaving behind the cart horse to squeal in anguish.

***

135

Estoban didn't recognise a single shrub around him, and strange trees loomed above. The sunlight was unable to penetrate through their thick leaves, yet the ground teemed with all sorts of green foliage. He was able to stretch out his neck and appreciated the cold wind on his skin.

He imagined a small fleck of snow but then realised that the canopy would have to be covered entirely in a thick layer before any snow fell to the earth below. It was as if he was cradled in a protective cave of green. He marvelled at the creation of his God when the horses trotted away, pulling him at an unusually fast pace.

Belarus jogged with a slight limp. His feet were bleeding, and Estoban expected to be stabbed in the arches of his own with a similar sharp rock. The terrain was rough and unstable; he stumbled more than once over thick tree roots, cutting open his exposed knees.

The horses pulled him a few feet before they slowed, waiting for Estoban to regain his balance, then pulled away at a faster pace than before. He found himself in a light run by the time the canopy overhead thinned out. The horses slowed to a march, allowing him to catch his breath.

Belarus was sweating as much as he was and made no eye contact with him whatsoever. Estoban felt his pain and the disappointment he had caused the tribe.

A scream then echoed through the trees. Estoban looked around him, but no one else seemed to have heard it. Estoban heard it again, but this time it was most definitely closer, and it sounded more like a little girl than a trapped animal. A musty odour emanated from the green forest floor evaporating moisture from a small creek nearby.

The trees stopped abruptly, and all Estoban saw was a clear rock face in the distance speckled with lights. The steep slope evened out to a smooth path trodden flat by dozens of horses. Limestone cliffs kept the rising sun at bay, showering the clearing up ahead in dark shadows. Estoban strained his eyes to see past the horses in front of him. The sight robbed him of breath.

An enormous wall loomed above them covered in green moss. A large opening in its centre boasted an intricate iron gate; it must have weighed more than six tons. The iron bars created a spider web protecting its sacred heart. Men dressed similarly to his captors looked down at them, spitting in their direction and yelling obscenities.

They marched through the gateway into a large, empty clearing. Above the vacant courtyard, the fortress of Romulus the Great boasted its splendour. Numerous openings were cut out of the rock to create a fortress unlike any Estoban had ever seen.

A young boy rushed to his side and quickly pulled a foul black sack over his head, screaming at the horsemen. "You should have covered their eyes! Our location needs to remain secure!"

"They are not going to live out the day to see their own rescue, squirt." The warrior laughed at the young soldier. "No one is coming for these men. They are all that's left of a race that was never meant to be born."

The remark stunned Estoban. *No one is left of my tribe. Did all the men fall on the battlefield? What of the women? What will happen to the women?* Fear engulfed Estoban's mind as terrible thoughts pummelled through his head threatening to squash his hope. He collapsed and vomited into the bag, nearly suffocating in the process. The men pulled him up and dragged him into the belly of the beast looming above him.

The sour stench pushed him to more convulsions. Phlegm and blood flowed freely from his mouth, dripping down his torso and leaving behind a trail to his feet. Estoban was about to collapse when the sack was removed and his head shoved into a barrel of salty water. He gasped for air before they dunked his head down again, holding it there for a few counts before repeating the process.

Satisfied that the puke was properly washed off, they shoved him headfirst into a small cell. Estoban fell over the threshold and tumbled into a pile of hay strewn about the floor. He turned over and stared at the ceiling, happy to be alive and no longer running through the underbrush. Grabbing his left wrist, he stroked the mark of the covenant, praying silently for the safety of his wife.

"Get dressed!" the guard yelled, throwing a piece of linen towards him.

Estoban stood up from the floor and collected the garment. It was mostly ripped and barely resembled a tunic. Blood stains covered the material that was evidently never washed. Estoban was thankful to clothe his naked body and find a little warmth in the cold cell.

The room was carved out of a single piece of limestone with no separate walls or even joints that he could see, and the bars of iron were drilled deep into the rock. There was no way of escape. The keyhole was intricate; Estoban came closer to the lock to inspect it when the guard yelled at him.

Estoban didn't even see the man hiding around the corner standing alert at his post and guarding the tunnel to his left. He retreated to the back of the cell and lay down to rest when the door slammed open.

"Estoban!" Belarus screamed excitedly.

Estoban turned to see Belarus being pushed into the cell with him. He nearly collapsed on top of him. Estoban embraced the man he longed to see. Belarus was alive.

"I thought they killed you?" Estoban questioned, looking the man over.

The scar on Belarus' side was hardly healing; pus and water leaked from the wounds. Estoban ripped a shred of material from his tunic and wrapped it around Belarus' chest to cover the wound.

"I am sorry." Belarus failed to find the right words to tell Estoban how terrible he clearly felt.

Estoban could see the guilt Belarus carried.

"You could have kept on fighting, yet you handed yourself over to the enemy … you gave your life for me," Belarus mumbled.

"You would do the same for me, Belarus. You are my friend. I would do it repeatedly if I had to." Estoban looked at the man before him. Belarus looked defeated, and his body shook.

"Belarus, look at me," Estoban ordered.

Belarus looked at him, and he attempted to exude only acceptance and forgiveness in his emerald eyes.

"You are a mighty man, Belarus. Yahweh loves you so much. No matter what you feel you've done, nothing is too great for Him to forgive. We might be the only ones left in this hellhole, but we are alive, and we will conquer. Give God the glory He so deserves. This is not the end; eternity awaits, and the followers of Yahweh have an everlasting covenant of peace with Him. Just like the mark you wear on your arm, He wears one on his heart. God will never leave you nor forsake you. Put your trust in Him. He will make himself known to you. Allow the God of peace to settle your heart and embrace the love He has for you. Then you will know what it means to be absolutely loved."

Estoban nodded, and Belarus could do nothing but nod in return. Night sounds echoed through the dark dungeons as screams and metal workings ceased. Estoban lay on his back dreaming of his wife. Love was sweet, and the thought of her waiting for him encouraged his faith. Mia would wait for him and keep true to her promise to thrive and to survive no matter what happened.

***

Drums, tambourines, and flutes echoed into the valley far below. Mia listened as voices echoed in a serenade of honour and tribute to the fallen heroes. She loved the celebrations of life and was happy to hear the women singing despite the sombre occasion.

Mourning had robbed them of joy, but the celebration lifted their spirit to celebrate the lives of their men and honour the bravery with which they fought. Millions of stars illuminated the night sky.

Mia sat beside the small lake bordering the forest and running along the western flank of the village, gripping Estoban's armour tightly against her chest. The stars gleamed on the still surface of the lake, creating a perfect reflection of the flawless night sky. She gently stroked the edges of her beloved's armour, dreaming of his touch in the small of her back and the tender kisses he so lovingly bestowed upon her.

"Estoban, I miss you. I vow to bring you honour all the days of my life. I will find you and we will be united again. Love is stronger than death, and I will fight to bring you back to me."

Mia closed her eyes and tilted her head towards the sky. "Lord, I hear you in the trees. Guide me, lead me, and make me strong to lead my people. You are my king, and I submit my will to yours."

Her heart ached for her companion. He was out there, and she knew it. Romulus was a brutal and heartless man; Mia knew what he was capable of and dreaded the thought of Estoban facing her tormentor. If Romulus found out who he was, the pain inflicted on him would be far worse than any other captive Romulus had ever seized. Blood was the only sacrifice of worth to the Angra Mainyu. The mighty Aveston would settle for nothing less. Mia feared for her love.

"Abba, Father, I pray that you will protect Estoban and shield him from the pain to be inflicted upon him. May he be brave and bring you honour, even in his death," she whispered softly, still clinging to the armour.

Mia looked out towards the Eurotas Valley. The moon spread a warm glow over it, and all seemed at peace, though her heart was in a mess. It made no sense to her that Estoban and Belarus would be taken and all the others slaughtered.

She expected that Romulus might not have found what he was looking for and settled for the leader of the regiment instead. In spite of the pain she carried in her heart, Mia was glad that her father was not on the battlefield, for she would have lost both her husband and her father. She had to find a way to infiltrate Romulus' keep without being seen.

An unsuspecting band of women would be more than enough to rid the world of the vermin that spread death around every corner. Mia was certain that if Romulus would find nations beyond the reaches of the known world, they too would fall victim to his hatred and be pursued until they were wiped from the face of the Earth.

"Mia," a gentle voice called behind her.

Mia turned to face the young scout who bowed on one knee before his Polemarch.

"I am sorry to bother my lady, but they are waiting for you," Elias announced.

"Thank you, Elias. I will be joining them in a moment."

"Yes, my lady. Shall I escort you?" he offered.

"You may go; I will follow shortly," Mia assured the scout.

Elias bowed low before his princess, walked quickly, and disappeared into the thick forest, allowing Mia to have the personal time she needed.

***

The moonlight was bright and the breeze fair. The snowfall had dissipated, allowing for the women to make a safe and speedy journey to the battlefield. Elias was shocked when he saw the open field boasting its slain warriors.

The traumatic discovery of the bodies was overwhelming; the image still sent shivers down his spine. There was no time to bury dead Persians, so a bonfire was set in the centre of the field where flames could devour human flesh. The smell was hardly bearable, but Elias stayed behind until every bone was burnt beyond recognition. Even the dead deserved respect.

Stroking his left forearm, he longed for a mark of covenant now more than ever before. His heart ached for Astrid. He was about to ask for her hand in marriage when the announcement came, but now her father was gone, and the burden of his loss was far too great to ask her now.

Elias was certain that somewhere in his future, if he was not slain and buried, he too would finally carry the mark of love on his arm as he carried it on his heart.

16

Belarus was lying dead still next to Estoban on the cold, stone floor of their shared cell. His breathing was irregular as dreams ripped through his mind, and he was mumbling continuously as his body quivered.

A flash of white burnt his eyes. Belarus was standing in the middle of the clearing wearing his white wedding tunic and white sandals. He held Ariana's ring in his right palm and turned it around in his hand, admiring the ruby that shone like fire in the bright light.

His heartbeat quickened when he saw the white stallion moving around the tree line. His bride was radiant. Her white tunic laced with sparkling jewels touched the ground as the magnificent horse galloped towards him. Ariana's dark curls bounced around her face, the flower garland holding her veil in place. He shuddered. Something about the vision was not quite right.

As she approached, he saw a large red stain running from her neckline to her lap. Her throat had been slashed, and blood tainted her dress. He ran towards her but stopped short. Her eyes were vacant, robbed of life. She passed him and he turned to run after her, but he was suddenly alone in the clearing.

He screamed loudly, his voice echoing off the limestone cliffs a few hundred yards away. He then heard an echo of laughter coming towards him. Mia and Estoban clambered from the tree line intoxicated with wine. They were laughing as they came up to Belarus.

"We honour you, our mighty Aveston!" they said in unison and bowed in prayer before him. Belarus pulled them up from the ground.

"No! You live for Yahweh and no one else!" he yelled at them.

They stared at him in wonder and suddenly burst out laughing. They walked away from him, supporting each other in their drunkenness. Belarus was angry; he felt a hatred burn inside of him he had never realised.

"Belarus, someone is coming." Estoban shoved him awake.

"No, not yet!" Belarus shook violently as he tried to bring his mind to full consciousness.

"What do you mean, 'not yet'?" Estoban questioned.

Belarus sat upright stunned, staring at nothing at all and breathing hard.

"What do you mean, 'not yet'?" Estoban repeated the question.

"I expected that we would at least live until sunrise, allowing for a rescue party to reach us," he uttered, still confused.

"You know that there were no survivors, Belarus."

Fresh tears rolled down Belarus' cheek. "I am sorry, Estoban."

"Don't worry, my friend; it was not your fault." He consoled him.

To be called in the dead of night could never be a good thing for a hated prisoner. Belarus rushed at the bars, leaning with his full weight, but the metal remained in its cradle unmoved. He rammed the gate again, dislocating his shoulder in the process.

He cried out in pain. Estoban rushed to his side, beating at the strong arm until it reverted into its socket. The crack of cartilage echoed through the chamber, numbing their heavy breathing.

A faint light started to grow brighter as four soldiers with their swords drawn approached their holding cell.

"Wake up, watchman!" the soldiers yelled at the gate keeper as he fumbled awake. He saw the soldiers and immediately searched for his keys stashed beneath two layers of clothing. The cold set of keys jingled. He twisted the first key into the lock and was surprised that it did not fit. Laughing nervously to himself, he tried the next key and the one after that.

Impatient, the burly soldier shoved the gate keeper away and unlocked the cell himself. He walked into the chamber as the door swung open and readied his weapons for a quick assault should the prisoners protest like before.

Belarus and Estoban stood still; no one dared to utter a word. The tallest soldier approached the cell and tied both men together at the wrist with a thick rope that chafed their skin.

They were led like lambs to a slaughter, half dragged and half shoved through small alleyways and stairwells leading to a broad landing. A large door stood directly to their left with another door swallowed by a narrow stone alley to their right some distance away. The door to their left opened suddenly, revealing a lavish chamber.

An emaciated figure emerged dressed in a dark cloak. His back was hunched over as he pulled the hood over his eyes, not wanting to be recognised. Deep scars could be seen on his hands and chin framed by long, stringy grey hair. He closed the door silently and as quickly as he had opened it. The dark figure moved close to the wall as he jostled by Estoban to descend the stairwell they had just come from. The smell of ether was strong in the air surrounding him. Belarus caught a whiff of the pungent odour that passed him followed by a faint smell of sulphur dragging behind it.

The burly soldier shoved Estoban and Belarus into the narrow alley to their right towards the other large black door. Another soldier stationed at the door opened the heavy latch and shoved the men inside, forcing them to kneel in the doorway.

The room was large and brightly lit by hundreds of candles placed around the room. A big chandelier hung over a wooden bench stained with dark smudges. The soldier pressed his dagger hard on Estoban's neck, allowing a thin trail of blood to seep from the cut. The large soldier did the same to Belarus but allowed no harm to come to his skin. The men closed the heavy doors, shutting out the guard stationed outside the chamber.

***

Red velvet hugged Romulus' shoulders. He loved the red cloak woven from camel's hair and wore it proudly. He turned to face the men brought into his personal torture chamber. Two pairs of eyes stared in bewilderment at the man that held their lives in his hands.

The surge of power was far too strong to contain, and Romulus burst out in laughter. The need to conquer a human being was starting to grow on the inside of him. Imagining the blood that would flow was a glorious aphrodisiac.

"Achaos." Romulus smirked. "This moment will be the last of your life. What do you have to say for yourself?"

"You can take our lives, but you cannot take our dignity," the one called Estoban spoke confidently.

"Your dignity? Then how about your trust, mighty man?" Romulus baited.

"I believe that there will always be a remnant of our people, and you will never rest until you find them. We are stronger than you think, Romulus."

"It's *Emperor* Romulus to you, boy!" Romulus fumed, grabbing Estoban by his hair and lifting his knees off the floor.

Estoban spoke calmly. "We are a loyal people, reaching out to those in need, to those you have bruised. We will grow and we will fight another day."

"Yes, reaching out to those who you do not know, a pitiful weakness," Romulus seethed.

"No, that is where you are wrong. We respect one another, and without doubt we will be the victors," Estoban protested.

Romulus sniggered, releasing Estoban to fall back to the floor. He withdrew a small dagger and sliced through the thick rope tying the two men together. He stood back and looked at Estoban. He rubbed his wrist where the skin had torn under the pressure.

***

Belarus stared at the floor, unmoving. The tall soldier then released his grip on him, cutting his wrists free.

"Rise, Bijan," Romulus ordered.

Belarus, now being addressed by his real name for the first time in months, remained kneeling for a moment before he stood. He walked towards Romulus and bowed down onto one knee before the man with his head bowed in respect.

"You have done a great deed, mighty Bijan. You will receive your place of honour as promised. No man shall bear a greater honour than that of the man that brought me the heart of Achaos." Romulus motioned for Bijan to stand beside him.

He moved slowly and turned to stand beside his emperor. Like a thousand tons of stone, treachery crushed Bijan's heart. Unable to look at the man he betrayed, he simply stared ahead. The tall soldier brought him a blue velvet cloak to cover his bruised body and a chalice of wine to quench his thirst.

***

"Belarus ..." Estoban called in a defeated but firm voice.

Anxiety ripped his heart from his chest, and Estoban just stared at the man he had known as Belarus, lost and broken. Words could never have enough meaning to describe the pain in his heart.

"Betrayed are you," Romulus burst out in glee. "You are a weak tribe! You are a so-called warrior, and yet you failed to see the simplest of truths. You should have seen the tide turn when there

147

was no pursuit after your wretched princess returned. Her escape was no surprise to you? Did you really think that I would just let her go after her incessant mockery? Achaos needed to be purged. Sending Bijan, one of our own, to infiltrate and lead your men to ruin was to be the only way. You fully trusted a man that was not known to you. That is your weakness. It has always been."

"No." Estoban boldly challenged Romulus. "That is our strength. Unlike you, we have mercy and forgiveness." He turned his eyes to Belarus, engulfing him with shame.

"You didn't even know where he came from, and yet you accepted him as your own brother?" Romulus exploded.

"We honour people and trust in who they can become."

"Foolishness!" Romulus raged.

"Foolishness is following your own selfish desires. You are alone, Romulus. You have always been alone, fuelled with hatred and imposing fear on your followers. No wonder they despise you so much." Estoban jerked back as a fist hit his right cheek, sprawling him on the floor to his side.

Romulus lunged on top of him, prodding his dirty, fat fingers in his face. Grime smeared over the broken gash in his cheek, spreading pain into his skull.

"You brute! How dare you make such a claim! My desires are my greatest strength. You are right; I am very powerful, and my subjects adore me for it. I will show you my power. I will annihilate your entire tribe. One by one I will pull them apart!"

Enraged, Romulus kicked Estoban in the face, spewing blood in all directions. With a sudden impulse to protect his face, Estoban pulled his arms over his eyes, revealing the mark on his forearm.

Romulus stumbled back in surprise as if the mark had slapped him. In a dazed fit of rage, he stared at the palm of his hand. He pulled the semi-conscious Estoban to sit back against the wall.

Twisting Estoban's left arm to face him, Romulus stared at the mark in comparison to the one brandishing his palm. He mumbled something Estoban could not understand.

Bijan was stunned at the sudden change in the room. His emperor cradled his palm as a sharp shriek erupted from his throat—an inhuman sound of terrible anguish.

Bijan saw the mark in the palm of the emperor's hand. It was identical to Estoban's covenant mark, but the mark on Romulus' palm had repeatedly been cut, creating a jagged blue scar.

"Guards, bring me the iron!" Romulus rumbled. "Bijan, pull him up."

Bijan lifted Estoban's limp body off the floor, searching his eyes. Bijan placed both arms over his shoulders, allowing Estoban to lean on him.

Estoban whispered into his ear, "I forgive you, brother."

The four words pierced Bijan's heart. Tears welled up inside of him, breaking every piece of composure he had left. Unable to respond, he simply nodded in agreement and turned his face away from Estoban. Romulus shoved Estoban from Bijan's shoulders, allowing him to lean back against the wall. Bijan pushed himself into the wall, wanting to disappear from the sight.

Romulus took Bijan's arm and motioned for him to stand beside him next to the large wooden bench stained with old blood and tar. Deep cuts in the table were filled with rotten flesh—small pieces torn from its previous victim.

Thick, red candlewax was still prominent on the table surrounding a missing shape. Bijan could see by the outline of the shape that it was indeed a small body, probably that of a young girl tortured for sacrifice.

Two soldiers dragged Estoban to the bench where he was tied down like a pig ready for slaughter. A third gangly man pulled an iron cart behind him filled with burning embers. He took a heavy metal object and placed it among the embers.

The iron started to glow in the coals. After a few minutes, he withdrew the object, holding it with a thick piece of wet cloth in order not to burn his hands. Bijan could see large blisters and scars on the man's hands where he had been burnt many times before. Romulus stopped the man just before he could singe the flesh on Estoban's arm.

"Stop," he ordered, turning to leave the chamber.

The room stood still in suspension. The man waited for his next order, holding the hot iron a few feet from Estoban. The man breathed heavily. The object weighed more than ten pounds, and the weight increased by the second as his arm shivered under it. Bijan watched the man, marvelling at his strength and obedience to wait in that exact position. He knew that if he dared to move, the iron would be used on him instead.

Romulus shoved the man from behind, throwing him off balance. The iron object fell from his hands and landed on Estoban's thigh. Skin started to burn, and the putrid smell of burning flesh sickened Bijan. Estoban screamed, his voice echoing off the walls.

The soldier grabbed the iron object, burning his own hands, and removed it before Romulus had time to bash him with it. The soldier retreated and placed the object back into the coals to reheat once more.

Romulus said nothing; he only stared at Estoban as sweat ran down the sides of his face in anguish. The sight clearly brought joy to his heart. Bijan could see the wrinkles around Romulus' eyes squish together. He was smiling. Bijan had never seen his emperor smile before.

Romulus untied a small dagger from its worn brown cloth. The red blade was made from glass fretted together with a substance Bijan did not know, giving the dagger its red glow. The weapon was not only sharp but deadly. Upon contact, the additional substance seared flesh, eating it away like acid.

150

Holding down Estoban's wrist, Romulus carefully placed the blade on his skin. It made a searing sound as the blade cut down vertically along the edge of his forearm, cutting a thin portion of the skin out.

***

Romulus lifted the blade from his skin when the entire covenant mark was removed. Estoban bit down hard, gritting his teeth loudly as he refused to cry out in pain; he refused to show Romulus any weakness. A single tear rolled down the side of his cheek. The pain was so horrible that it threatened him to faint.

A sliver of hope helped Estoban to keep his eyes fixed on Romulus. The man from hell itself held the skin from his arm up to the light. Estoban saw every line and curve that reminded him of his wife in the hands of his enemy.

Belarus just stared at the skin in Romulus' hands and protectively held his hand over his own tattooed covenant mark.

"She will be mine!" Romulus belched out in delight.

Estoban knew precisely what Romulus was about to do. He tried to free himself from the metal chains that held him down.

"You will never have her!" he screamed in revolt.

The red dagger burnt the bottom of his chin where Romulus held it, searing the flesh from his throat. The burning sensation overwhelmed him.

"I will ravish your wife, and she will scream in anguish. She will curse the God that made her and allowed her husband to be tortured. I will send a message to her written on the skin of your arm."

"She will never denounce our Lord!" Estoban protested.

"What? I cannot hear you. Your breath is futile. Your attempt to protect her failed, just like your God has failed you!" Spittle foamed at his mouth as every word was intended to poison Estoban's heart.

Estoban looked intently in Romulus' eyes. "She is stronger and more powerful than you believe. Mia lives without fear; she lives with God. God will protect my wife. You will never win."

"I disagree, Estoban. I will win, and I will have my woman of victory. She escaped me once; I will never let that happen again."

"She has already eluded you, Romulus. Do not be deceived. You cannot mock God. He will turn this unfortunate victory of yours around, and you will not live to see another one!" Estoban breathed out his last breath as Romulus thrust the red dagger through his throat.

***

Thick, red blood gushed from the wound and flowed over Romulus' hands and feet. He looked at the man on the table in disgust. In his rage, he shoved the table on its side, letting the body sprawl onto the floor, its hands and feet still clinging to the table like an insect to a leaf.

Romulus grabbed the sword from the soldier to his left and ran around the table. He kept hacking at the body, his eyes as black as death itself. Flesh and blood covered the entire room.

The image of his master unnerved Bijan. His knees became weak, and he collapsed on the floor. Bijan knew that he was unable to leave the room, lest he face the same fate as Estoban.

Even the soldiers turned with their backs to Romulus, unable to stomach the rage and dismembering of Estoban's body. Bijan stared at the floor, following the streams of blood as they covered the stones.

The hacking stopped when there was nothing but bone and sinews left of the man who forgave him. The pain of death was far more pleasant than the pain he had to carry in his heart. He jerked upright when he heard his name.

"Bijan!" Romulus yelled.

Bijan stood quickly to look at the man who slaughtered his best friend.

"I am pleased. You have done well, and your success will be known throughout the keep. You will be general and shall take your place beside me at the banquet tomorrow in your honour. No luxury shall be denied you, and no treasure shall be refused." Romulus looked at Bijan. His face was covered in blood speckled with fine pieces of flesh.

"Thank you, my liege." He bowed deep and took the hand of his emperor, shaking it but failing to kiss it—the smell of blood drew him to convulsions.

Romulus grabbed his chin before he could withdraw and pulled Bijan close to his face.

"Where was Glaucus?" he questioned.

Bijan was afraid to disappoint Romulus. "I never met him. To my knowledge, he will be wintering in Athens with Amyntas I. Your revenge will be all the more satisfying when Glaucus returns next summer to find his tribe vanquished. You will have your final victory then."

"Victory? You speak of victory, yet this is but the beginning, Bijan. We will do remarkable things together." Romulus' black eyes sparkled like two shining obsidians.

"You said you would let Estoban live. Why kill the man that could lead you to their hiding place?" Bijan questioned.

"That is why we sent our best man. We do not need him; you led us to them already. They will run to you, and in turn you will lead us to their place of safety. Within a matter of days, they will all be wiped off the face of the Earth," Romulus gurgled.

"Yes, my lord."

"I would have had your head if you did not bring Glaucus. But the enjoyment I got from torturing the husband of my ever-hated enemy was the one thing that saved your life." He spat in Bijan's face as he spoke. The stench of his breath was even worse than that of the blood.

Romulus finally released the grip he had on him.

"You will be taken to your own special quarters as soon as those ghastly markings are removed from your arm."

The thought of the covenant mark being removed pulled at Bijan's heart; it was the last thing that made sense in a world of chaos. He bowed his head and turned to leave. Two soldiers reproved him and led him to a small chamber adjacent to the torture chamber.

He sat down next to a hot bed of coals crackling in the fire. The same iron object that was going to be used on Estoban waited in the cauldron. A skinny man wearing a dark cloak then entered the room. It was the same man he saw coming out of Romulus' chamber. Bijan didn't recognise him immediately, but as soon as the man reached out to him, he knew who he was.

"Rosenduz, what do you want with me?" he asked defeated.

The scrawny man moved faster than Bijan remembered, for he seemed to hover instead of walk. The old alchemist was not a man to be reckoned with. His grey hair fell in thin strands around his scarred face; the deep gashes made by Romulus reminded Bijan that even Rosenduz had to bow to the emperor.

"I seek no trouble, mighty Bijan," Rosenduz said slimily. "All I ask is a favour."

"I cannot make a deal with the devil," Bijan responded.

"Oh, but I object. You sold your soul to Romulus a long time ago."

"What do you want?" he pressed the issue. Nothing was ever easy with the alchemist. What he desired was not something one was meant to get involved in. His magic was far too powerful.

"I seek a certain person for my own."

"You can take anyone you wish," Bijan said.

"I seek a lady to serve in my chambers as an assistant. I will protect her from Romulus, and she will not be harmed." Rosenduz paced slowly. "I seek a woman with a pure heart.

Honest and brave. The only one I know who could serve me is the woman who won your heart."

Bijan looked at the man. His dark pupils rimmed with gold seemed to be moving like smoke in a stone chamber, swirling around the openings that fed them with oxygen.

"You will never find her! She is mine, and she will never serve you!" Bijan screamed. He was about to grab the old man and break his neck, but he restrained himself.

"She will no longer love you, Bijan. You have betrayed her tribe and her trust. She will not forgive a man who would choose his own life over that of her tribe, but I can protect her when Romulus brings them here. He will not kill her. I will make sure of that."

Bijan could do nothing but stare at the man. "Do you promise that she will be safe?"

"You have my word," Rosenduz promised.

"What is the favour you require?" Bijan wanted to know.

"I need a small trinket to secure the spell."

"Which trinket?"

"The amulet you carry around your neck will do." Rosenduz waited patiently for a reply.

Bijan grabbed the necklace Ariana had given him, removing it from his neck. It was the only thing he had left that signified their union. He observed Rosenduz and believed that he would do as he promised. He looked at the amulet for the last time; the silver chain hugged the covenant seal. It shimmered in the firelight.

He handed the necklace to Rosenduz.

The alchemist's eyes lit up, and he smiled broadly. "I will not disappoint you, my brave general."

Rosenduz bowed low and vanished as quickly as he arrived.

Bijan closed his eyes and laid his arm on the armrest, ready for the searing of his flesh. The soldier removed the hot iron from the cauldron and pressed hard on his arm. Bijan did not make a sound but cried quietly as the mark that gave him his identity was ripped from his life.

17

Words swam in discord before her eyes. The truth was far too painful to write. Mia inhaled the crisp winter air spilling in through the open crevices under her cabin door. With a fresh resolve, she returned to the parchment with determination. She reread the note to her king, signing it with dark red ink.

Mia knew that her father would only trust the name in which she signed. Herione was the name given to her by her mother, Isemene. Only her father ever used her full name, in letters and reprimand. The tribe had merely known her as Mia, the joyful heir to the throne. Mia felt nothing of that joy as she sealed the letter with her amulet. The silver carvings of her covenant mark etched their double into thick, red wax.

"May you find your master in good health," she whispered to herself.

The knock at her door startled her. She rose quickly to unbolt the lock, and a slender man with fine features stood in her doorway.

"Tobias, come in." Mia invited the scout to sit by the fire.

"I came as quickly as I could, my lady." Tobias stood by the small alcove in front of the open fireplace. The cabin was warm and inviting. Mia led him to sit by the fireside on a thick blanket where her papers lay scattered. Bunched up scrolls covered the soft blanket like a minefield.

Mia shoved the balls of paper aside and cleared a spot for Tobias. "Please sit a while."

"Thank you," he nodded.

Mia handed him a bowl of sweet soup served with three soft bread rolls baked only a few minutes earlier. Esmeralda—her trusted servant—left the cabin, not wanting to disturb her during dinner.

"You must be hungry," said Mia gently.

"Famished." Tobias uttered a quick prayer before he scoffed down a fresh bread roll daubed with butter and still warm to the touch.

Mia watched the young man with wonderment. His long, blond hair, neatly braided, fell to his waist, and he wore a bright blue tunic with a dash of red at the hem. His hands were clean and well kept. Tobias had the features of a Greek God, and Mia knew of the whispers among young girls whenever he passed them by. He was an eligible young man, and Mia had hoped the war would not claim him.

"I have called you here for a great purpose, Tobias," she said sternly.

Tobias swallowed a mouthful of soup.

"I need you to take a message to the king. Only I am privy to his location. He will winter at Ostia Antica, the harbour city of Rome. This scroll will tell of our recent misfortune, and I know that my father will return immediately. He is our only hope, Tobias. You must hurry to his side and comfort him when he receives the ill news."

"I will do my best, my lady." Tobias nodded slowly as she placed the small scroll sealed with her covenant mark in his hands.

"You know the abandoned Citadel in the northern mountains?"

"Yes, my lady," he replied with vague recognition.

"That is where my father will find the remnant of Achaos." Mia walked to the window unsettled.

"My lady, I do not think it wise to send me away. There are only a few fighting men left to protect the village," Tobias protested.

Tobias was a slender man but he was strong, and Mia knew that he would defend his people until his death. She sat down beside him and took his hands into hers. Mia looked into sincere eyes.

"I need you to find my father. I cannot trust anyone else. You are my best scout, and you have served me well. It is in our best interest that you bring back the only man that can lead his people to safety. In the meanwhile, I will ensure that we flee to this safe haven where we will be protected by God. The winter will be our ally. No one will pursue with snow fuelled against them." She hugged his shoulder and placed a red velvet bag in his hands.

"Here is my gold. Now ride. Take the short route to Rome. When you reach the port of Katakolo, they will deter you from sailing. The seasons have turned, and no one will lean support of their vessels; however, show Auraleas your treasure and I am certain that he will take you across the turbulent seas. But be careful; do not let slumber overtake you lest he kill you in your sleep."

"I will do as you say, my lady. May Yahweh protect you in the perilous journey to the mountain sanctuary." Tobias bowed low in honour to his Polemarch.

***

Tobias finished his soup and bread in silence as they both stared at the fire. Its warmth cradled them, blinding their horrible fate in a wash of pretence. Tobias set the plates aside and turned to Mia. She was radiant, and he could fool himself for a moment into believing that the loss of her husband had not tainted her heart. But the tragedy of their loss outweighed their hope.

He took her small hands in his and kissed the soft skin gently. This show of affection was not uncommon to the people of

Achaos. They loved their princess and showed their affections openly whenever she passed by. A grand wave or the kiss on her wrist was seen as an honourable tribute to their beloved. Tobias chortled softly.

He looked into her eyes and made a promise in his heart to find his king and to lead him to their sanctuary no matter the cost. This was his new purpose, and he would fulfil it, even if it cost him his life.

Tobias stood and bowed one last time, offering his respect. He then turned quickly and closed the door behind him, leading his life and purpose to a greater calling. The young scout ran to the stables to prepare his knapsack for a speedy journey.

Tobias packed light, carrying only essential clothing and food for the twelve-day ride to Katakolo. Exchanging his blue and red tunic, he dressed in dark brown and green. Tobias would blend into any forest should he need to hide from his enemy.

His legs and arms were covered in thick, leather armour layered in thin strips to allow for movement. His bronze breastplate was replaced with a leather copy displaying the same lavish imprints boasting of Yahweh. His feet were shod with fine leather straps covering his entire foot to protect against the cold winter chills that often riddled toes with frostbite.

A broadsword tucked into its sheath would be his only weapon; a swift horse with a light load was far more valuable than a metal-clad warrior.

Tobias pulled his dark cloak tight around his neck, tucking it into his leather belt. He pulled his long braids into the hood of the panther fur cloak and faded into the darkness.

He chose the fastest horse and mounted the animal. The black stallion stirred under his weight, ready to run into the night. With one last look, Tobias greeted his village in a sad farewell, praying silently that he would return to the lush Eurotas Valley.

***

The room was sparsely decorated, the walls covered by dark soot from a thousand candles burning late into the night. The absence of light threatened Bijan. His books and personal effects were neatly arranged on the small bookcase by the window.

A simple leather divan stood askew in the opposite corner, grabbing the last sunlight to filter through the dense tree line to the east. The sun was setting on another day lost to life.

Bijan paced around the little room stroking his left arm. The pain was unbearable, but he hoped to feel the stinging pain until his life was taken from this world. He betrayed the only man he ever trusted completely.

The sacrifice had not only secured Bijan his position as leader of the entire army but allowed him the respect he had always dreamed of. He had once admired his emperor and knew that no matter what he had to do, he aspired to be like the man he served. However, he now realised that all his childhood hopes of aspiration were squandered on a broken dream that could offer no peace.

He hated the man he had become. He reached for the amulet around his neck but found only an empty void; Rosenduz had taken the last piece of dignity he had left. All he could think of was Ariana and the fact that she would never forgive him. How could he go back and pretend to be the man he was not?

The anguish was too much to bear. Bijan ran to the bookshelf and pulled it over, spilling books, scrolls, and gold onto the floor. He dropped down on one knee attempting to pick it up when he heard a voice.

"If you dislike the order of the room, I will gladly fix it, my lord," the maidservant said, running to his side and picking up scrolls and loose papers.

Bijan studied the young girl. The left side of her face was bright red with finger marks still showing on her cheek. Braids covered her head but ended abruptly where scissors cut it short. She was certainly not a plain girl—her eyes were chestnut brown, and she smelled of vanilla. Her skin was almost translucent, and he couldn't prevent himself from touching her cheek. She froze. He pulled his hand away quickly.

"Forgive me; I don't know what came over me," he apologised.

"Please, my lord, you may do anything you wish with me. I am your servant; if you need me to satisfy you, I will do so gladly."

The words stung his heart. He could never imagine being touched by any other woman than his wife, Ariana. The prospect of her offer was as offensive to him as the brutal murder of his best friend.

"No!" he shouted as he straightened and turned towards the window.

"Forgive me if I displeased you." She crawled to his feet and hugged them tight, kissing the tips of his boots. "Please do not send me away; this is my last opportunity to show him I will be good. I promise."

"Stop doing that!" Bijan ordered.

She squirmed away from him into the corner, looking about her in horror. She rubbed her cheek violently, apparently wanting the mark to disappear and for her life to make sense.

Bijan bowed down next to her and held her shoulders tight, forcing her to look into his eyes.

"Look at me," he ordered.

Her brown eyes were void of hope, and the only emotion he sensed from her was fear and total bewilderment.

"I won't hurt you; I promise you that much."

She looked at him puzzled. "He told me if I do not serve you in any way you wish, he will have me tortured and drowned in my own blood."

"Who told you that?"

"Rosenduz."

"The alchemist?"

"Yes. He told me that if I should fail in my mission to win your heart that he would not only kill me, but he will abuse my body in ways that it was never meant to be. My organs would make for great magic potions, he said." She just stared straight ahead as the reality of her predicament dawned on her.

The girl started to shake violently, and all Bijan could do to calm her was to hold her tightly against his chest. Her breathing started to quiet down when the door suddenly burst open.

Romulus, followed by two very nasty-looking men, crashed through the door. He saw Bijan kneeling with the girl in his arms and was about to pull her away when Bijan grabbed his wrist. Astounded, Romulus just stopped his motion and attempted to pry his hands free.

Bijan stared at the dark, lifeless pupils of his emperor.

"Do not touch her!" he ordered.

Romulus did not reply. He straightened his back as Bijan released his grip.

"She is mine, and no man is to lay a hand on her. Do you understand?" Bijan belched towards the soldiers trying to look away.

Bijan released the girl, and she ran into the corner, picking up the scrolls and replacing them in the bookcase. Bijan then walked to his emperor and kneeled beside him, taking his strong hands in his, and kissed the palms of his hands as was custom.

"Forgive me, my lord, for the outburst. I was told that I could have whomever I choose, and she is my choice," he offered.

"Of all the beautiful women in our possession, you would choose the youngest daughter of Nimrod?" Romulus questioned with a frown. "You realise Daelia is only fourteen. A little young for your taste, is it not?"

"Since when did that stop any of us before, my liege?" Bijan kept calm, not wanting to show his surprise.

"But of course, Bijan. Who am I to protest?" Romulus teased. "Your time away has changed you."

Romulus turned to the young maiden and studied her nervous eyes. Bijan knew Romulus loved it when his subjects showed respect in the form of fear. That was the only emotion he was able to control, and which allowed them to be controlled. He could likely smell the fear wafting from her.

"Daelia, leave us," he ordered.

"Yes, my lord." She curtsied and moved quickly to the door.

"Oh, Daelia," Romulus walked in front of her, stopping her a mere foot away, "please go to the alchemist and tell him to give you the effects of the Athenian princess. If you are to be the concubine of my general, you at least need to look like a princess."

She bowed again but said nothing, quickly exiting the room.

Romulus turned to face Bijan, and his dark eyes studied him from a distance. Bijan could not tell if his emperor was pleased or not. The thought of disappointing him now would lead to the certain death of all he held dear. The fear he felt emanating from every servant in the keep was strange and uncomfortable.

He had grown up in the courts of his mighty emperor and knew the ways of man, but the few months he spent away seemed to have increased his hatred for all he had come to know as valiant and true.

Bijan had been reaching his sixth birthday when he set out with his father Darius to serve as a blacksmith's apprentice to Romulus and his defected army. It was an adventure he had dreamed of since he could remember, shaping blades and daggers for the generals of Romulus the Great.

He often entered the emperor's tent in secret to listen to talk of war and plunder. The thought excited him like no other adventure ever could. He served with his father for many years until one day the great emperor summoned him himself.

"Mighty Bijan, I have seen you lurk around the tents of meeting," Romulus said.

His heart beat faster, afraid of this mighty man.

Romulus laughed. "Do not be afraid. I am in need of a personal blacksmith, and I have heard that your skills far outweigh your age. Is that true?"

"Yes, my lord. It would be a great honour to serve you."

"I will teach you great things of battle and women." Romulus burst out laughing again at seeing the young boy blush bright red.

Bijan remembered the day he entered into the service of the emperor. He had worked hard, and in return Romulus allowed for him to sit in on important meetings and learn all he could from his personal guard. It was not long before he was of fighting age and joined the special legion in service to his emperor.

Working as a personal blacksmith and soldier was a job he had to juggle fiercely, but his wisdom and uncanny ability to adjust to any situation did not go unnoticed. It was the greatest honour to be released of his duty as blacksmith and appointed the youngest third general in Romulus' personal guard.

Romulus startled Bijan out of his memory as he squeezed past, walking towards the opening in the wall. He stared at the empty courtyard for a moment too long before he drew the thick velvet curtains shut. Candlelight illuminated the room in a soft golden hue.

He looked around for a soft seat to sit in, and when he realised that there was none, an urgent call echoed through the hallways. A young soldier appeared almost instantly with a lavish wooden chair similar to those of the kings of the north. A permanent keepsake, Bijan was sure.

They brought a second chair for Bijan and removed his small couch by the window. It was not lavish enough for a general. Romulus bid him to sit down.

"Wine!" he belched.

A servant girl ran in, almost spilling wine over Bijan in the process. He rose to help her but saw the glint of surprise in Romulus' eyes. He sat down quickly and scoffed in the servants' direction. This action received more satisfaction from his emperor, and Bijan simply nodded in respect. He took the goblet to his mouth, drinking deeply. The smooth, salty liquid numbed his lips and throat, momentarily taking his breath away.

Romulus laughed loudly, spitting droplets of wine all over his black velvet tunic. Gold and silver threads were woven into the garment's hem. Romulus was dressed for a celebration, with his dreadlocks pulled back into a tight knot tied with thick, golden clasps.

Tambourines and drums could be heard in the courtyard as merchants made their way into the keep carrying braised meat, wine, and breads. Musicians came together in a celebration of victory held by all the allies of Romulus the Great.

"Tonight's celebration is special, Bijan. Not only did you deliver the husband of the one woman who I hate more than anything else, but you have given me a way to settle a dispute long forgotten."

"Forgive me, sire. What do you mean?"

"Glaucus." The name slithered from Romulus' lips like a snake readying to trap its prey.

Bijan understood the true motivation of his mission for the first time. It was not about Mia and her escape, but a far greater purpose of hatred and vile torture rooted deep in the heart of his emperor.

"Have I ever told you of my confrontation with my first sacrificial lamb?"

"No, sire." Bijan was surprised at the openness with which his emperor now approached him.

"I was eleven when I reprimanded the first Jew to vomit on the mighty Aveston. I grew up in Persepolis, the ceremonial capital of the Achaemenid Empire. I was strong and valiant and pursued the Aveston as long as I remember. It gave me my first surge of power when I took the young boy. He was an exile from Israel; I never knew his name, but his blood flowed into the ravine by the side of our house. It was a moment of complete resolve."

The man beside Bijan trembled with delight unlike anything he had ever seen. Recounting the graphic slaughter of the youth sent chills down his spine.

"I cornered the boy on the local playground," Romulus continued. "He was only two years younger than me and boldly proclaimed that Yahweh would rescue them one day and I would be lost and sent to hell for my torture of innocent animals. He believed that I could be swayed by such evil confessions of an imbecile. The audacity to believe that I would let such mockery slide! I grabbed him by the head and stuffed my shirt sleeve into his mouth so he was unable to scream.

"I dragged him behind a large tree hidden in the shallow river covered with moss and slime. I had carved the tree out to create my own special cave in honour of the Angra Mainyu. I tied the boy's hands and feet together behind his back, exposing pale flesh untouched by the sun. I hung him upside down on a makeshift lever, making it more difficult for him to breathe. I slowly started to carve a pattern out on the skin of his stomach. The thin lines of blood soon became streams flowing over the boy's face. He tried to scream but no one was able to hear him. The gurgling started soon after the blood flow.

"The sensation of warm blood dripping on your toes is quite exhilarating. A prayer was whispered in offering to my God for his abundant wisdom and power. At that moment, a dark cloud formed around me. Incantations escaped my lips as the last of the boy's breath escaped his. In that moment, a bright flash of light and thunder rode through the sky, lighting up the valley in an unexpected uproar.

"Inexplainable power filled my heart with such a burden of purpose. My eyes darkened from a light brown to darkest black, and all my senses were enflamed with a lust for more. I loved it."

Romulus stared ahead, stroking his heart and eyes misted over with thoughts of a long-forgotten joy. Bijan stiffened in his chair, looking at a man in total rapture. The image disturbed him.

"Did it happen again?" he asked slowly.

"Nearly." Romulus took a slow breath and continued. "I was reprimanded and sent to Pasargadae, the capital of Cyrus the Great where I served in the king's kitchen as punishment for the next five years."

Silence filled the chamber, deafening the faint whisper of a drum beat far in the belly of the stone giant beneath them.

"I nearly killed Glaucus Solon. If my power had fully grown, I might have had the chance then. It was a chance meeting in Pasargadae."

Bijan stiffened at the mention of this meeting. Estoban had told him once about his father-in-law. Before he met Yahweh, he had had an encounter with a boy who wanted to force him to serve an idol made in the image of a man with horns. Glaucus escaped with his life, which ultimately led him to the lush Eurotas Valley, serving the God of Israel with fervour and passion.

"Thanks to you, I will indeed have that chance. After I take his daughter as ransom, he will have no other option than to face me." A guttural laugh escaped the emperor's throat, filling the chamber with its eerie sound.

A sharp rap at the door broke the tension in the room.

"Sire, the banquet is awaiting your imminent arrival." The man bowed deep and left the room.

"Come, Bijan. Let's celebrate our victory!" Romulus jumped from his seat with a newfound excitement rushing at his heart and a fiery satisfaction he had long ago felt.

Bijan was finally alone, pondering the hatred that filled these halls—death, decay, and lust for revenge. He was unable to bear it when he saw her in the corner of his eye. She was radiant.

Daelia was dressed in a fine blue silk dress revealing her curved middle. His heart skipped a beat. It was not lustful, but rather a strange desire to hold her like the sister he never had. The sudden urge to rescue this frail girl out of a nest of debauchery filled him with a new purpose, one with which he would counter death and bring back life.

18

Purple clouds threatened the valley with another premature snowstorm, and cold winds circled through the open field in the centre of the village. All was quiet as dusk faded into evening. Today was the first day without hope of returning heroes.

The dead had been claimed and buried in the small cemetery a mile away from the village. It was a day of mourning. Lamp lights faded early, shutters were closed, and wailing ceased. The valley was deathly quiet. Voices could only be heard in a shallow murmur resounding from a solitary limestone hut. The meeting house was shrouded in darkness.

A faint golden hue escaped the edges of dark wooden shutters closed against the cold onslaught of the wind; the torches had difficulty chasing the darkness away.

The fireplace brimmed with life as flames licked wood in an array of splendour. Ariana would normally be seated by the side of the comforting warmth, but the arguments around her made her uneasy. Her attention shifted from one face to another. Ten people crowded the small room, including her.

Mia paced by the door. She was dressed in a dark velvet tunic, hugging her fur coat tight against her chest. Evelyn sat quietly in the corner busying herself with wool and knitting needles, her grey locks in disarray.

Eve stood tall behind the seated elders. Her hair was taken back into a tight braid that seemed to pull her face backwards. Her eyes glowed brightly, ready for the fight. Ariana's uncle, Justus, sat hunched over, tugging his frail hands beneath a warm woollen blanket. Jacobien sat next to him but seemed stronger than the times Ariana had seen him before. He was regal and fuelled with purpose.

Ariana did not know the other two women in the company but was impressed with their silence. They sat beside Jacobien and hardly moved as arguments chased one another.

Elias and Dumbrorin guarded the doors leading outside. They were dressed in Achaean military style with breastplates fixed to strong bodies. Elias was tall and slender with blue eyes that revealed his Germanic heritage. He had a rugged appearance but was indeed very handsome.

Dumbrorin reminded her of Belarus. He was just as tall and strong with si milar dark hair that spread over his shoulders, but the ever-constant smile on his face betrayed his joy. Belarus hardly ever smiled, but when he did, he lit up and made Ariana laugh even more. The memory of her beloved surprised her in light of what was going on. She kept the thought to herself, refocusing on the debate at hand.

***

"We cannot expect the women to fight, Mia!" Justus yelled in anger.

"We fight or we die, Justus. Romulus will stop at nothing until we are not only captured but slaughtered for his evil God!" Mia protested.

"Uncle, she is right. I will not allow our family to be lost forever because you are unable to understand the magnitude of our situation," Ariana interjected.

"Hold your tongue, young lady," Eve reprimanded. "We are all afraid, but we cannot risk another bloodbath. I already lost my husband, and my son barely escaped with his life. I will not walk into death blindly."

The room stilled at Eve's outburst. Mia paced around the room.

"I believe that Mia is right," Evelyn spoke for the first time. "Romulus captured most of the territories around us and left only a few survivors to tend the fields and gather for his men. Our only allies lie far to the west, and by the time the king should return, it will be too late."

Everyone in the room seemed to digest the information, everyone except for Eve. "We should leave for Athens in the morning. He can follow all he wants; we flee before he gets here."

"Fleeing for Athens will do no good. The winter will claim your body before you even get close." A voice came from behind them.

Eyes turned to Elias standing by the door. He was a scout, not an elder to give advice. Eve smirked at him, brushing off his comments.

"Elias is right," Mia answered. "But so are you, Eve."

Acknowledgement of her outbursts surprised Eve. She turned to sit beside Ariana when Mia continued. Mia sat down on the floor in the middle of the room and drew a map in the collecting dust.

"Here in the northern mountains lies an abandoned Citadel. We do not know who built it, but I have explored its cave system more than once. It is well insulated and will keep everyone warm. There is ample space, and it is secure. The water supply is good, and it's protected by the mountain itself."

As one, they all stared at the map laid out on the stone floor.

Jacobien and Evelyn were the only elders who knew about the existence of the Citadel. They looked at one another and knew exactly what to do next.

"We will make sure that everyone reaches the Citadel safely," Jacobien assured Mia.

"The fighting might come to Achaos, but if we leave by sunset tomorrow there will be enough time for the early snowfall to cover the tracks, and Romulus would never think of venturing into the dangerous limestone cliffs during winter," Evelyn agreed.

"By the turn of the season, my father would have returned with fighting men alongside him. I have already sent word," Mia added.

The news startled most of them.

"Tobias would probably be a day's travel away by now, destined for Rome," she continued. "If he should be set back, leave for Athens after the first summer rains. You will be safe and well taken care of by our allies. Dumbrorin, how many scouts do we have left in the village?"

"Twenty-two strong fighting men, my lady," he answered.

"I'm certain most of the men would join our plight for a battle, but I must insist that most of you remain with the tribe during the winter. You will be their only protection should anything happen."

"I understand. We shall protect them." Dumbrorin bowed in respect of his Polemarch.

"What do you mean *your* plight for a battle?" Eve inquired.

"I am setting out against Romulus before he has time to pursue us. He will come for us, and I am not about to let him win," Mia said, determined.

"Who will fight with you?" Eve was astonished at the audacity of their so-called Polemarch.

"I will make an announcement by first light. Those who would like to join me can do so at their own will. The rest will follow orders from Jacobien and Dumbrorin for the evacuation and resettlement in the Citadel."

Dumbrorin looked surprised when Mia mentioned his name. Jacobien looked in his direction and nodded in approval.

"Dumbrorin will be in charge of all security, and he will act as Polemarch in my place under the supervision of Jacobien."

"A noble choice, my lady," Jacobien added, nodding his approval.

Dumbrorin blushed and gave a slight nod in appreciation of Mia's trust.

"I trust you will have plenty to do before the morning assembly?" she asked, directing her gaze at Jacobien.

"Yes, we will make haste and be prepared to leave with enough supplies for the winter by nightfall tomorrow," Jacobien stood from his seat and straightened his brown cloak. He bowed deep and held Mia's hand for a moment; she saw tears well up inside his eyes, and she felt a deep sense of compassion for him.

"You are a brave woman, Herione. We honour you and pray that Yahweh will protect you."

Mia wiped the tear from his cheek and smiled at the portly man still holding onto her hand. Jacobien cleared his throat and motioned for Dumbrorin to follow him towards his home.

The two men left quickly, swallowed by the night. Everyone except for Elias, Ariana, and Evelyn followed. Mia collapsed in front of the fire. Ariana was about to comfort her when Evelyn stopped her.

"This is a burden she must bear alone, child," she whispered in her ear, just loud enough for Mia to hear.

Ariana studied the woman's eyes but said nothing in return. She collected her blue cloak and retreated to Mia's home to wait for her there.

"You can also leave if you like, Evelyn." Mia strained to speak.

"No, dear." The old lady bent down to sit beside Mia and pulled her close. "Tonight we pray, and we call on God for His guidance and deliverance."

Mia hugged the wise woman, tightly pressing her face into her bushy hair. She finally broke down and cried tears for her husband, her father, and her tribe.

19

A cacophony of drums, flutes, and tambourines droned out over voices screaming at one another. Goblets clanged and wine spilled over marble, silk, and melted wax. The banquet had reached a high point of drunkenness and revelry.

Debauchery was the word Bijan would use to describe the macabre scene before him. Women dressed in strips of linen and silk shook their bodies in circles on dirty leather laps of men overcome with lust and alcohol. He was repulsed and took another bite from the meat on his plate in order to keep the nausea at bay.

The banquet was a treat for all the warriors of mighty Romulus, a celebration of their latest conquest. He was seated on a high throne embellished with red velvet and gold. Romulus was surrounded by young women, all barely covered. He loved the attention each and every one gave him—food and sex on a silver platter.

***

Valah stood in the doorway leading to a long corridor that ended in the outer courts of the keep. A cool breeze made its way past him as a storm gathered in the distant valley. Valah could smell the sleet that was about to shower the keep in early frost. Winter was coming quickly.

He shivered not from the cold but from the image before him. His men were enjoying themselves to the full. They had conquered the Achaean army in battle and lost many brothers and sons, but the feast would cover their grief. Valah loved to be a general in Romulus' army. He might not always agree with his methods, but he respected the man.

Valah studied the men as they had gone from respectable to outright inebriated. He was not a man longing for wine — alcohol never touched his lips. He laughed as he watched them. The girls attending to the men giggled at one another and knew that lust might reign, but the capacity to copulate would fail them.

Valah realised that if no man were to have sex with them, they might actually escape torture for a night. He felt sorry for them in his own way as he remembered the girl that clung to his back all those months ago. Her eyes had been filled with hatred and fear above all else. He spent many sleepless nights trying to eradicate the look on her face, forever etched into his memory. Valah could not disguise the fact that the smiles were counterfeit and the affections enforced.

He turned his attention to the man beside his emperor. Bijan perplexed Valah. He was dressed in black leather, strapped tight around his chest. He was a big man, standing a full head above the men in his regiment. His hands were tough and his attitude tougher.

Black hair hung straight to his shoulders, and a thin scar ran across his neck; Valah could see that it was fresh. His left wrist was wrapped in a white cloth but revealed a red stain on the inside of his arm. Bijan kept stroking the wound with his other hand as if he stroked the hands of a beloved.

His face was shaven clean, and his hands hardly got dirty from his meal. It was custom to eat with one's hands, yet Bijan managed to make a skewer with which he ate his meat and fruit.

Valah tried to recall the man who led the army to many victories over the years. Bijan had been untouchable. He felt no pain or remorse and cut down men and children alike. Numerous campaigns allowed Valah to study the mighty warrior, and he dreamt of becoming as strong and determined as this man, but the Bijan that sat next to his emperor was a different man. He shied away from drink and kept the women at bay. He looked with sympathy rather than dominance at the men before him. He brought the entire army of Achaos to their knees, and he showed remorse rather than conquest. Valah could not understand the change in his demeanour and thought it best to study him in more detail before he approached him.

***

Bijan stroked his forearm and winced. The pain was nearly uncontainable, but he refused to drink the bitter potion Rosenduz had offered him. Bijan wanted to feel the pain of his loss. He instinctively reached for his amulet, forgetting the space on his chest was empty.

He swore softly to himself for giving Rosenduz the trinket. He was confused, and a world that should feel welcoming was choking him. The pain of defeat hung over Bijan. He could not explain the emptiness he felt inside of him, as if the Earth opened up and swallowed his last bit of integrity into an abyss of torture.

"Bijan." He suddenly heard his name whispered faintly.

"Bijan." Again he heard it, but this time it was louder.

"Bijan!" Romulus shouted, hitting him on the side of his head.

Bijan jerked to his left and realised that Romulus and seven young girls stared at him awaiting an answer.

"I am sorry, my lord. I was drifting in triumph." He smiled, raising his half-full glass.

Bijan saw Romulus smile and then laugh. He felt like a fool for dreaming of remorse when all he had ever wanted lay before him. Romulus promised fame and gold in abundance, and since his return, Bijan found it to be true. He did indeed enjoy having his own special quarters and was grateful to Romulus for keeping his word.

"Bijan, do you really long to have only one girl be yours instead of all the precious beauties our dungeons have to offer?" Romulus pointed to Daelia sitting silently by Bijan's feet.

"I do. She will make an example of servitude and, might I add, give indispensable pleasure," Bijan chuckled, feigning levity.

He could see that Romulus liked the remark and clapped his hands in triumph.

"And what of the Achaeans? Are they as ravishing as the harlot my men allowed to escape?" Romulus probed.

"Like Mia?"

Romulus nodded with an expression of disgust and longing intertwined into one.

"Yes, they are quite exquisite," Bijan ensured his emperor.

"I will be glad to take Mia and many like her for myself, see if they cry at the onslaught of pain like their young boys did in battle," Romulus guffawed.

"I believe these women will cower more than you can imagine." Bijan shivered at the thought.

"Then I look forward to riding out at dawn to claim my prize," Romulus belched out in triumph and the soldiers replied as one, not even knowing what the cheer was for.

"Tomorrow?" Bijan was stunned.

"But of course. Why give sustenance to men without a greater purpose in mind?" Romulus was affronted.

"I am sorry for my outburst, sire, but those women will be useless to you at a time like this."

"What do you mean, Bijan?" Romulus questioned.

"They have just lost all they held dear. They will be weak and broken, and there is no fun in breaking down an already broken woman."

Romulus thought about the statement for a long while. He enjoyed the screams and protest—fear and retaliation were the pinnacle of his euphoria. He looked at Bijan and spoke in a hushed tone.

"I do enjoy breaking down every last bit of resolve they have before I cut them down ..." Romulus' breath reeked of dead flesh.

"Fine, we will give them some time to get themselves back together. Valah would be most indebted to you for giving the men a few days of rest in their own beds." Romulus jabbed him sportily on the shoulder.

"I think it a wise decision, my emperor." Bijan bowed his head in respect and kept a cool face that looked ready to devour something, but in his heart he hoped that the women would flee at the first word of their loss.

Bijan knew the strength that exuded from his wife and knew that the same fire burned in the hearts of the other women in her village. They would not back down from the fight, and even though they lost all their men, they would never succumb to fear of annihilation. They believed in a God that was not made from wood and stone, idols shaped my human hands, but in a God that gave peace and strength like Bijan had never seen.

He didn't quite understand the security in something one cannot see, but he saw in the lives of every Achaean that same satisfaction and joy that came with the love of their redeemer.

He bowed his head in defeat and stood abruptly, catching Romulus off guard. Daelia followed on his heels.

"Are you going so soon?" Romulus asked.

"A desire I long to satisfy bids me farewell for the night." Bijan pulled Daelia closer to him and shoved her towards the exit.

Romulus laughed and pulled his own servant closer for a long, disgusting embrace.

Bijan grinned through clenched teeth and bowed to Romulus who paid him no more attention but grabbed the poor young girl in a vice grip between his legs.

Bijan gently ushered Daelia through the crowd and looked with intent at a few men who dared touch his property. The men laughed and apologised profusely before grabbing another woman close at hand. He walked quickly and passed by Valah standing in the doorway. Bijan bowed his head and Valah responded.

***

Valah watched Bijan and his concubine exit the banquet, and he stared after them. Bijan eventually let go of Daelia and spoke softly to her with the fondness of a brother. Valah shook his head and reprimanded himself for looking down on a man who was to be his superior.

He then looked to his right and saw a ravishing young maiden in red silk beckoning to him. His former doubts about the ladies' imitation vanished from his mind as he allowed her to seduce him.

20

The sun was bright on this cold autumn morning. Just over 2000 faces looked at Mia as she tried to explain in detail to them the decision that had been made. Some pointed fingers and murmured while others nodded in agreement. She felt alone and scared. Her heart was racing, and there was no way to escape the announcement she had to make. She was certain her father would have done it differently. Mia believed that Yahweh would turn the misfortune around, but relaying the message was far more difficult.

"I will not let my children be slaughtered and tortured. It's for freedom that we have been set free—free from Greek rule and the oppression of the senate. We are free to live and to love Yahweh as He deserves to be loved. We can no longer ignore the threat from the enemy. Our choice is simple—life or death. I choose life, a life that's worth preserving. Our life is God's life. Our husbands and fathers sacrificed themselves to protect us; are we just going to give up and quit? Or are we going to stand up for what we believe in?"

The crowd murmured.

"I know the man that sets out to destroy our tribe. I have met him, and I have seen his hatred. Romulus will stop at nothing until he has ruined your life. He will slaughter your boys and take your girls for himself to torture and rape. I have seen the things he does to young women. It's horrific." Tears started to roll off her cheek as the crowd quietened down.

"I do not expect you to understand what he did. All I need to know is that you will trust me, that you are with me."

Mia looked at Jacobien who smiled at her. He was indeed her father's best council, and this time he did not deter her from reaching out to the warriors inside each one of the women. Jacobien no longer doubted the strength Mia had in her heart, strength so resolute that it withstood the evil that lurked inside of Romulus—a monster who would ravish and kill as his heart desired. Jacobien reassured her that should the crowd crucify her, he would gladly go down with her. He too believed that an attack could no longer be avoided.

Dumbfounded, the women just stared at Mia. A single hand then suddenly shot up amid the crowd, followed by more and more until the entire crowd raised their hands in agreement. A slow cry started in the centre and built up to a giant roar. The women started to sing an anthem that stirred Mia's spirit.

"We will fight, and we will survive!" a young girl shouted in the first row.

"Yes, we are with you, Mia!" another voice rang out.

A sudden repeated "yes" echoed through the valley as women started to dance and sing in anticipation. They would follow their Polemarch to freedom.

"For Freedom!" Mia hollered.

"For Freedom!" the reply rang out in unison, shaking the forest floor.

***

Mia felt relief wash over her as the crowd dispersed to prepare for the day ahead. Carts would be filled with supplies for the winter months in the Citadel. Women, children, and animals would all make the long journey this very night, taking only what they were capable of carrying. A swift and clean escape was their only choice.

Mia watched the women scatter, leaving her standing alone in the open clearing. A snowflake settled on her cheek, and she felt the cold spreading deep into her bones. An unexpected warm breeze then touched her cold skin, sending shivers down her spine.

"Will you be alright, my lady?" Elias asked.

Mia spun around, surprised. She looked into his tender eyes. Elias' pale and textured skin was a testament to years of warfare and torture. He preferred to wear a beard that glimmered like bronze to cover his bad skin. He was one of very few who understood what it felt like to endure hours of torture, barely able to survive.

"Elias, I will be. But I need a favour."

"Anything, my lady," he answered without question.

"I want you to escort the people to the Citadel," she ordered.

"Dumbrorin is more than capable of carrying out the request. I will not leave your side," he protested.

Mia took his rough hands in hers and looked at the man before her. The sudden attention made Elias uneasy. She looked at him the way a mother might look at her son.

"I have seen your commitment to my husband through all the years. You haven't failed at a single request—"

"And now you expect me to fail this one?" he interrupted, jerking his hand away.

"I understand your allegiance to the crown, but what of your own life?" Mia wanted to know.

"My life has no meaning outside of my commitments, Mia."

Hearing her name called out so bluntly stunned her.

"Forgive me, my lady. I have sworn an oath to your husband, Estoban, to protect our village and to ensure our survival. I am not about to leave my princess without the proper escort she needs to a battle," he said gently.

Mia stood motionless for a moment and changed her approach.

"I respect your commitment, and I thank you for it. Estoban would have been proud of you. But do me one favour and please announce your affections to Astrid."

The mere mention of Astrid's name evidently made his pulse quicken. An image of her filled Mia's mind—Astrid had copper hair like that of Elias' beard, and Mia had seen her bringing him baked goods and any sweet thing she had made, dropped by the barracks to him and him alone. Mia knew he adored the maiden and longed for her hand in marriage.

"I have seen how the young women look at you. You don't seem to notice the stares of adoration, do you?"

Elias blushed profusely.

"This might be your last day in Achaos. Don't let it linger and leave a young maiden in distress over her heart. She longs to be courted, and even though her father is no longer with us, I will give my blessing as I have wanted to do for many years."

Mia looked at him and saw his resolve turn from embarrassment to determination.

"What if she declines?"

"I can almost guarantee that it will not happen." Mia punched his shoulder. "Go and see to it that it is done. We will leave at first light."

"Yes, my lady. I will gladly do as you ask." Elias' face lit up as he smiled.

Mia watched him go in a flurry. The day had gone by much too quickly. She not only witnessed how her fellow members were able to pack an entire household within hours, but she saw how much love flowed through the streets of Achaos. By dusk, the tribe was ready to leave.

***

Elias observed Astrid tying down a bundle onto the cart as the sun disappeared behind the mountains. Her mother had loudly instructed her precisely the order in which their household items should be packed in order not to break or fall from the cart, and she'd rolled her eyes at her mother, paying little attention.

She was still smiling at her mother's comment when Elias walked around the corner towards her. He studied her as he approached, his hands tucked deep into trousers worn only for battle. He was tall and held his head high, hoping she would not see the uncertainty in his eyes. She walked around the cart and slowly approached him.

Elias stopped in his tracks when he saw Astrid advance. Her strawberry blonde hair waved about in the breeze and resettled around her face. Smooth skin like alabaster was shaped around deep aquamarine eyes. She was dressed in fine white linen embroidered with green patterns across the midsection of her tunic. Her fur cloak lay aside on a small bench she still had to tie down on the cart.

"Elias, what's the matter?" she asked urgently.

He watched her, unable to utter a word.

"Elias, come on, has something happened?" she asked again.

Her eyes were filled with worry, and all Elias could do was take her hand in his, saying nothing.

Astrid just stared at him as he held her hand securely but gently, stroking the soft skin on the inside of her left palm. He bent down to kiss her arm and smelt deeply, her skin the scent of vanilla. All Astrid could do in response was tuck her hand into his thick bronze locks and play with his hair. He froze for a moment and let go of her hand. He stood straight, uncomfortably stepping back a little.

Astrid moved closer to him and stood almost against him. She looked up at his face as he froze staring into her eyes. She reached her hand out and stroked his short beard, and he trembled under her touch.

"Elias," Astrid spoke in a soft voice, beckoning him to speak to her.

"I was wondering, when this is all over, would you consider …" His voice trembled.

"I am yours, Elias. I have always been," Astrid giggled. "My heart has long ago been given to you. I was waiting for you to ask me, but I guessed you weren't interested."

"No! I love you, Astrid. I was afraid you might not …" he trailed off.

"Not what? Love you in return?" Astrid smirked and gave him a little shove. "Don't be silly!"

Astrid jumped into his arms and embraced the man she longed to love her entire adult life.

"Promise me something, Elias," she whispered.

"Anything, my love." Elias stretched out the last word.

Her heart grew faint within her, and Elias could see her finally able to release the passion she had stored up for a long time.

"Return to me, my valiant warrior. Slay the beast and come home," her eyes pleaded.

"I vow to love you all the days of my life, Astrid. If it is God's will, I will return."

Elias took her face into his hands and kissed her lips gently. His world came to a standstill when his lips connected with hers. He had never kissed before. Raw emotion flooded his veins; he drew her closer and embraced her with strong arms. Astrid allowed him to shower his love on her, for she knew that this might be their last chance.

When he finally let go, she ran to the cart and shoved her hand deep into the pile searching for something. She pulled out a satchel and rummaged through its contents. Elias watched her with silent anticipation. He had never felt more alive than this moment. Astrid pulled a small pouch from her satchel and held it in her hands for a few moments before she gave it to Elias. He opened the leather pouch and tucked his hand inside, retrieving the jewellery that lay at the bottom. A large, circular amulet the size of Astrid's palm lay in his hand. He gave her the pouch and turned the amulet around. It was a carving of her family's seal set in fine silver, a rare commodity in Achaos.

"It is the symbol of my parents' union. A replica of their covenant seal." She looked at the emblem in his hand. "With this amulet, I promise to honour you and wait for your return. Take it with you and remember me, Elias."

"For the last eight years I have carried the image of you with me into battle and every quest I have undertaken. Why would I not remember you now?" he chortled.

He hung the amulet around his neck and allowed it to drop to his chest. Astrid touched the amulet and settled her hand over his heart.

"I love you. It will be my honour to become your husband." Elias smiled and hugged her again, not wanting her to see the tears of joy that spilled from his eyes.

***

Mia watched the pair embrace from a distance. She enjoyed the show of affection, missing Estoban more than ever.

"Mia!" someone yelled.

Mia turned around to see a flustered Eugo running up to her with Eve following not far behind.

"What's wrong, Eugo?" she asked.

"My mother won't let me fight!" Tears started to form in the corner of his eyes, threatening to spill over the brim.

"You barely escaped from the battlefield in one piece. Your hands are still raw from the sword, and your leg might not be strong enough. She is right, Eugo," Mia tried to console him.

"I will never abandon the women who fight heroically for our tribe's survival," he protested. "God is with us, Mia. I've seen His mighty army fighting on our behalf. We will return with no more enemies to pursue us."

Eve finally caught up with them; she puffed and her face was red with fury.

"Mia, I will not let my only son die like his father did!" Eve shouted.

"Calm down, both of you," Mia ordered.

Eugo refused to let his mother touch his arm. He shuffled away from her, and her expression changed from anger to rejection. He spoke with such intensity it brought tears to Mia's eyes.

"I cannot rebel against my mother, but this one time I need to choose for myself. Mia, I saw what those monsters did to my father, the men, the boys I was with. They have no heart, and I won't let you face them alone. I believe our army is far superior to theirs. I have trained alongside Estoban, and I can help you on the battlefield." Eugo rushed his words, but his intentions were clear.

Eve just stared at her son at a loss for words. Mia turned towards her.

"Eve, I need you to think about Eugo. He lost everything, including his father. You cannot expect him to flee into the mountains along with women and children. He will never be able to deal with the regret in his heart for not giving it his all."

"But I lost everything too, Mia. I cannot lose my only son." Eve sat in the dirt and sobbed violently.

Eugo bent down beside his mother, anger evaporating from his heart.

"I love you, mother, but you need to let me go. I must find myself, even if it is on a battlefield."

Eve looked into his eyes and saw genuine compassion for her. She knew she had to let him go and become the man Demetrius knew he would.

Eve took his face into her hands and wiped the tears from his eyes. "Fight and come home."

"I will, mother. I promise," Eugo said as he hugged her tight.

Mia knew that a promise like that was filled with empty sympathies. Battle was uncertain and the outcome unpredictable, as was proven a week ago. Mia embraced mother and son and blessed them. Eve nodded to Mia, and she returned the gesture knowing that the sorrow Eve felt could never be consoled.

***

A total of 1931 individuals made their way into the overgrown path leading into the mountains. Dumbrorin was closely followed by Justus and Jacobien, riding into the unknown. Elias stood beside Mia as carts filled with precious commodities were pulled by oxen and donkeys. The horses remained in the village, ready to take the warriors in the opposite direction.

Mia bowed low as Evelyn and her granddaughter Meriba passed them by. Mia loved the vibrant old woman and was sure that the children would be in good hands. Eve cried as Eugo ran to her to give her a last farewell kiss on the cheek. She stood proud as she walked away, but Mia understood the anguish with which she left her beloved behind.

Young children ran along the carts playing, unaware of the treacherous path that lay ahead. Hands waved and women saluted their daughters and mothers as they walked along the road, filled with courage and hope.

When all the villagers were gone and the sun gave off its last bit of light, Mia gathered the remainder of Achaos together. She spoke in a strong, confident voice, encouraging the women seated around her.

"As it is written in the book of Isaiah the prophet, the word of the Lord says: 'In that day, the Lord Almighty will be a glorious crown, a beautiful wreath for the remnant of his people. He will be a spirit of judgement, a source of strength to those who turn back the battle at the gate'."

Women bowed their heads in respect and prayed to Yahweh for His deliverance.

"We are followers of Mighty Yahweh, and even though it seems lost, He will not let us be defeated and wiped away from the face of this Earth. Let His light shine upon us as we go to fight a battle that has been predetermined for a time such as this. Do not lose heart. Be strong and courageous. We will not be afraid."

Mia studied the faces of all the young women around her. They were strong and well trained. She did not fear for their courage, and she was proud to lead them.

"Tomorrow we will ride out to meet our enemy. I want each one of you to be ready—well rested and alert. Take your husbands' armour to the blacksmith's quarry and shape it to suit yourself. Take up any sword and spear you can find. Archers can get supplies from the barracks. Tonight we dine, for tomorrow we ride."

The group cheered and danced as they played their instruments with a joyous noise.

***

Fire pits billowed late into the night as each breastplate was reworked to fit snugly around thin middles and petite bodies. Bronze metal shone in the moonlight as Mia walked through the village clearing. Fire pits were stoked with fresh wood, and meat smoked in the fire. *A banquet fit for warriors*, Estoban would always say.

Mia smiled and sat amid the crowd next to Eugo and Elias.

She stroked Estoban's name inscribed on the inside of her breastplate. Mia polished ash from the corners and held it tight against her chest; it fit perfectly. Mia would wear her husband's armour with pride the few days she had left to breathe. She looked out at the crowd gathered around her in the clearing spurring one another on.

There were 112 women that remained to face Romulus in the mountainous Parnonas Valley, in addition to Elias, two scouts, and a very eager Eugo.

21

Dark grey clouds covered the valley as far as he was able to see. Bijan pulled his dark fur cloak tighter around his middle. The leather around his chest felt constricting and gave very little warmth; he longed for the light tunics he had grown accustomed to wearing in the beautiful valley due west of his current location.

Bijan pushed open the thick, velvet curtains as far as they allowed. The window let in a gush of cold air preceding the strange clouds building in the distance. The shape of the clouds seemed unnatural, and he had never seen anything like it. His chamber was dark, as dark as the night he abandoned his wife for a promise of riches and glory. Bijan remembered the moment he sacrificed an entire nation to greed.

He had heard the call not long after he had fallen asleep. Ariana was sleeping peacefully, her body draped over him. He loved her smooth skin hugging his tightly. Her arms were strong, and he had to pull her from him to get up. She lay still, crouched into a little ball, when he left the room. Ariana had stolen his heart; she was indeed his first true love.

He paced through the living room and quietly exited the cabin. He dropped down to the ground, disappearing into the foliage. Bijan specifically requested for his home to be situated along the eastern perimeter for this exact purpose. Estoban had not questioned him for a moment, expecting him to want the location to keep a good lookout for any assault to the village. Little did

Estoban know that Bijan had already dragged destruction into the heart of Achaos.

Three men cloaked in black awaited him in a small clearing a mile out from the village. Bijan could see the outline of the three, like claws protruding from the earth. He turned towards the men and was about to protect himself and kill them. They would be unable to deliver news to his emperor and Achaos would be safe, but loyalty to his master bid him into submission. He raised his arm and allowed the man on the right to pull a red dagger from a white cloth and dig it between his ribs.

The sacrificial blade seared his flesh as it cut deep into his body, nearly piercing his lung. He kept quiet, tolerating the burning sensation that swept over him. Adrenaline rushed to the wound and made his head spin. As quickly as the blade entered his side, it was removed and placed in its covering and the men gone. Bijan had played his part to perfection, drawing out the full strength of Achaos and sending them to their deaths.

A sudden knock at his door ripped him from his thoughts. Six women slithered into his chamber. One lit the candles as the others bowed at his feet. Bijan ignored the intrusion and kept his eyes firmly focused on the approaching cloud formation.

It glowed purple and churned around violent lightning. The rumble could be heard echoing through the valley. He became acutely aware of what was happening around him. Hands caressed his legs and arms. A wave of warm breath in his neck sent shivers down his spine. His heart started to race as adrenaline heightened his senses.

He didn't notice that his cloak was removed and the leather straps holding his garment in place loosened. His leather coating fell from his shoulders, revealing tanned skin filled with scars and old wounds.

A hand touched his left forearm, and he jerked it away. The girl again took up her position and was about to kiss the palm of his hand when he hit her squarely in the face, spinning her backwards to the floor. The room froze for an instant before Bijan realised what had happened.

He cowered to the side seeing six pairs of eyes on him, undressing him, wanting him. He screamed in terror as all six again approached him, all crawling on hands and feet and not wanting to stand over him. The girl wiped away the blood from the corner of her mouth and again bowed to kiss the same palm that injured her moments before.

Bijan's scream echoed through the chamber, like an animal trapped in a nest of vipers. The soldiers outside his chamber looked at one another and grinned—each one of them feeling the euphoria of the thrill. The doors burst open suddenly, spewing out young maidens half-dressed and frantic. They rushed past the soldiers down the hall before they were able to respond.

"After them, you idiot!" the man shouted.

The soldier jumped to attention and ran after the six slaves, hoping to gather them before anyone else noticed. The remaining man approached the chamber slowly. He peered inside to see Bijan hunched in a corner, his fists red with blood. He was half naked and shivering. He looked up at the soldier, his eyes vacant. The man retreated slowly and closed the door behind him.

Bijan cried in shame. He finally stood when all his energy was spent and his tear ducts dry. He cleared his throat and poured red wine into a glass chalice by his bedside. His door burst open again, but he paid no attention.

***

Valah watched the man standing in the middle of the room gulping down a glass of wine. His fists were encrusted with dry blood. Valah was about to turn when the man spoke.

"Are the women alright?" he asked.

"They will be," Valah responded.

"Please come in, Valah. I have been meaning to have a conversation with you." Bijan gestured for Valah to sit down on the lavish leather divan.

Valah was slightly uncomfortable but sat facing the man as he poured another glass and drank it in one smooth gulp. Bijan was back to his old self, and Valah felt a strange sense of peace knowing that whatever tormented the man was far more potent than the visions he himself had seen.

"Have you ever felt lost, Valah?" Bijan asked.

"Yes," Valah replied, studying Bijan.

His shoulder-length black hair hung in tassels around his face. He thought for a moment that he saw a tear on his cheek but shoved the thought to the back of his mind.

"Why do you ask, Bijan?" Valah pressed.

"I have this recurring feeling that all I have ever wanted robbed me of the one thing I actually needed." Bijan spoke in a muffled voice, an eerie sound that gave Valah shivers.

"I do not understand what you mean, sir," Valah responded.

Bijan looked at Valah with a surprised expression. "Why are you here, Valah?"

"I take pride in knowing where all my charges are at all times. I sent six women in my care to your chamber on request of our emperor. He told me that Daelia was of no use to you. She is only a trinket of purity. He was certain you would keep it that way."

Bijan shuffled uncomfortably at the last comment.

"I admire that," Valah continued. "But Romulus insisted that after two days you needed the accompaniment."

"He was wrong!" Bijan shouted.

Valah sat still, allowing the rage to pass before Bijan sat back down opposite him on a similar divan.

"I only wanted to see if you were alright. The women said you were possessed and chased them from the chamber."

Bijan laughed. "Possessed is not nearly a strong enough word, Valah. I have countless sleepless fits driving me to convulsions. I see the faces of women and children I have slain in cold blood all in the name of a demon that claims to guide our emperor. The Angra Mainyu doesn't exist. None of it does. We are just here by chance to do Romulus' bidding. There is no greater purpose. No God, only idols and dreams of deities that promise freedom and liberation."

Valah watched as Bijan returned to his wine, this time taking the bottle instead. He understood what Bijan meant; he himself had often pondered the same thing. Valah sat quietly with Bijan for nearly an hour before he stood to leave. He turned to Bijan.

"I am sorry for your loss. I can see that a heart ripped apart like my own could never recover. I also don't want to see the faces of the tortured again; it plagues my dreams. I had thought that you'd changed somehow, but I can now see it is only the realisation of your true self that drives the change in you."

***

Bijan said nothing as Valah left his chamber, leaving him to sit by himself. He didn't understand the turmoil in his heart and mind. He was lost and broken, numb and lifeless. Fear and frustration threatened to choke the last breath from his lungs.

He kept his eyes on the dark rolling clouds approaching the keep. His heart churned inside of him. What was he thinking? Estoban was a good man—he loved him like a brother. He lost all thought of containing his emotions, and a deep, hungry growl escaped his mouth and echoed off the walls as he collapsed to the floor.

The clouds were moving faster now. They entered the small window cut from the gleaming limestone wall and filled the room with intense cold. Tears blurred his vision as hands grabbed him from all directions, pulling him limb from limb. The pain that shot through his heart was unbearable.

Each thought jerked him farther into the dark clouds overtaking him and wrestling with his heart. His mouth pulled in a skew spasm as his whole body contorted into a seizure. The wine bottle fell from his hands and shattered to pieces, spilling wine over the stone floor. A word wrestled from his mind, but his body would not relent.

Bijan pushed with all his resolve past the restriction in his throat. The word escaped in a rasp from his lips, "YAHWEH!"

With the speed of lightning, the pain was gone. He opened his eyes to see his chamber in shambles as his fists had connected with objects around him. The Egyptian cotton sheets were torn and ripped to pieces, strewn about the bedpost. Could he have done this? His mind was reeling at the prospect of his own rage.

Heat started to run up his spine, and an opening appeared in the wall to his left. There was no door he knew of, for each secret passageway was known to him. A male figure dressed in white approached him from the opening, glowing like the sun. Bijan narrowed his eyes to prevent the light from blinding him. He held his hand by his face, shielding it from the bright light. The man held a fiery red coal in his hand. He raised the coal to Bijan's mouth and placed it inside.

Heat and fire exploded inside his head, but he wasn't consumed. The man stared at him with eyes blazing like fire. A voice emanated from him with the sound of rushing waters that exploded in Bijan's ears.

"any avhb avtk bny, shbhrty"

He tried to understand the meaning of the word but failed as power surged into his body, a force that made it impossible to stand. He fell prostrate before the man, and his world went dark.

It seemed like an eternity wrapped in darkness before he awoke. His room was dark; candle wax soiled the floor beneath the candle holders, and the dark clouds still hung in the distant horizon. He was lying in his bed, and everything around him was back to normal—neat books on the shelf to his right by the window and his clothes arranged over the leather divan brought in by Emperor Romulus.

Had it all been a dream? It seemed so real, so tangible. He fell back into the soft sheets, confused, and allowed sleep to overtake him as exhaustion set in.

***

Despite the frigid wind blowing in from the south, the sun reached down from the horizon to cover the valley in shimmering gold and red, chasing away the grey morning. Mia recounted her strategy for the battle to herself. She was certain that every possible contingency was planned for.

She tied the last leather strap to her knapsack like she had done a week before. She smiled at the thought; she never expected to pack a small bag, carrying only the things she would need to survive for herself.

Mia looked at the armour lying beside the knapsack. She remembered laying out Estoban's armour on their last morning together, and her heart ached for her beloved once more. She pulled the shin guards tight and wrapped material around her wrists to protect them from chafing against the protective metal guards. She looked at her covenant mark one last time before she covered it in material followed by strong leather encased in bronze.

She gave one last look around her cabin to see if she had missed something. She walked towards her mirror and stared back at the woman in the reflection. Her skin was pale and seemed to elongate her face. Her high cheekbones were red from the cold. Clear blue eyes were framed by golden locks in disarray.

She pulled her hair back in a twisted hairstyle, keeping loose strands from her face. She took a small crown woven in a similar pattern to her covenant seal and placed it on her head, binding it along with her hair.

Mia set the breastplate in place and twisted to her left to attach the leather straps to its metal clips and then did the same on her right side. She would wear the armour as a great honour to her fallen hero. She was about to leave when she remembered something.

She ran to her closet and pulled out Estoban's chest. She rummaged for the small amulet she had given Estoban on the day of their betrothal when she heard the rap at the door. She stood quickly, expecting word from one of the few scouts she had left.

Mia opened the door to see Eugo and Danelle, both dressed in military style, awaiting her.

"Good morning to you both, mighty warriors," she greeted.

They giggled.

"We thought it best to escort our princess to the procession," Eugo stated.

"If you would please follow us, my lady." Danelle gave a slight bow, looking ridiculous in the patchwork of armour Eugo had made her the night before.

Mia pondered again over her decision to allow anyone who was willing to fight to join her cause. Danelle seemed so small, fragile, and inexperienced in the world, yet she was about to face beast men in the heat of battle.

She shrugged off her restraint. "If you would be so kind as to give me five minutes; I just need to get a few last things."

The duo bowed in honour and stood beside the door, as if guarding it with their lives.

Mia retrieved the amulet from the chest and closed the lid on all the precious things that gave Estoban's heart joy in this world. She placed the amulet around her neck, allowing it to drop to her breastplate and chime as metal connected with metal. She scanned the room. Confident that everything was in place, she threw her satchel over her shoulder, placed her father's sword next to her golden dagger in its sheath around her waist, and exited the room, leaving behind all its memories.

Elias was standing beside Mia's horse awaiting its charge. The amulet around his neck was shimmering in the early morning light. Mia pointed towards the amulet, and all he could do was smile in return.

"You were right. There is nothing like the promise of young love." He laughed, trying to hide the flush in his cheeks.

Mia smiled as he tied her satchel down and held out his hand, ready for her to mount her horse. The trail of warriors behind her gave her a serenity she did not expect. The atmosphere was filled with anticipation, and Mia understood for the first time what it felt like to the valiant men who had gone before her. Although there was no music or falling flower petals to greet them, she felt a sense of pride and accomplishment as she set out into the forest.

The village disappeared behind the trees, and women, dressed like the best warriors Mia had ever seen, marched their horses in perfect silence. Mia looked towards Elias flanking her left side. She bowed her head and allowed the scout to ride ahead, showing them the route to follow.

22

"I set you as a seal upon my heart, as a seal upon my arm," a voice whispered to him. Bijan looked everywhere for the sound and saw a woman sitting in the centre of Achaos' clearing, enveloped by a lavish chair woven from branches and beautifully decorated with white blossoms.

He recognised Ariana and ran to her side. She was smiling and whispering their vow continuously, humming to herself. Her left arm was slashed and the covenant mark removed; a hole gaped in her chest where her heart was supposed to be.

Bijan didn't understand but knew that a physician might be waiting in the meeting house, so he picked up her body and ran towards it. The large wooden doors opened as he approached. Upon entering, he saw an altar for burnt offerings in the centre; the altar resembled one he had seen in the temple of Dionysis.

Bijan looked around the dimly lit interior and saw the shape of a man seated on the simple throne. Romulus raised a chalice to his face and drank deeply from the black liquid. The firelight created twisted images on his face; the look of a demented man swam in every one. Bijan froze in the doorway.

"Sacrifice her." Romulus pointed to the altar.

Bijan laid his wife on the altar, powerless to his sudden submission. He looked at the dark eyes of the man that was about to take everything from him again—they reflected no emotion.

"Sacrifice your wife and receive a prize worth far more," Romulus said with benevolence.

Bijan was unable to move, his feet locked into the stone floor. Ten girls about the age of seventeen appeared at his side. They were sparsely dressed and covered with black markings that ran along their arms and legs. They started to caress his thighs, then moved their hands to his chest and ran their fingers through his hair. Romulus handed him a golden goblet.

"Drink, mighty warrior, and receive your portion," he sniggered.

Bijan drank the dark liquid and nearly spat it out. It burned his throat and his stomach, enflaming his entire body. The girls whispered into his ear, their breath carrying the stench of death. He wanted to cry, but a strange desire burned in his mind.

Romulus walked to the covered window and drew back a black veil to reveal Estoban with his head hung downwards on a cross made of timber. The man had been mutilated and his covenant seal removed. Bijan was unable to hold the sadness in his heart. He shut his eyes.

A gentle voice made him open them again. He was back in the village. He cautiously followed the voice to a door and braced himself for what he would see this time as he opened it. His kitchen was just as he left it. A pot hung above the fireplace, and the aroma of rabbit stew welcomed him in. Ariana stood by the pot, stirring. Relieved, Bijan grabbed her from behind and she turned towards him, but the woman he saw was not his wife. The woman's dimpled cheeks smiled. His mother stirred the pot again and motioned for him to sit down. Bewildered, he just followed her orders.

"She was naughty. Your father and I removed the evil that dwelled inside of her." She smiled brightly as she placed a bowl of hot stew before him.

Bijan jumped up and ran to the stairwell. He took three steps at a time, hastily wanting to reach Ariana's prayer room. She lay on her side—her belly was ruptured, and her intestines covered the floor. She held their son in her arms. The baby was shrivelled and blue and didn't breathe. All Bijan could utter as he collapsed next to his family was "No Ariana, not my beloved!"

A voiceless scream erupted from his throat as he sat up straight in his bed. Bijan looked around the room; it was dark and musty. He threw the Egyptian cotton sheets off the bed and ran to the covered window.

He pulled the red velvet curtain aside and gulped fresh air. He felt dizzy and vomited in a corner. He pushed himself against the restraint of his muscles. He breathed hard, trying to make sense of the dreams that evoked anger inside of him.

Bijan stared at the horizon for a long time before he realised that his extremities were growing numb. He grabbed his velvet cloak and pulled it tight around his body. Tears ran down his face as it all came back to him.

The love he felt in the village of Achaos, the betrayal of his first and most loyal friend and ultimately the demise of the only woman who loved him more than life itself. Bijan shook with fear as he again saw the image of his wife, ripped open from her naval to her chin—blood and intestines twisted in a congealed mess. He needed to fix what he had broken. Bijan tried to find the answers, but reasoning failed him.

He ran to the hallway, nearly collapsing on the tiles as he rounded the corner. He knocked on the door to the storage room just to the left of his chamber, a privilege for the general's concubine, they called it. But the thought of Daelia locked in a storage room with no window enraged him more.

***

The knocking on her door stirred her awake. Daelia instinctively grabbed for something to cover herself with but then realised that she was safe. She reached for the candelabra and lit the wick; the small room was engulfed in light. It was cramped and housed only a basin of water on a stone pedestal, a bed half the right size stuffed with straw and covered in a thin blanket, and a rail on which hung her new wardrobe specially chosen by Bijan himself. She walked to the door.

"Who is it?" she asked politely while grabbing a dress from the rail.

"Daelia, I need to tell you something!" The urgent voice of her general sounded frail and muffled.

"The key is by the doorpost." She shuffled into a yellow dress she liked very much and tried to straighten her short hair, attempting to look ravishing and presentable.

The key turned in the lock and Bijan shoved the door open. He was ashen white and covered in sweat. Daelia took her sleeve and cleaned his cheeks. He seemed bewildered. Taking his face into her hands, she forced him to look her in the eye.

"What happened to you?"

"I have done things that are as terrifying to me now as they will be to you when you hear them."

Daelia looked at him, unsure what to make of his portrayal of remorse. She had grown to like him, and ever since she met him he was more of a guardian than a monster taken into service by Romulus. She shivered at the thought.

"Tell me, Bijan. Tell me everything." She gave a slight smile, and it seemed to ease the guilt-ridden warrior.

Sitting beside the fireplace in his chamber, Bijan recounted his journey from the time he was able to remember. The fire was welcoming; the fur skins absorbed most of the cold stone beneath her as Daelia sat opposite him, close enough to hear his soft voice. His voice creaked, and she could see his mind run through memories of long ago.

He was five years old when he moved with his father. They were living in Barazjan when Romulus called his men to arms. It was time to leave the empire behind for better and greater things.

His mother named him Bijan, 'hero' in Persian. While he was still in her womb, Anousheh believed that Bijan was going to change history. She had died during childbirth, leaving his father to tend to him. Darius Khalili was an excellent blacksmith and one of only two to be enlisted by Romulus.

Romulus served under the leadership of Cyrus the first and was promoted to the king's personal guard, receiving great reward for his skill in battle. But despite his great power and influence, his attempts at revenge on the Jewish nation failed due to the Great Edict of Restoration written by the king to release all Jews from their exiled captivity. At the succession of Cambyses the second, his long-time friend, Romulus believed that their great bond and mutual hatred for the Jews would bring about the change he longed for, but Cambyses remained true to his father's reign and continued the release of the Jews from exiled captivity.

Due to confusion and internal succession struggles within the royal family, Romulus was dejected as the new general. Frustrated and filled with a rage that was uncontainable, Romulus defected from the Persian army and broke away to seek vengeance on his own. Romulus was exiled by Smerdis of Persia, the successor of Cambyses the second. Romulus vowed to destroy and annihilate all the Jews and those who believe in their God.

Bijan spent most of his youth making swords and armour for Romulus' soldiers. He loved the craft more than his father did and was soon noticed by Romulus. They had arrived at the abandoned stronghold in the Parnonas Mountains and settled in the keep after seven years of travelling. Belarus started to work as Romulus' personal blacksmith, a position he was fashioned for. He soon sat in on important meetings and learned about fighting and conquest.

Four years later, he requested his admission into military service. He was remarkably successful and quickly ascended the ranks. He was promoted to leader of the regiment and second only to Romulus himself. He was denied no luxury, and for ten years he served his emperor faithfully and grabbed at the opportunity to be the one to bring Achaos to its knees. After the escape of Mia, crown princess of Achaos, Romulus sent Bijan to infiltrate the tribe and gain their trust, a job he had done to perfection as the man named Belarus.

As Bijan recounted the numerous missions he had done on behalf of his emperor, the tears rolled off his cheek. Murder, slaughter, rape, and plunder were the only things he ever did. Romulus called it conquest of a nation that deserved no pity. Pride and greed drove Bijan beyond the reaches of dignity. He had sold himself to a cause that was hopeless and savage. The hatred his emperor had for followers of Yahweh far outweighed any position of purpose.

Bijan never allowed religion and idolatry to abuse his mind. It made him weak and his purpose cloudy. He preferred to kill and gain the renown he came to own. The pain he now experienced crippled his resolve.

When Bijan spoke of his beloved Ariana, Daelia slumped and hoped for a love as strong as the one they possessed. Love broke down all that he had come to know as true. Now it was all gone, a tribe betrayed, and the love of his woman forever lost. How could any man take the life of another?

Daelia watched him as he told her the tale. She saw no glint of pride or accomplishment in his eyes, only sorrow and a deep longing to be forgiven. She longed to give him the release he yearned for, but she knew that only a higher power could deliver such forgiveness. Instead, she moved beside him and allowed him to rid himself of the tears.

She secured him in her embrace, holding him close until his sobs became only slight tremors and finally subsided. Her own tears were hidden from him. She needed him to be at peace, not burden him with more guilt. Men like him were responsible for her capture, the rape of her mother, and torture of her father, the pain unabated.

She longed for freedom and escape but knew that her fate would be ever intertwined with the man she held in her arms. She had to help him release his pain.

"A nation divided against itself cannot stand," she finally said out loud.

"What do you mean?" Bijan sat up, looking at her.

His eyes were those of a defeated man, long ago ruined by evil.

"If we can create a plan to break down the unity within the keep, we can overthrow it," Daelia stared straight ahead, her mind working silently behind mahogany brown eyes.

***

Bijan took note of the change in her demeanour. She was no longer the plain servant; instead she burned with such purpose and intensity that she was far more attractive than Bijan had noticed before.

His mind spun as she laid out a plan to devour the enemy from the inside. She proposed an assault by all who opposed the emperor and, in that notion, bring him down from within. The prospect of freedom built inside his heart. If such a thing was even possible, Bijan needed help from above. He saw the vision again—the coal in his mouth, the renewal in his strength, and the purpose with which his mother named him.

'Hero' kept repeating in his heart. Daelia then shook him hard, and he refocused on her pretty face. She stared at him, dumbfounded. He said nothing as he stood, dropping the cloak from his naked body. She shied away as he dressed and looked at him only when he spoke.

"There is something I have to do first." Bijan waited for her to collect herself and follow him.

He closed the door to her chamber after she entered, locked it, and whispered through it. "I will come for you, and together we will rid the world of Romulus and his evil heart."

And then he was gone.

The passage scraped his leather covering in a hushed fumble. Bijan ran as fast as he could without drawing attention to himself. Soldiers paid little attention to the man as he drifted past, nodding in their direction. He needed to get out. The tunnels closed in on him, suffocating his resolve. Pain threatened to crush his heart.

He had to stop for a moment to catch his breath and allow his mind to settle. He stood beside the last chamber in the tunnel before he was in the outer courtyard. Bijan heard moaning, and he leaned closer to listen. He heard Valah but failed to identify the woman he was singing to. He moved closer, placing his ear next to the door.

***

A chant escaped Valah's lips, repeating over and over. He placed his hands beside the image carved from stone, nestled on a stone pillar surrounded by small candles lighting the face of Nabu, the God of Wisdom. The representation looked down on Valah.

His horned cap and clasped hands represented ancient priesthood. His power over human existence was so strong that Valah could feel the surge flowing through his hands. Nabu had the ability to increase and diminish, at will, the length of human life. Valah longed for his God to write his destiny on a sacred stone tablet.

The stone and the hammer remained in place. Valah tried to plea again for his life to be written, but the tools did not move. Filled with rage, he shoved the idol to the floor, cursing it as it shattered. Valah fell backwards, unwilling for his God to remain silent. Nabu never spoke, but whenever Valah bowed in worship, the power that filled his heart was unquenchable. He waited for the anger of his God to kill him, but nothing came. He lay motionless, looking at the soot on his chamber's ceiling.

A sudden shuffle beside his door broke the silence. He jumped up and rushed at the door, grabbing his sword and scabbard. A person ran from it as he pulled the heavy latch open. A lone figure ran across the courtyard towards the stables, and Valah pursued the man. Silently he waited as the figure saddled a horse and mounted the beast; only then he saw his face.

He saw Bijan look around the clearing, seemingly to make sure he was not followed. Satisfied, he then nudged the horse forward and told the guard to open the secret passage beside the iron gate. The guard opened the door, allowing Bijan to ride his steed into the night.

"Where did he go?" Valah inquired after making his way to where the guard stood.

The guard spun around to look his general square in the eyes. He fumbled over his words.

"A secret mission for Romulus, my lord." The guard bowed low, fearful of reprimand.

Valah said nothing but gazed until Bijan disappeared out of sight.

***

The full moon cast shadows through the heavy canopy, lighting armour in a dazzling array of sparkles. The steep climb through the underbrush was slowing the pace, and deep grooves in the ravine made crossing near impossible.

The early snowfall hardly penetrated the forest canopy, but when it did, mud and debris massed together to create darker mud that sucked limbs into the deep. Every 300 yards, a clearing offered some time to rub off the mud and regain strength before trudging through the next section of forest. Groups of thirty marched no more than ten feet apart, each group led by one of the regiment's scouts.

Elias ran to Mia and whispered softly. Mia gave the signal, and the entire regiment froze and disappeared in the underbrush. A distant winnow of a horse could be heard.

"Another three miles northeast, my lady," Elias confirmed.

"How many stationed outside?"

"A mere twenty. I do not believe they are expecting company. The passing groups number three at the most. I have seen many travellers coming from the surrounding villages south of Sparta, a long way to travel to have business with the emperor," he relayed.

Mia scoffed at the mention of Romulus. "He is no emperor, trust me. He is nothing but a vile, deceitful man filled with greed and an unquenchable lust for blood."

Elias remained silent until the horses disappeared in the distance. For the last three days, Mia and her army avoided the main route that cut through the valley. Horse-drawn carts and men's feet cleared a narrow, irregular path through the underbrush.

Marching parallel to the beaten track made their progress tarry. Every morning, Elias and three scouts investigated the route ahead and ensured that no traps were laid for the army approaching from the west.

"We continue for another two miles before we rest," Mia instructed.

"Yes, my lady. This way."

Elias led the group due east for half a mile and turned sharply north for a further mile. With only half a mile to go to their destination, the route to their left grew wider and less bumpy. Mia longed to tread on level ground but knew that a simple mistake as small as that could destroy the element of surprise and ultimately lead to failure. A mile from the keep, Elias led the group into a sharp ravine that allowed for shelter and warmth against the cold breeze drifting through the valley.

When all the soldiers had settled in, Mia, Ariana, and Eugo accompanied Elias towards the keep. With little baggage, their journey was swift. The underbrush gave way to smaller shrubs, allowing for better footing.

When the trees cleared enough to see the mound ahead, Mia's heart began to beat faster. She recognised the sharp incline and knew exactly what the keep was going to look like.

Like a vivid dream, the keep surprised Mia and rendered her speechless. The large, circular outer wall seemed twice as high as she remembered. Green moss emanating a sour stench covered the wall, making a climb near impossible. An approaching enemy would be spotted a mile away in the open field surrounding the green wall. She was amazed that they had initially missed her with arrow and spear when she fled, a thought that gave her a slight assurance of their incapacity to handle surprise.

"We will attack at dawn while everyone is still deep in their stupefied slumber," Mia said as she smiled.

"Which direction do we take?" Ariana asked.

"To the left of the large gate, near the bottom of the pucker beneath the drawbridge, is a small sewage entrance. We go in from there."

Ariana twisted her nose at the thought of rummaging through a service tunnel probably reeking of dead flesh and garbage. Mia noticed her expression; she suppressed her laughter and looked at Eugo instead. His eyes were wide with wonder. He had probably never seen a sight such as this. He was knowledgeable about architecture in Sparta and its grandeur, but it was still unremarkable compared to the keep cut away in moss-covered limestone.

Retreating to the hidden ravine, Mia knew that many questions would await her; she pulled Elias aside.

"I will need some time to myself to pray. Can you keep a lookout for the regiment?"

"I will do as you wish. Keep safe and do not go too far from the ravine. The moon is about to set over the mountains, and darkness is fast approaching. We will need our rest before we attack at dawn," Elias warned.

"I will do as you say, sire." Mia saluted the scout and laughed while retreating into the overgrown forest.

***

Elias stared at the tree line, hoping to see where his princess had gone. She disappeared, camouflaging with the forest in the blink of an eye. He would remain at his post until she returned before he rested with the rest of his regiment.

23

Hooves sloshed through ankle-deep mulch, and horse and rider swerved to the left and right, missing trees and leaving sharp debris in their wake. The clearing nearly startled him when he entered it. Pulling hard on the reins, the horse revolted, nearly throwing its rider into the thicket just beyond the clearing.

"Shush, be calm."

Bijan stroked the neck of his stallion until it calmed, trotting on the spot. He jumped off the animal, still stroking its neck and whispering into its ears. Plumes of steam gushed from its nostrils as its heart calmed from the run. Satisfied that it would keep quiet, he tied the horse to a nearby tree and he made his way to the clearing's centre.

The moon shone wildly in the open sky, snow clouds momentarily blown aside.

"Where are you when I need you?" he yelled. "Estoban spoke of you before he died. He fell into the hands of Romulus, tortured and ripped apart, but still he forgave me for the treacherous villain that I am. Why will you not hear me? I have raped and ravished countless women. I murdered infants ripped from their mothers' wombs for money. For fame and respect I plundered, robbed, and killed in cold blood, sporting for my emperor."

Bijan walked in circles screaming the deeds out in plain sight, not bothered by anyone hearing him.

"They say you are the only God. Why call to idols and things made by man when we have the true Almighty in our midst? Estoban told me tales of you … fabrications of his mind, I thought. But I was wrong. I am a pitiful show of a man. How can I decide which life to take? It's all so precious in your sight. My brave Ariana loved me without question; she bestowed on me all kinds of kindness a murderer does not deserve. I am pleading with you, Lord. Take this burden from me. Take the pain away and renew a clean spirit within me. I want to follow you. Come into my heart; change the man I have become."

The moon then vanished from sight, but nothing else happened. Bijan fell onto his knees and into the mud as darkness surrounded him. He was lying on his stomach, spent from the fatigue that permeated every piece of his body. Bijan pushed himself from the mud; the soft earth squeezed between his fingers as he sunk deep into the mulch.

The smell of raw earth and fresh snow surrounded him, engulfing him in a cold embrace. He didn't know how long he had lain there sobbing into the night. He had no words left to say, and whenever he spoke, his words made no sense to him, as if something willingly drew him back.

"God Almighty, Yahweh hear me!" he uttered, completely defeated.

The silence was deafening. Bijan was about to give up when he heard a faint whisper.

"Bijan, my beloved."

"Forgive me, my Lord." Bijan let go completely, exhausted from the turmoil in his heart.

Those four words ripped the heavens open, and a bright light illuminated the clearing where he waited. The trees gave way to a grand auditorium filled with a mix of spectators all looking down at him. They were smiling and humming. The noise of the crowd sounded like water spilling off the side of a cliff. The rumble increased as the same man from his vision dressed in pure white walked out of the crowd towards him.

The man took Bijan's face into his and looked into his eyes. The sight was breathtaking. Bijan felt the warmth permeating from this man. His eyes looked like they were on fire, and yet his smile showed no disapproval. Bijan felt his knees weaken.

He was unable to hold the stare, as the sheer power of the man overwhelmed him more than anything he had ever experienced. The man knelt along with Bijan and kept his face firmly in his hands. His voice was like a thunderous cloud, yet soft and gentle.

"I love you, my son. I forgive you, my beloved. I have given myself for you. I am He—the alpha and the omega, the first and the last. There is none but me. You are my beloved, and you are mine."

Tears overflowed and ran down Bijan's face, gushing like a waterfall. He felt the pain and remorse lift from his shoulders, and a sense of awe and lightness filled his body. A renewed strength far more intense than his vision filled his bones. His body felt alive and on fire.

Words of affirmation and love overwhelmed him. He recognised the same love Ariana had bestowed on him, but this was far more permanent and laced with grace. He closed his eyes, unable to keep them open in the rapture of his rebirth.

"Bijan."

Bijan felt as if the earth had swallowed the man he was and birthed a new man, filled with compassion and the ability to love completely. Bijan could hear the faint whisper of his name on the wind. Forgiveness and redemption had come to him at last.

"Thank you, Father." He bowed his head in respect and prayed.

Suddenly a twig snapped, and his eyes opened abruptly, searching for the perpetrator around the clearing. He unsheathed his dagger as he crouched, ready to attack anything that came his way. His eyes searched the dark shapes of the trees looking for the attacker.

"You can lay your weapon down, Belarus."

At the mention of his deceiver's name, he dropped the blade and raised his hands. He remained standing where he was, waiting for arrows to pierce his legs, his arms, and finally his heart.

Mia strode into the clearing as the moon vanquished the cloudy covering. Her armour glistened in the moonlight. Her hair was taken back into a strong braid that twisted to keep her small crown in place. She was as radiant as if he saw her for the first time. A peace that he didn't understand overwhelmed him.

"Forgive me, Mia. I have done a terrible thing." Bijan fell on his knees before her, arms still raised.

Mia walked to him and knelt beside him. She took his face in her hands and forced him to look in her eyes. Despite the dark hour, her eyes shone like luminous sapphires. She looked at him with compassion and the grace he had come to know this fateful night.

"I forgive you, Belarus." A tear slipped from her eye as she embraced him tightly.

Bijan could do nothing but return the embrace, a relationship restored.

"I am so sorry for letting you and Estoban down. I didn't know how lost I was until I finally found Yahweh."

"I saw everything. I know what you have done." Mia released her embrace, stood up, and walked to the centre of the clearing.

She tilted her face towards the sky and took in the beauty of the moon. It was completely round and shone brightly. The moisture in the air caught its light and granted the moon its halo. Bijan heard her speak a soft blessing over her departed Estoban. She clung to the covenant symbol around her neck dangling on its silver chain.

"I loved him more than life, but Estoban is one with the Lord. He will no longer have pain or remorse," she turned towards Bijan, "and neither should we."

He swallowed hard.

"What do we do now?" he asked.

"Now we pray."

Mia bowed her head and started to intercede for her tribe and their deliverance but prayed loud enough for Bijan to acknowledge every request and stand in agreement with every spoken word.

When the duo finally reached the limit of their strength, they stood in awe of their creator. The deep void in Bijan's heart was no longer there. It had been filled. He understood for the first time what it must have felt like for Ariana to succumb fully to the love of their God on their wedding day.

She had tried to explain the unity she felt, but he failed to grasp the wholeness of God, until now. The covenant seal — a symbol of unity between husband, wife and God — finally became a reality. This covenant could not be severed, no matter what happened in this life.

"Mia, I need to show you something."

Bijan pulled up the sleeve of his shirt to reveal a broad blue scar on his right forearm.

"What happened?" she asked, curiously studying the disfigurement.

"You gave me this scar by the iron gate the day you escaped from the keep. You nearly severed all the muscles. I was lucky to regain enough strength in my arm to heal completely."

Mia gasped in surprise. "That was you?"

"Yes. It reminds me of who I once was — angry and filled with hatred and contempt for anyone who did not submit to our ways. But you and your God changed me. I am no longer that man. I am a new creation. I no longer live with malice and deceit. Let me make things right, I beg of you."

"You already have." She smiled at him.

Mia pulled her dagger from its sheath and laid it in the palm of his hand.

"I believe this belongs to you."

Bijan stroked the gold-encrusted blade inscribed with Persian writing that his father had given him on his sixteenth birthday; he remembered the day well. He felt the blade become one with him as he twisted it in various directions. He then shoved it towards Mia.

"I believe you have earned the right to become its new master."

***

Mia blushed at the sentiment. She could see that he no longer desired for anything from his past to soil his new life. He would face many tribulations, but God would turn around the tragedy for good.

"I have come to know you well, Belarus. I also know that you are not a man without a plan." She eyed him curiously as his mind appeared to turn.

"A valiant young girl reminded me of a very wise saying. We need to divide the house. It cannot stand if it falls from within."

"How do you suppose you will be able to catch Romulus unguarded?"

"Use his weakness against him," Belarus assured her.

Mia pondered for a moment and realised that all she really knew of the enemy was his desire for blood.

"His trophies are his weakness, Mia," Belarus continued. "Romulus keeps the royals alive at all costs. He once held a Nubian princess captive, raped her, tortured her, and broke her down. There was barely anything left of the princess when he executed her three years later. That is why he has such a deep hatred for you, my lady."

"I never gave up ..." she whispered to herself.

Mia realised that her resolve might have been broken if she was held for another three years, even if her instincts wanted to say otherwise.

"I am second only to Romulus. My treachery has awarded me the treasure I thought I always wanted. If the daughter-in-law of Amyntas and I can work together, we can make it happen."

"She is still alive?" Mia was excited for a moment.

"Yes, the Athenian princess will live if her resolve keeps her alive. As soon as she gives in, Romulus will lose his desire for her, and her fate will be sealed. I have many soldiers loyal to me, and most of them have a deep hatred for Romulus. Most would want to see him fall. There is only one man, Valah, who I need to secure for this plan to succeed. His disdain for the emperor is evident."

"Two days. We will be ready," Mia assured him.

"May I ask one favour?"

"Anything I can do to help."

"I will send a young girl to you as soon as our plan is set into motion. Her name is Daelia. Please take her into your care. She is just a girl in need of a family like yours."

"I promise to take care of her," Mia replied without hesitation.

"May Yahweh protect you." Belarus bowed low, still holding her hand in his palm.

Mia placed her hand on his head. "And may He be with you."

They parted with a firm shake, and Mia watched the man she had come to love as a brother depart through the thicket. She looked towards the sky and prayed that his plan would succeed and that Romulus would be defeated once and for all.

24

Bijan sat upright, eagerly awaiting the rise of the sun. He felt a sense of satisfaction as he stared around his chamber. He waited for Daelia to come to his bedside with his breakfast. He hardly ever slept late and expected her to be as swift as the sunrise on this fair morning.

Everything about him had changed. The meeting in the forest was not only an escape but a rebirth of a new life he had never known. Fervour accompanied his every thought, his motives as clear as the daylight engulfing the keep.

It was rare for the sun to shed its light amid the sharp crevices in the valley. Deep gorges and ravines twisted and turned to reveal this gem. The keep was hard to reach and near impossible to find.

He barely heard the short rap at the door.

"Enter!" he yelled.

Daelia entered dressed in a green tunic rather than one of her usual silk dresses. The garment was loose fitting but still shaped around her body to reveal every voluptuous curve. Bijan understood for the first time why the men gawked at her. He hardly noticed her until now. She placed the tray on his side table and turned to look at him. She froze. Bijan waited for her to say something, but she remained quietly petrified.

"What's the matter? What happened?" Bijan quickly moved to her side, shuffling with the sheets tangled around him.

Bijan was very aware of his naked body and thought it best to keep himself covered. Ariana would be the only woman to ever set eyes on him again.

"You've changed," she said, surprised.

"What do you mean?"

"I can see it in your eyes, in your body language."

Bijan sat down beside the tray. "It's that obvious?"

He looked at his hands as if seeing them for the first time. Daelia sat opposite him on the divan, staring in utter amazement.

"You will not believe what happened."

Bijan then recounted his vision in the forest, not leaving out a single detail. He explained to her the release he felt and how much he was forgiven. He tried to relay to her the peace he experienced, but it seemed lost on her. She looked at him with interest, but behind her eyes he could see her scepticism.

"It's all true, I promise you. I feel more alive than ever before. It's as if I see everything for the first time. Take you, for instance. You are so beautiful its overpowering."

Daelia looked at him with scorn, showing hurt at his ridicule.

Bijan saw the pain in her eyes and rested his hands on hers.

"God loves you, no matter what happened to you or who belittled you to feel unworthy. He wants you to turn to Him and give everything to Him."

***

As Bijan waited for her to respond, Daelia pondered the sudden openness with which he addressed her. She felt exposed for the fraud she was. She pretended to be happy serving as the general's concubine, keeping up appearances, prancing around like a little harlot only to remain unscathed from the stares of the other men in the keep. She wanted to scream her anguish but knew that it too would be futile. She would only receive a slap for her outburst.

She looked at Bijan. This man was indeed no longer the man from last night. He was filled with courage, and all the fear and regret she saw before was gone, as if buried six feet under with his ego and his reputation. She looked at him and studied his eyes. They revealed nothing but the truth, and she knew that it was indeed the truth.

"Would you like to ask Him to do the same for you?" he nudged.

The mere thought of talking to an unseen God made her shiver. She remembered when she was but a girl how her aunt used to talk about Yahweh. Her father refused to listen and forced her from their home. He had no regard for the blasphemies of pagans.

Nimrod knew that only the Angra Mainyu could keep all the other Gods in check. How could she propose that it was just a man-made religion only filling the ravenous void placed by Yahweh in order for us to seek Him with our whole heart? She claimed that there was only one God, and He was the Almighty, Yahweh Himself.

Her aunt had whispered in her ear, "Seek Him child, seek Him with all your heart. Devote yourself to Him and He will take care of you."

Her aunt smiled and was gone. That was the last time she ever saw her. Daelia studied Bijan as he ate fruit and legumes with such desirable intensity that she longed to feel the intoxication he felt.

"How does it feel?"

"How does what feel?" he asked.

"How does it feel to be totally free of your guilt and your pain?" She studied him, trying to spot a hint of betrayal in his answer.

"I was dead; now I am alive. I was heavy laden with remorse, suffering daily with guilt seeing the faces of the ones I killed. They plagued my sleep; I never rested," he paused, "but now I see such sweetness and grace. It's overwhelming."

"I want what you have." Defeated, she fell at his feet pleading for forgiveness.

"Don't do that, Daelia. It's simple; just repeat after me: Lord, please forgive me for my sins. Come into my heart and make me your child. I long to serve a God that is true and just. Please deliver me and make me your own."

Daelia repeated the words after Bijan. She paid close attention to every word she spoke, making sure that she didn't miss a beat. She waited for the vision of the man in white to come, but nothing happened.

"Where is He? Why didn't He come?" She started to look around frightfully, expecting that God didn't want her.

Bijan took hold of her and hugged her tight. She calmed.

"God works in mysterious ways, Daelia. He will come to you in His own way, a way that would make sense to you. A way you will understand. You are His beloved, and He is yours."

Daelia looked at him. Bijan was strong, and she loved to be in his arms. She realised that she didn't long for him physically, but he was like the brother she never had. Always looking out for her, caring for her, keeping her from the hands of the enemy.

"Promise me something," Bijan whispered.

"Anything," she said softly.

"When it all goes down, flee the keep, run as fast as you can, and find Princess Mia. She is expecting you."

"She is?" Daelia was surprised.

"Yes. She will be looking out for you."

Daelia hugged him again and stood, not looking in his direction. When she came to the door, she turned.

"Thank you, Bijan. I will be forever indebted to you." She turned and left.

***

The morning sunshine streaked through the overhead canopy. Elias sat at his station, ready for the onslaught that he expected would come. Mia had spoken to him and him alone about her meeting with Belarus; she had recounted his supposed journey to God and the plans he had made to fight from within.

She was excited and called for a day of rest before they set out to battle. Elias thought that the element of surprise would be lost. He didn't trust the man, and after his betrayal to Estoban and Ariana, Elias feared Mia would be stepping into a trap specially laid for her capture.

"You seem upset, Elias."

He spun around to see Ariana holding a bowl of fruit out to him. Her hair was pulled back into a neat braid revealing her slender neck and small ears. He hadn't noticed them before. He couldn't remember ever seeing her with her hair tied back.

"You look different," he said sheepishly.

"In a good way, I hope ... Danelle's idea of a warrior's hairdo." She laughed with a slight edge to her voice.

"You look great, my lady." Elias bowed his head in respect.

"Why do you do that?"

"What, my lady?" Elias looked about him, searching for the cause of her remark.

"Bow your head and not call me on my name?"

"It's a form of respect to my leaders, my lady," he replied.

"Call me Ariana, please. I am not accustomed to such a show of honour." She shied away, sitting beside him on the large boulder.

"I am truly sorry that you do not see yourself in the position in which you have been placed. The women not only look up to our Polemarch for leadership; they look to you for comfort and guidance as well."

Ariana was stunned to hear of the respect that overflowed from Elias' lips. She seemed suddenly aware of her posture and the way she responded.

"Thank you, Elias. Your respect is much appreciated." She straightened.

He bowed his head again. "You're welcome, Ariana."

He smiled and returned to his bowl of fruit.

"Can I relieve you for a moment?" she asked.

"That would be fantastic. I need to stretch my legs."

Elias entered the crevice and to his surprise saw the extent of the clearing. Large limestone pinnacles erupted from the muddy ground, creating a maze of ragged teeth ready to digest a crippled animal.

Soldiers were taking shelter in between crevices that lined the entire opening. Many bundled together for heat around small, inconspicuous fires preparing breakfast. Elias realised that he no longer marched besides women, but he was indeed in the company of heroes.

Each lady was strong, well able to wield a sword, and lacked no skill in warfare—a trait taken from the Spartans. Not only did the boys learn from a tender age to fight, but the girls were raised with the same set of laws.

Women were never permitted to go to war but were rather well trained to guard their own territory in the absence of a full garrison—soldiers as well trained as their husbands. What they lacked in experience they made up for in passion.

Elias understood the battle that raged in each of their hearts. Many sent off daughters, mothers, and sisters to hide in the Citadel. Only 118 were brave enough to follow Mia into the wilderness.

A strange urgency drove these women, something Elias barely understood. He grasped that men had to go and fight for the provision of their families, be it in the vineyards, the groves, or the battlefield. But what made women as fierce as their male counterparts?

"Good morning, Elias," Mia called from the back of a small crevice.

He walked closer to inspect her small shelter. Her knapsack had heaved its contents onto a small blanket. Mia sat back, sipping a cup of green tea and basking in the sunlight that would certainly fade within the hour.

"It's all clear, my lady. The path does not stir with visitors today. Ariana gave me leave a while," he reported.

"Thank you, Elias. Please sit and join me."

He bowed.

"Clarissa, can you please bring us another cup of tea?" Mia asked over her shoulder to the girl sheltering the fire beside her.

Elias studied the young maiden. She reminded him of Astrid. She had the same cherry blonde hair and about the same length. However, she lacked the aquamarine shimmer in Astrid's eyes that made his knees weak. He relished the memory.

"What have you decided, Elias?" Mia questioned.

"I beg your pardon?"

"Do you think I have made a wise judgement in trusting Belarus to make good on his promise? Or do you suggest we should return as the elders have often tried to persuade me?"

Elias thought about the question for a moment. He rechecked his heart and spoke without question.

"I believe you will always do what is best for your people. I do not question your authority; neither do I think you unwise, Mia."

She smiled at his informality.

"I am glad that I can rely on you. I expect you will do as Estoban trained you to do during battle."

"What is that precisely, my lady?" He looked at her questioningly.

"When we fail, flee with as many survivors as you can and reach safety to fight another day," she said plainly.

Elias sat up stiffly. He knew that he had no other choice but to agree, and he bowed his head in response. Mia smiled, returned to her tea, and sat in peaceful quiet, face turned towards the sun.

"May I speak freely, my lady?" Elias was uncertain if he was allowed such trivial talk.

"Please."

"I understand the need for men to battle for the tribe's provision, but why do women fight the way they do? What do they fight for?"

Mia looked at him and answered without having to think too hard.

"We fight for our families' survival. While men fight for protection and provision, we are still the keepers of peace and order in our households. Women are the glue that keeps them secure. Without the respect and sacrifice of a mother or wife, our heroes will be defeated. We honour our men, and they love us in return. It's simple really. We fight for love." She chuckled, deep in thought.

Elias sat back, pondering hard.

"Does this puzzle you?" she asked.

"Yes, it does," he acknowledged.

"It is for freedom that we have been set free. God loved us first; that is why we love Him. We are devoted to Him. He is the master provider. All we need to do is be good stewards of the things He had placed in our lives. For men, it is to provide and to shelter his beloved family. For women, it is to love and care. We cannot allow the enemy to come and wipe his feet with our hearts. We have a need to fight for our right to live."

"I am he who will sustain you. I have made you and will carry you; I will sustain you and I will rescue you." Elias quoted the prophet Isaiah.

"It's exactly as Isaiah puts it; the Lord will sustain us and rescue us. Our situation will be turned around for good. You will see. With God, there is always a way."

Elias felt satisfied with her answer and sat back, returned to his tea, and twisted his own face towards the sun.

25

Twice Elias tried to relieve her of her watch, but Ariana dismissed him. The third time he did not relent and ordered her to step down. He handed her a bowl of rabbit stew, but she refused to eat, claiming her mind was far too occupied and her body too queasy.

"We have only a few hours until the sun sets to rest properly. By nightfall we will start the final preparations to set out," he reminded her.

"I will be ready." She smiled unenthusiastically.

"Are you certain you will be alright, Ariana?" Elias asked again.

"Yes, I just need to take a walk and clear my head before I head back," Ariana assured him.

"I expect you to return by sunset." He bowed his head and settled himself on the boulder overlooking the forest surrounding their hiding place.

Ariana gave a low bow and laughed as she disappeared into the thicket. Elias laughed in return, refocusing his mind after an afternoon spent discussing the future and the battle with his Polemarch. He was again reminded of Mia's strength and perseverance in the face of danger. She was very much like Estoban, and Elias liked that. She was determined, focused, and lacked no encouragement. Dawn would bring a frightful day for all, including him.

Ariana walked through the forest as if on a lazy noonday hike. The afternoon was shrouded in light snowfall barely able to moisten the earth, but the wind cut to the bone. She was thankful for the animal skin shrouded over her shoulder. She approved of the panther fur Belarus had made for her.

He had spent a whole day in search of the feline lurking about the grove of olives. She had made her den near the western border of the grove in a small cave only familiar to the farmers. She had three cubs of about a month old.

Belarus waited for her to return with a meal, trapping her in a simple cage. It was a magnificent animal. The cubs were sold to a merchant from Sparta on the lookout for rare precious animals, and the mother made for an interesting soup that Ariana disliked very much, but the fur on the other hand was as beautiful as the creature itself.

She stroked the black fur hugging her neck and pulled it closer to her chest. She walked for about a mile before she stopped to listen to the forest. She heard no birds; it was a strange valley without the usual sounds.

Creeping insects could be heard at night as they came out to feast on small mice and cockroaches, disgusting little things that crawled up unnoticed on one's leg until they scratched one's knees. She had slept last night with little rest due to the creeping things.

She was about to return when she heard a soft voice singing. It sounded ominously sweet. The hair on her neck stood upright, telling her to run and go back the way she came, but her curiosity got the better of her. She approached a small clearing to her right.

She thought she saw something stir but could not make it out due to the deceiving light of dusk. She approached softly, placing each footfall securely away from broken branches or any other fallen debris. Her pace was slow and steady; the clearing was just beyond a row of trees. She stopped and listened again for the sound.

A scrawny figure dressed in a red cloak sat with its back to her, rocking slightly. She knew very well not to reveal herself, but she could not avoid the urge to speak to this person. She walked into the clearing the same moment he stopped and turned to face her.

She squinted to get a better look at the man. He reached out his hand, luring her to his side. It was covered with deep scars and boil-like blisters. She wanted to run and hide but felt his presence luring her closer.

"Come closer. I don't bite," he said in a frail and elderly voice.

"Show yourself," she ordered without stepping closer.

The man pulled back his hood to reveal his face. It was as scarred as the rest of his body might be. She noticed that he wore no shoes and carried a leather satchel over his other arm. His skin was pale and tattered and reeked of almond oil.

He seemed very old, yet his eyes revealed no such thing. They were black rimmed with gold and had the appearance of an eagle's. They moved about, searching her body for any sign of revolt. Ariana moved closer to him but remained out of reach of his hands.

"They call me Rosenduz, but you can call me whatever you like," he uttered slimily.

"I am Ariana," she replied.

"I have been expecting you." He called her to him.

He looked at her stomach for a moment too long and smiled. She mistook his motivation for staring. Her armour shone brilliantly despite the darkness that crept closer. She stroked her beloved's breastplate absentmindedly.

"What do you want with me?" she prodded.

"I am here to suggest a simple exchange—a life for a life."

"What do you mean?" She was uncertain and wanted to run, but she moved a step closer, eager to hear more.

Rosenduz wiped the stringy grey hair from his face and looked at her. He turned towards his satchel and retrieved a silver chain Ariana knew too well. Her heart skipped a beat as she froze; she had difficulty breathing. He turned towards her and saw the surprise that painted her face a deep crimson.

"You know this amulet well?" he asked, waiting patiently for her to catch her breath.

"It belongs to my husband. How did it end up in your possession?" she screeched.

"Shush, the guards might hear you."

Ariana instinctively covered her mouth but ran towards Rosenduz, ready to grab the amulet from his frail hands. The man moved so fast it surprised her. As she was about to grab the amulet, he stood, twisted in a spin, and ended up right behind her. He grabbed her from behind with his left arm, holding her in a strange embrace while dangling the only object she had left of her beloved in front of her.

"Let me go!" Her deep voice echoed in the clearing.

"Take it easy, girl," he whispered in her ear.

Ariana calmed, and she watched the amulet swing just out of her reach. If she wanted to get back the covenant necklace, she needed to be more cautious in her negotiations.

"Let me go. I will not do that again. You have my word."

Rosenduz let her go and returned swiftly to his seat on the fallen tree trunk. She stumbled backwards and nearly fell to the ground. She managed to steady herself and sat down on her haunches, ensuring that her balance would not fail her this time around. They studied each other, frozen in time.

"I will give you the amulet and hand Romulus over to you shackled and tortured, in exchange for that which is in your womb." Rosenduz pointed at her stomach.

Ariana reached for her stomach. She stroked the spot that gave her the urgency to vomit every few hours. *I am barely married a fortnight. Could I be pregnant?* she thought to herself.

"Yes, you are with child," he said without looking away from her stomach.

"It cannot be. It is too soon," she protested.

"But alas, young maiden, it is as I say."

Ariana stood and paced around the clearing. Rosenduz turned his focus to his satchel, and Ariana watched as the alchemist rummaged through its contents. Her mind was reeling from the possibility that she might have something far more valuable than the amulet inside of her, a piece of her beloved that could never be taken.

"You will never have my child," she sputtered.

"What a pity. Bijan said you would never surrender."

"Who?"

"Ah, forgive my insolence. I meant your beloved Belarus." He slithered as he said his name.

"He is alive?" she asked without thinking.

"A little more than alive I would say. He sits at the right hand of our mutual disgraceful enemy, Romulus the Great."

The revelation hit her like an avalanche taking with it all the steadfast trees. She recounted his different demeanour to that of the tribe. She remembered his rough hands which he swore were from farming, but in her heart she knew they were scars from years of handling a sword.

The gash on his right arm he assured her came from a farming implement could have been the clear line of a broadsword or dagger. He was far too tall to come from the southern regions, and his strange longing was unnatural to her. She should have known that she was tricked.

"Surprised? You should know that the hands he laid on you have shed much innocent blood, lured you in to slaughter your men and to deceive your princess."

Ariana just looked at him, shocked to the core. She heard Belarus' voice whisper sweet nothings in her ear, felt his embrace as strong as death. Her mind wanted to be angry at his deceit, but her heart failed to find fault in the man. She loved her husband, and she would fight for him as long as she lived no matter what he had done.

"You cannot have my child!" she screamed as she pulled her dagger from its sheath and shoved the blade towards her stomach.

"No!" Rosenduz yelled.

The frail man moved fast, but this time she was prepared. She shoved the dagger towards him and caught him broadside, slicing through his skin just below his ribs. Rosenduz screamed like an enraged animal, fumbling with the blood gushing from his side.

He twisted to look her in the eye for the last time. His expression was that of a dead man. All life departed from his eyes, and his skin seemed to sink even deeper into his skull. He then suddenly turned and was gone.

Ariana attempted to pursue but stopped short. The trees where Rosenduz exited stirred once again. This time she took out her sword and prepared for his vengeance.

"Please don't hurt me," a soft voice spoke just beyond her sight.

"Reveal yourself!" Ariana shouted, not wanting another surprise overtaking her.

A young girl dressed in a loose green tunic came out of the forest. She shivered in the cold, barely covered by the lavish material. She had short brown hair and radiant eyes. She was plain yet extraordinarily beautiful.

"Are you Mia?" the girl asked.

"Who are you?" Ariana questioned, not lowering her weapon.

"My name is Daelia; I followed the alchemist through his secret passage. I was locked up in the keep for several months. I was a servant and concubine of General Bijan," she replied timidly.

The mention of that name made Ariana lower her sword. Conflicting images swam through her head. *This young girl is barely fourteen, and she served as my husband's concubine?* The thought threatened to make her faint, but Daelia rushed to her side, supporting her weight.

"Bijan never laid a hand on me; he protected me from the others. He ordered that I be his concubine to ensure that no other man had authority to claim me as his for the night. I swear that to you. I was abused by the other men, but Bijan saved my life. He led me to the Lord."

Ariana pushed the girl back and looked into her eyes.

"What did you say?" she ordered.

"He never touched me," she assured Ariana.

"Not that. The last thing about the Lord." She looked at the girl, wanting to rip answers from her mind.

"This morning at breakfast he returned from a harrowing ride through the night. He claimed to be born again, from death to life. I asked him to share that with me and he led me in a prayer. I confessed my sins and I found peace unlike anything I have ever known," she said, smiling wildly.

"Where is he now?" Ariana wanted to know.

"You cannot follow Rosenduz. He will capture you and torture you. You will live until there are no more lungs into which to draw breath." Her voice was cold and heavy.

Ariana looked at this brave girl and hugged her tight. Daelia relaxed into her embrace and started to sob.

"My name is Ariana."

Daelia let go of the embrace and wiped away her tears.

"You are his wife, aren't you?" She spoke with sudden excitement.

"Yes. I am the wife of Belarus, but I gather you know him as Bijan." Ariana smiled for the first time since her encounter with Rosenduz.

"He spoke so much about you the past few days. He loves you!"

"I know he does." Ariana knew for certain.

"He told me about the betrayal and how the guilt devoured him every moment of every day. But I can promise you that he no longer carries that burden. Yahweh has restored him completely. He is a new man, and you can be proud of him." Daelia touched Ariana's shoulder.

Ariana took her hand in hers and led her back to the tribe.

***

Tambourines, cymbals, and flutes clanged in unison as Bijan stepped out into the courtyard. He held his head high as he approached his emperor seated on a lavish throne in the middle of the clearing.

Romulus watched as hundreds of men started to beat on their shields and cried out their salute to their general. The musicians stationed on wooden tiers surrounding the keep wall played with such intensity and passion that one might have thought for a moment the cacophony of instruments might actually sound good.

Hollering overpowered the instruments as Bijan approached the throne. He knelt on one knee and allowed Romulus to place a red, velvet cape adorned with a golden chain around his shoulders. The material lay in pools around his feet.

The music and shouting stopped suddenly, and a deafening silence engulfed the courtyard. Hard breathing was the only sound emanating from the crowd.

"Today we honour our general, for he has found favour in my eyes." Romulus studied the crowd as he delivered his momentous speech.

"Today I announce my successor! I have searched for several years to find a man valiant and purpose-driven enough to fill my shoes, and here he is. Rise, General Bijan." Romulus raised his hands for Bijan to stand.

His heart was beating like thunder, the echo of the cheering crowd lost in his ears. Bijan breathed through his nose, not wanting anyone to see the distress that raged in his heart. He had just been acknowledged as the successor to a man he loathed more than life. Bijan despised his motivations for murder and hated himself for succumbing to Romulus' every command. He was a changed man, and he no longer wanted to be part of this mockery of life.

Bijan swallowed his disgust and stood tall, facing Romulus. His emperor held his gaze for a moment, smiled, and bowed on one knee before the successor of this vast army. Unsure what to do next, Bijan turned as if showing off the emperor's most prized possession. He held his hands out in a fanciful display, accepting the praise that was lavished on him. As he turned, the crowd erupted in cheerful glee and the music again engulfed in rapture.

When Bijan had almost completed a full turn, he spotted Valah standing in the alleyway leading into the keep. It was the same exit Bijan had fled through the night before. Valah didn't clap or cheer along with his fellow soldiers. His eyes fixed on Bijan; blue stones judged the new successor, and Bijan understood why.

The man was strong, and he served as first general while Bijan was away on his infiltration. Valah never denied his emperor anything. He followed Romulus like a dog followed his master, cleaning up vomit and crumbs as he marched. Bijan had taken Valah's rightful place.

Valah must have harboured great jealousy. If only Bijan could explain the burden placed around his neck, Valah might look at him with more than eyes of judgement. Bijan bowed his head in respect, not expecting Valah to return his gesture. He was right.

***

Valah watched Bijan turning in a show of grandeur, a moment that should have belonged to him. He despised the man dressed in royal red with its chain glimmering in the faint sunlight. He wanted to see Bijan come to ruin, but at the same time he felt a sense of awe about him.

Bijan was tall and valiant. He had indeed infiltrated the heart of Achaos, the only hateful burden Valah himself could not lift from his emperor's shoulders. Bijan deserved the crown of a victor.

Valah had observed him when he was but a young lieutenant in the army. Bijan was strong and determined, never coming home without a prize for his master. They all longed to be as strong and brave as he. Valah had grown to respect the man and followed his every decree. When Bijan set off on his biggest mission yet, Valah was certain that he would not return without the ultimate prize, therefore ensuring his succession to the throne.

But Valah was wrong. Even though Bijan did come home a hero, he was no longer the same man. He lacked bloodlust, a trait that could be seen in his eyes. Bijan had taken special liking to Nimrod's youngest daughter. Daelia was but a girl, yet she possessed the poise of a queen. A worthy challenge for a man like Bijan, but instead he treated her like a daughter of his own, protecting her against any man that had a mind to hurt her.

It was not lost on Valah that she had been missing all morning. Daelia was nowhere to be seen, and that unsettled Valah quite a bit. Bijan didn't go anywhere without her following close by.

Locked on his gaze, Valah saw the eyes of a hero and a servant. The man was filled with compassion, and Valah could see the strain of an immense burden rest on his shoulders. He could see that Bijan wanted to do nothing but escape the hell he found himself in. Valah had seen it in the eyes of women he raped and men he tortured.

Something was not right. Valah had difficulty placing his finger on it, but something was certainly amiss from the charade that played out in front of him. He needed to seek guidance from the Aveston. Tonight, he would lay bare that which was hidden. Valah turned around and disappeared in the tunnel behind him.

"Mighty Bijan!" the crowd cheered.

Romulus stood beside Bijan as he completed his turn and embraced him like a father would his son. Bijan was uncomfortable in his arms but hugged back with the same intensity the emperor used. He had still to find the ability to forgive as Estoban forgave this man in the face of certain death, an ability he was certain would be hard to find.

***

The celebrations moved from the courtyard as the sun set over the mountain tops. Sentries posted on the outer walls cursed the oncoming winds as the banquet was sure to sport great meats and women—something they all longed for out in the dead of night. Nothing ever happened on the outskirts of the keep. The road was hard to tread, and the season for traders had passed. The onslaught of cold nights filled with a flurry of snowfall would be their only company until the turn of the season.

26

The valley was shrouded in darkness as clouds converged together, the full moon shedding no light. Freezing winds moved about the limestone outcroppings trying to cover the final words spoken by Mia.

"Tomorrow is the day we have all been waiting for. Yahweh will protect us. His promises are true. As He says in Isaiah, 'I will go before you and level the exalted places, I will break in pieces the doors of bronze and cut through the bars of iron, I will give you the treasures of darkness and the hoards in secret places, that you may know that it is I, the Lord, the God of Israel, who calls you by your name'."

The group raised their hands in agreement, punching their fists in the air. Tonight would be spent preparing and praying, humming songs of courage as they readied their armour, sharpened their swords, and prepared for war.

An hour before dawn, they set out to a nearby clearing Elias and Mia had scouted out the day before. They had a clear height advantage on the army that was assured to march beneath them. Deep trenches were dug and filled with debris and other sharp objects to cripple horses and riders as they set off in pursuit.

Elias stationed the horses two miles down the slope, ready for retreat should Romulus and his army overtake them. Ten warriors were stationed near the horse pen ready to respond when they heard the call. Elias called his scouts together and ran through the battle strategy again. Two scouts would run towards the next selected clearing when Elias gave the order, readying the traps laid in the centre of the clearing. Fire would consume any enemy soldier who dared escape by that route. The other four, along with Elias, were stationed on the eastern flank where the rising sun would hopefully blind the enemy, catching the first of the foot soldiers off guard.

He watched as thirty bodies ascended trees, taking their aim through strong bows and arrows. The vantage point not only gave a clear shot of the open field but afforded great camouflage against any comeback.

***

Mia positioned herself close to the centre of the clearing behind a large fallen tree. The shallow snowfall that covered their tracks blended with a haunting mist that remained in the clearing. She watched Elias as he took his position in the opening of the clearing. Mia knew that over a hundred bodies surrounded the clearing, but save for Elias she couldn't spot a single one. Her father had trained them well to disappear into their surroundings, a skill that ensured countless successes in battle.

Dawn was shrouded in cloud cover, something Mia anticipated. The success of their mission depended on sunlight coming out at just the right time to blind the enemy and ensure the element of confusion among them, diverting the ranks and causing them to lose focus.

Mia waited for a long time, hoping that Belarus had made good on his promise, but as time passed, she knew that something had gone terribly wrong. She whistled softly, and within minutes Elias was by her side.

"I think something happened," she whispered quickly.

"My thoughts exactly; I am going to inspect the trail ahead and send a man behind just to make sure we are not surrounded and set in a much larger trap than the one we laid." Elias disappeared in an instant.

Mia looked at Eugo nestled high above her in the nook of a tree. He looked down at her and shook his head—nothing, not a single disturbance in the forest. Mia had been disturbed by the shouts of hundreds of men banging on shields the day before. Her soldiers all readied themselves and waited for the onslaught she thought would come, but it only subsided, and upon inquiry Elias reassured her that it was but a feast held in the outer courts of the keep. Ever since hearing the thunderous roar, her nerves were on edge.

A long whistle echoed through the underbrush. Mia looked up, stunned. The warning had come from Elias. No one was setting out from the keep. The call also meant that their plan had been discovered. Thirty warriors scattered from the trees, and many more appeared from the thicket. Mia motioned for them to fall into rank and to follow in formation to the hill surrounding the keep.

***

Ariana dragged her hopes behind her. She had expected that all would work out and that she would be home in the arms of her beloved by week's end. The call to march meant only one thing— their plot had been discovered. A new approach would be needed, one that surely would not be in their favour.

The crest loomed overhead as the army converged between the trees. Ariana heard the stunned cries run through the crowd. She pushed her way through fearful women, with Daelia scurrying right behind her. The young maiden had taken quite a fancy to her. Ariana did not mind; she found solace in the fact that they could talk about the same man and feel loved by him in different ways.

Ariana stopped short when she crested the hill. Before her lay an incredibly large fortress. Its surrounding wall was at least ten feet high and sported wooden poles every five feet. On these poles hung mutilated bodies, some missing heads and torsos, others impaled. Blood and insides gushed from their stomachs and heads, mulch dripping down the wooden sides. Ariana regressed slightly when she realised what had happened.

She looked over the bodies and counted about twenty-eight women and girls, stripped of their clothing and their lives. Nineteen soldiers hung upside down on makeshift crosses—all traitors. She followed Mia's gaze and settled her eyes on the main attraction. Next to the impaled bodies were two cages arranged beside a grand throne. The cage to its right contained the daughter-in-law of Amyntas, King of Athens, and the other contained her beloved Belarus.

Belarus was unable to speak. His face was mangled, with bones threatening to jut out of his skin. The skin on both his arms was slashed, and the bleeding hadn't stopped. On his chest was a large carving of their covenant mark, gashed deep in his olive skin. Ariana wanted to run to him, to hold on to him, but Daelia pulled her back, her eyes filled with the same tears that ran down her own cheeks. Ariana crumbled and cried.

***

Mia watched as Belarus bled out from his wounds, sorry that she had laid such a heavy burden on him. The young princess she had seen the day she escaped was but a weak resemblance of her former voluptuousness. She was thin to the bone, and her beautiful golden locks had been cut short against her skull, revealing numerous scars of the whip and fist. She would not survive the day.

***

Romulus rushed from his meal when report came that the army was approaching. His scouts had served him well. He draped himself in a black cloak rimmed with gold; thick black fur hugged his neck. He tied back his disorganised dreadlocks with a thin leather strap and made his way towards the defence wall. Soldiers all bowed when he passed, showing him newfound honour and respect. Romulus walked up to his throne and sat down beside the cages. The Athenian princess pleaded for mercy, but Romulus only ignored her. She had finally given up.

Romulus waited to see the so-called army, but he only saw trees clouded in dense fog. He motioned for Valah to move closer.

"Have they arrived yet?" Romulus asked.

"They are just out of reach, my lord. They arrived less than an hour ago."

Romulus stood from his throne and addressed the unseen ghosts.

"Mia, I expect you to be out there. An assault on this keep is futile. We are far too strong for a band of fighting little girls. My men will squash you in mere seconds. But it does not need to be like this." He studied the tree line, waiting for any sign of their presence. It remained deathly quiet.

"Ladies, do not listen to Mia," he continued. "This is what I say: make peace with me and come out to me. Then every one of you will eat from your own vine and olive tree. I will take you back to your own land, a land filled with grain and new wine, a land of bread and vineyards, a land of olive trees and honey. I will make a peaceful covenant with you. I will give back what this man has taken from you." He pointed to Bijan who tried to say something, but his face was far too damaged to speak.

"Choose life and not death."

***

The women started to stir, whispers of a promise and a new life. Mia turned to the crowd and saw the women hovering between the reality of their situation and the promise of peace.

"Do not fall for his words. Do not be deceived. He will only torture you and kill you like those poor girls hanging from the wall," Mia pleaded.

"We can go back home!" one woman said.

"I can be united with my daughter!" another protested.

"Don't be silly! He will never let you go!" a young girl spoke with passion.

The quarrelling started soon after that. Some women pleaded for the fight while others had already given up, surrendering into the hands of their enemy. Mia heard accusations thrown her way buffeted by defences from others. She did not know what to do. She was no longer able to keep her warriors together. She held onto the eldest of the women and pleaded again.

"You cannot bow down to Romulus! You will not see the day come to an end before your life is snuffed out. Think of your daughters and your mother back at the Citadel!"

"I *am* thinking of them, dear Mia. It would serve you well to do the same. We are not warriors; we are women," she protested and released herself from Mia's grip.

Mia fell into a heap and cried for the futility of their venture. She knew that they were far more passionate and stronger than any of them could ever think, but her efforts were in vain. More and more gave up, not wanting to fight any longer and their hope and their purpose spent.

***

Romulus saw the first girl come into view. She was barely twenty and dressed in full body armour, followed by two more. He could hear the quarrelling grow on the wind. He knew he had struck a nerve, but he did not expect the surrender to occur as quickly as it did. He ordered the gate to be opened.

"This could be a ploy to weaken our defence, my lord," Valah suggested.

Romulus knew that it could not be true.

"Impossible. These frail women have lost everything, including their courage. They will all come to my side and beg for mercy, unaware that I will cut down one after the other," he chortled with glee.

***

Mia moved towards the edge of the clearing, her resolve set in stone. She would never surrender to the vile man that gawked in her direction. She could see the deep folds of his skin, smell the stench of his breath. He would have to pursue to claim hold of her.

***

Romulus watched as the Achaean women emerged from the tree line. Some ran in groups to safety while others dwindled, unsure if they were making the right choice. He smiled at them, not only to seem inviting, but he waited with anticipation to see Mia succumb to his power. Over seventy women were counted along with three men, scouts Romulus presumed. They were lean and fit, and they would make excellent eunuchs.

Romulus instructed Valah to see to the women and hurry them into the tunnel system led by the dungeon keeper, for there were far too many to house in the belly of the beast. He would have to rid them of some before nightfall. Valah then looked back at Romulus, seeming confused as to what he was still waiting for as most, if not all, the women were already accounted for.

Romulus stood still; his face had drawn taut, searching for something. He watched but saw no more movement. He then stepped aside and plunged his dagger deep into the chest of the Athenian princess. She screamed but was cut short with his second gash cutting her throat in half.

Still nothing moved.

The clouds had parted slightly, allowing for a beam of light to illuminate the clearing beyond the keep. Romulus saw the shimmer before he saw her. Mia stepped out of the tree line just far enough for Romulus to see her face. She stood defiant and bold, watching him as he stepped closer to the edge. The blood dripped from his hands and congealed on the lip of the wall.

Romulus burned with such intensity that he threw the dagger in Mia's direction. Still, she did not flinch. He screamed her name at the top of his lungs, sending phlegm and spit to droop down his face. He hated the very sight of her. The fact that she did not say a word or show an ounce of fear made his blood boil.

***

Mia watched as the gate closed behind the women. She cried in her heart for the torture and mutilated death that they would most certainly encounter. Romulus screamed her name and cursed her with obscenities, but she just watched as he spilled his rage and collapsed in fatigue, still pointing his bloodied hand in her direction. She felt only pity for the man. She had long ago forgiven Romulus for the pain she endured at his hand. She would never forget, and she would never surrender.

Mia disappeared in the thicket, and she was gone. Romulus collapsed to the ground, crying in the defeat that ripped his heart to shreds.

***

Silence engulfed the troupe. Thirty-two warriors remained, including Mia. She dropped to her knees and started to weep. Elias bowed down beside her, wanting to comfort her, when he stopped short.

"It is not worth it," Mia gasped.

"I implore you, my lady, not everything is lost."

"I cannot see that we have any other alternative but to flee to the southern regions, allow Romulus to pursue us until winter seizes either of us," Mia stated flatly.

"What use would that be? We will die in the winter storms. It's best if we return to the Citadel," Elias protested.

"And lead them back to the entire remnant? Are you insane?" Mia stared up at him.

"I suppose you are right. We cannot do that."

Elias felt his heart ache at the thought of leading Romulus anywhere near his beloved Astrid. He would follow Mia and lead the emperor away from his keep even if it cost him his life.

"We have warriors stationed two miles from here. We can take all 128 horses and lead them through the southern regions; we can throw Romulus off. He would never be able to guess our numbers. Tracking us would be easy, and the goose chase would render their forces numb and useless," he suggested. "Our horses are far swifter. It would certainly give us a head start."

"Let's get going." Mia wiped fresh tears from her cheek and broke into a light jog along the well-trodden path towards the west.

***

The keep was shadowed by dense fog. Ariana kept watching and listening. She heard Belarus give a faint cry of anguish, but it was cut short, probably by a blade. Her eyes stung from the tears that kept her vision locked in a blur. Her heart was torn, and she vowed to have her revenge when the time came.

A sharp tug at her left arm startled her. Daelia was urging her to follow the last few soldiers heading east, away from the keep, but Ariana wanted nothing more than the blood of Romulus on her dagger. She loathed the man more than she ever imagined. For the first time in her short life, she understood the burden Mia had to carry since her capture and brutal torture. Ariana wanted to cry not only for her beloved Belarus, but for her friend and her loss.

She turned and started to run with long strides, picking up her pace with every step. Daelia kept lagging; Ariana often dragged Daelia behind her. The girl was very brave but lacked the training Ariana was thankful for. She urged the young girl to keep running. Romulus was soon to pursue, and on foot they would probably be dead by nightfall.

***

The smell of blood met Mia long before she saw the massacre blocking the entire crevice ahead of them. This was the only place where the road narrowed dramatically to create a three-metre-wide gateway between two limestone cliffs. Elias had been cautious on their arrival, allowing enough time for the army to pass securely without being spotted.

Their horses were left 300 yards down the slope where it spread into a wide fan filled with more familiar trees as it broadened out into the Eurotas Valley. The steep hill was hardly visible beyond the wall of bodies blocking the way. A total of 128 horses were piled on top of each other, and winnowing and haggard breathing filled the valley.

Mia's own horse was lying on its side in front of the pile. She ran to it but realised that its throat had been severed, and the blood congealed into dark pools. There was no sign of the monsters who massacred their horses. Elias called out to her just off to her left.

247

"My lady!"

Mia ran to his side. Nauseated by the sight, she dropped to her knees, drenching her clothes with mud and blood. All ten soldiers were strewn on the floor before her. Mia could see their clothing ripped, hands tied to their backs, and legs spread wide. Elias removed his cloak and covered an abused girl. Tears welled in his eyes, and Mia saw the anguish that crushed his heart.

"We need to bury them," he said.

"Yes, Elias. Immediately," Mia tried to comfort him.

"What about the horses?" Daelia asked behind her.

Mia turned to see the young girl. Daelia was out of breath and visibly exhausted. She wore a plain tunic and handmade leather coverings. Mia was thankful that Ariana had another charge to take care of, even if it only helped her to deal with Belarus' death.

"Cut their throats. They are of no use to us," Mia ordered.

***

Mia handed Daelia a golden dagger that hung beside her left hip. It was large and felt clumsy in her hand. She was stunned as she walked closer. There was a fairly small horse to her right. Both its hind legs were cut, and the animal kept on trying to stand. Foam formed on the sides of its mouth.

Daelia raised the dagger but stopped next to its neck. She froze. She could feel the warmth of the horse's breath on her ears as its breathing thickened. She felt a hand cover hers and help plunge the dagger up to its hilt in the strong neck muscles. Blood gushed from the wound. She wanted to pull away, but the person behind her was too strong. Her hand was nearly disappearing into the flesh when she heard the whisper in her ear.

"Feel the warmth. Feel the pain ebb away from the animal. Feel its last breath as it relaxes."

Daelia waited until Ariana let go of her hand before she was able to pull the dagger free. She turned to look Ariana in the face.

The woman was fierce; her hands were drenched in blood as she stepped aside to plunge her broadsword into the chest of another horse. She said a quiet prayer and moved to the next animal.

Daelia watched as they severed neck after neck, releasing the animals of their pain. Ariana stopped to catch her breath and looked at Daelia to see her covered in blood leading from her wrist all the way down her right side. Ariana clearly felt sincere compassion for her.

"Death is inevitable. We are at war. As soon as you are able to use your weapon intended for its purpose, you will be able to protect yourself."

"I'm afraid." A tear cleared a smooth path in Daelia's cheek.

Ariana, enflamed with compassion, took two strides towards Daelia and hugged her as tight as she was able. Blood smeared on Daelia's leather breastplate, and she hugged Ariana despite the warm, gory liquid sticking to her neck. Daelia cried longer than she ever had before, shaking off the horror that overtook her mind.

***

The soldiers guarding the horses were buried along the cliff wall in shallow graves and the horses relieved of their misery. Mia looked around her to see faces smeared with blood and mud. No one even attempted to wipe it away.

She never felt more lost than right in this moment.

"It is better to turn up this pathway leading back into the mountains. Romulus would expect us to flee into the valley beyond the heap of decaying bodies," she uttered.

All the heads bounced in agreement.

"I have seen this short route. It's narrow where the cliffs come together. Horses will only be able to follow in single file. Swiftness will be to our advantage," Elias suggested.

"Do you know where it leads?" Eugo questioned.

"No. I haven't had the time to explore it farther than a few metres," he said.

"It is our only way. Elias, we follow you," Mia ordered.

"Yes, my lady." Elias spun around without asking another question.

Their eyes were quickly adjusting to the failing light. Soon nightfall would be upon them, so travelling would have to wait until morning. They needed to find a secure place to rest before Romulus and his violent army set out in pursuit.

27

Cold moisture formed droplets on the wall, and Romulus ran his rough hands against the sides of the tunnel. Screams and shouts echoed through the hallways as soldiers took their pick, bickering over the women. Bijan was not mistaken when he said that every one of these women was a vision, just like their crown princess.

Romulus enjoyed the echoes of torture. Thrilling tingles ran up and down his spine as he viewed the flurry of activity. The heads of the three Achaean men were neatly displayed at the entrance of the vast network of torture chambers and cells filling up faster than Romulus could count.

"How many?" he asked Valah.

"Seventy-four, not counting the three idiotic men that thought they were entitled to anything other than decapitation," Valah scoffed.

"Excellent," Romulus seethed.

"Shall I have some sent to your chamber for closer inspection, sire?"

"No. Take some for yourself and see if they are able to satisfy your need which has been lacking as of late."

"Forgive me, sire. I do not know what you mean?" Valah inquired.

"Ever since our return from the land of Pharaoh, you have not taken a single woman for yourself. Even Bijan, in his traitorous heart had taken at least one woman, even if only as a trinket."

Romulus stared at the man with such intensity Valah had to look away.

"I needed some time to recollect myself, my lord," Valah objected.

Romulus studied the man's unease.

"See to it that you are not slacking. A valiant successor like you should not be intimidated by something as foolish as a girl. They are nothing but tools to use, of no importance. Use them to satisfy and then focus on my command. Why do you think I have taken such great care to drag them to my keep? Is that clear, Valah?"

"Yes, my lord, absolutely. How could I imagine otherwise?"

***

Valah bowed low before his emperor. The mere mention of succession sent his mind in a spin. If he was to stand a chance of becoming the next emperor, he needed to find the emptiness that lurked in his heart and quench it. What good was a ruler if he was not complete?

Again, the thought of Bijan entered his mind. He had been so confident in their last meeting, and Valah was stunned to hear of his plans to overthrow Romulus. He had almost agreed to go along with him, wanting to see the filthy man dead just as much as he did, but the jealousy he had for Bijan far outweighed his hatred for Romulus. Jealousy was indeed as demanding as the grave.

Bijan had truly changed; Valah had seen it at the inauguration. Valah wanted to be free more than he liked to admit, but the audacity to think that he would succumb to his pride and follow Bijan was absurd. The charade had played itself out, and Bijan had made a dreadful choice in his approach. His plan might have succeeded if he had not revealed it to him.

Valah had found the way to secure his position, and he was not going to let fear deter him. He had decided to turn the play around and beat back against Bijan, and now the affirmation of succession was worth the discomfort of the emptiness that plagued his heart.

Valah looked up to say something more, but Romulus was gone. He had never seen his emperor as apprehensive as today. Women had been counted, shared, and revelry stirred in the men's hearts, yet Romulus was digressing.

Valah was slightly perturbed, but he shoved the thought swiftly from his mind as his eyes settled on a beautiful lady hiding in the corner.

***

"I wish I could see my mother one last time," Danelle sniffed.

"She will be okay, Danelle. Trust me," Eugo said comfortingly.

He held his best friend in his arms. Eugo loved Danelle and always imagined that his sister might have been as incredible as his best friend. Eve lost her daughter when she was five months pregnant and Eugo was only five years old. He pleaded with his parents for years, and when the news came of the arrival of a sibling, he was elated. Eugo counted the days. He longed for a companion to climb trees and scout the village with, but his hopes were soon shattered.

His father had gone to Sparta on a training mission when Eugo's mother fell. Eve had fallen face down, hitting her stomach against a sharp metal object. Eugo thought it must have been a kitchen utensil, but his memory failed him. Eugo had no way of understanding the consequences or the severity of her accident.

All he could remember was the blood and his mother's cries for her unborn child. Eve survived the fall, but her stomach had been severely cut and the child killed. The physician had to remove the baby. Eugo caught a glimpse of his sister's small hands and feet before they took her away. The baby had turned blue, and the red smudges of blood could not shroud it.

Eugo cried for days and hoped that a second child would be conceived, but Eve was no longer able to bear children. Eugo settled for matchstick men and horses made from fallen tree branches tied together with thin rope. He was a solitary child until he met Danelle. He was eight years of age and only a year older than she was.

He showed her the village and taught her everything about adventure she ever needed to know. He was proud of her today. It must have been terrifying to see her mother go away into the keep in hopes of survival. Danelle had been torn, and Eugo could see it in her eyes. They had spent the night talking with Daelia.

Eugo understood what would happen if one surrendered to Romulus; he did not need to imagine it. He saw what Romulus did to the men on the open field. This man was nothing but a murderous brute, and Eugo understood that making a deal with him was like making a deal with the devil himself.

Danelle shivered. Eugo pulled his short coat from his shoulder and placed it around her.

"Aren't you cold?" she asked.

"No," he assured her.

***

Eugo's smile comforted Danelle more than she could have imagined. She shivered more out of fear for her mother than the cold. Danelle replayed the morning's events over and over in her mind. Her mother, Olivia, tried to pull her away from Eugo at the clearing, but Danelle held on far too tight. She tried to explain to her mother what Daelia had told her, but Olivia would not listen.

Olivia's hair had been falling from the bun attempting to hold her short curls in place. Danelle looked so much like her mother; they had the same olive complexion and dark hair. Danelle preferred to keep hers long even though it became unkempt very quickly. Her mother was a whole foot taller, and Danelle often dreamed of becoming such a refined woman as she was, but resisting fear was never her mother's strongest virtue.

Olivia had struggled and nagged her daughter to follow, but at the seventh refusal, Olivia had to let her go. Tears flowed freely from her sparkly eyes as she gave Danelle a final goodbye kiss on the cheek and ran in a full sprint towards the keep.

Danelle dropped in a pile at Eugo's feet as her mother made her way towards certain death. All Danelle held dear was finally lost to an enemy beyond anyone's expectation. Were it not for Daelia's confession and warning, Danelle might have made the trip herself.

"I believe we will win this fight," Eugo said, distracting her from her thoughts.

"What do you mean?"

"In times of trouble, I look to the north and face the King of Kings," Eugo stated proudly.

"What?"

"The King of Kings, Yahweh Himself." He nudged towards the north.

Danelle looked in his direction but saw nothing but a few dwindling stars. It was pitch dark, with the moon nowhere in sight. The sides of the cliff where they took shelter were steep with barely enough room for both of them on the ledge. Danelle crawled closer to the edge, hoping to get a better view.

"I don't see anything." She finally gave up.

Danelle dropped back against Eugo and puffed out warm breath, billowing steam into the frigid air.

"I remember my father once told me a tale of a man. He was so afraid of the massive army that approached them. They were coming over the hill, and he asked his master what they should do. His master prayed and asked that his servant's eyes be opened."

"What did he see?" Her eyes widened with expectations.

"The man saw something he couldn't describe."

"What did he see, Eugo?" she prodded.

"Victory, my friend! He saw victory!" Eugo yelled with fists in the air. "All around him and his master was an army of heavenly beings. So numerous was this army that the servant had to turn around to get an idea of their number. They protected them, awaiting the battle that would ensue at any moment."

"Did they fight?" Danelle begged to know more.

"No, the enemy was so overwhelmed by the sight that they fled into the desert."

"Wow … but what does this mean for us, Eugo?"

"Everything!"

Danelle stared at the vacant valley before them, puzzled and unsure of the meaning of the story. Eugo raised his hand and spread it out over the valley ahead.

"Danelle, God has the victory already planned. You might see an empty battlefield and only a few of us, but I see the heavenly host spread out over this valley before us, ready to go to battle for us. Remember, Mia always told us that the battle is not ours …"

"But the Lord's." Danelle completed the well-known phrase for him.

A broad smile spread over his face as Danelle looked at him. She did not know how Eugo could be so sure that today they would have victory. The night was already passing by in a haze of excitement. He was satisfied that God was on his side. He lay back against the cliff-face and breathed deeply, closing his eyes to the night.

Danelle felt unnerved, but she knew deep inside of her heart that Eugo was right. She was filled with courage to stand in the frontline of battle by his side. The victory was indeed already theirs for the taking. All they had to do was have faith and watch what God would do in this place.

She looked out over the small field below them and sighed. Tomorrow would be the day that all her fears, dreams, and hopes collided in a flurry of strength to make her the warrior she had always aspired to become. She lay back beside Eugo, crawling slightly behind his shoulder, and slept.

***

Mia made sure that all her warriors had settled in for the night before she slipped away. The dark undergrowth threatened to swallow her legs in thick, watery sludge. She pulled her legs free at a slow pace. The ground solidified 100 yards later.

Mia dropped to her knees, defeated and tired from more than treading through mulch. Her eyes were puffy from tears that allowed no time to come slowly. Spittle and phlegm sputtered from her mouth as she cried. Nausea tried to fight its way into the mix, but Mia kept it at bay.

"Why, God? Why have you forsaken me? I call with all my heart; answer me!" she cried into the night.

Her voice rasped through deep breaths and slurred speech.

"You are my refuge and my shield. I have put my hope in your word. I know you are greater than anything I could ever imagine, but why have you taken everything? What have we done to deserve this?"

Mia felt a hole where her heart should have been. All that she held dear was taken from her. She wanted to give up and surrender herself to the monster who had taken every last bit of strength from her. Was it not for the look in Belarus' eyes, she might have done just that. She looked at him, caged and mutilated. He was but a sack of torn flesh, but his eyes still conveyed a hope she felt was already lost.

Belarus had found the only one that was worth fighting for. Yahweh had delivered him and sheltered him even in his last pitiful hours in that cage. She saw God in his eyes filled with mercy, love, and compassion. Romulus must have seen it. The man was dead, and nothing could salvage the ruins in his heart.

Romulus promised wealth and freedom to the women, but Mia knew for a fact that the moment they arrived in the belly of the beast they would be counted, divided among soldiers, and tortured. Some would be kept as slaves and others as harlots, ready to satisfy multiple men a night.

Mia's heart shattered at the thought of all those women. Not a single one of her warriors were older than forty or younger than fifteen, a special selection for Romulus. He would not have had it any other way. Three of Elias' scouts also turned themselves over, but Mia doubted that they would survive the night.

Drenched in tears and sweat, Mia finally broke down, her resolve squandered. Her head hung low when she heard the faint whisper. Her numb heart started to beat faster, revived by the breath of God. More tears welled inside of her, spilling their contents in strong torrents.

"You are my beloved," the voice spoke.

Mia shivered and wiped her face clean. She lifted her head but kept her eyes firmly shut.

"All is as it should be. Not a single hair on your head will fall unless I have orchestrated it. Be still and know that I am God."

Mia felt heat rush up from her knees and warm her entire body. She kept her eyes closed, unwilling to look at the angel of the Lord she was certain was standing beside her. Peace that was far beyond anything she could ever understand overwhelmed her. She felt alive and refreshed.

"Remember this—I am God, and there is no other. There is none like me. I make known the end from the beginning. I say: my purpose will stand, and I will do as I please. I am bringing righteousness near—it is not far—and my salvation will not be delayed. Do not fear, Mia. Your time is in my hands. I will satisfy you with long life and freedom for all the captives. I, and only I, can do this. Do not fear, for I am with you."

"Thank you, Father. How precious to me are your thoughts, O God. How great is the sum of them. Were I to count them, they would outnumber the grains of sand covering the earth. When I awake, I am still with you," Mia uttered slowly.

The heat vanished from her cheeks. She opened her eyes, seeing the night as if for the first time. She bowed her head once more and breathed steadily.

***

The room was cold and musty. Fear filled his every nerve. Romulus despised the chambers hidden deep within the limestone cliff. Rosenduz wanted his chamber as far away from the screams as possible; apparently it interfered with his meditation.

Romulus was pleased to place the alchemist as far away from him as possible. He loathed the man more than most, yet he was unable to resist the treasures he produced time and again.

Rosenduz played a pivotal role in Romulus' plan. Every potion and spell the alchemist laid on his table was a masterpiece. Romulus was aware of his movements and every ploy uncovered.

Disappointment had settled in when Rosenduz had finally broken the last tether of trust Romulus had for the man. Rosenduz had snuck out into the forest through his secret chamber only to fraternise with the enemy — Romulus had seen the new trinket Rosenduz carried, an amulet that resembled the markings of the Achaeans.

Romulus remembered the last words Rosenduz had spoken in an attempt to prove his uncanny ability to know everything. It fuelled Romulus' hatred for the man even more, and it had failed to purchase his life.

"The plot to overthrow your kingdom is as transparent as the deceit hiding in the centre of your prideful heart. Bijan is playing you like a toy. You are wretched, humiliated!" Rozendus had cried. "Bijan and his men will overthrow you from within. The Athenian princess and Bijan are in cahoots. The great Romulus will fall once and for all, and I will be celebrating over your dead flesh!"

The alchemist had cried in vain as the red dagger cut deep into his chest cavity, exposing his blackened heart. Romulus believed that it would be as black as pitch, but the red flesh surprised him. Rosenduz was nothing but a mere mortal man, unable to quench the vengeance that lurked in Romulus' heart.

Rosenduz had tried to say a last incantation, but his breath was cut short by the searing blade. In his hand he clenched the shiny amulet, now just a symbol of his treachery.

Even though the alchemist was dead, his presence was very much still alive in his lair. Romulus walked slowly around the worn black table in the middle of the room. A star was engraved in it with a sharp chisel. Around each of its five points, a circle was drawn, placing a smooth indent for a candle and its wax. Not a single piece of wax dirtied the table.

The walls were covered in shelves stacked full of scrolls, bottles, and animal skins. Nobody but Romulus ever entered the chamber. Rosenduz tortured his subjects in the dungeon and took only the body parts he needed for his potions. Romulus never questioned him about the content of his mixtures for fear of the answer; he desired to hear no ingredient in the potions and salves Rosenduz so often applied to his wounds and ailments.

Romulus wanted answers, and the only man able to entice him to his liking was ripped beyond recognition and already fed to the pigs. Romulus spun around, taking in the room one last moment. He thrust his arms onto the table, shaking it with a sudden thud. He pulled with all his might as the first of the four shelving units came down. In his rage, the other three followed soon after, engulfing Romulus in a haze of chaos. Potions and powders collided in a flurry of fantasy. Romulus wanted to scream, but his throat closed up instantly. His breath had evaded him more than once in this quiet chamber.

Out of the ashes rose a solitary figure. It was Romulus' first victim—the young boy he slaughtered in his youth. He pointed towards Romulus and laughed joyfully. He was then joined by an entire chorus of voices ringing out in stupefied laughter. The noise was so overbearing that Romulus had to grab his head in order for it not to explode.

The laughter then stopped short, and the sound reverberated off the cold limestone walls. All was silent. The last fumes and dust settled in on the rubble. A large man blocked the doorway leading to the keep.

Romulus tried to focus his vision, but recognition failed him. It was only when he spoke that Romulus recognised who the voice belonged to—his father, Javad Farhad. Romulus cowered at his father's voice. The only man who ever dared to teach him a lesson was again standing before him, pointing and belittling.

Romulus hated the man. His heart pounded louder as he jumped over scrolls and debris to choke the only man he hated more than himself. Stumbling over rubbish, he knocked his knees against a sharp object that drew a stream of blood. The vision was gone; it rendered Romulus motionless on top of the rubble, bleeding profusely.

Haggard breathing filled the chamber. Romulus grabbed for a bottle lying just within reach. He took hold of the lid and pried it open. A pungent odour filled the entire room, but Romulus did not care. He dug his hand deep into a soft grey mixture and pulled enough free to cover his wound.

Heat spread faster than Romulus had ever felt; his entire body was on fire. His back started to convulse in strong arches, sending Romulus flying to the floor. His body contorted in positions he was not aware it was still able to do.

He cursed the alchemist under his breath. Even in his death, Rosenduz would finally have the revenge he so desperately longed for. Romulus strained to keep his eyes open, but the pain was far worse than anything he had ever experienced.

The Angra Mainyu stood above Romulus, screaming in his face. Romulus opened his eyes to narrow slits but failed to focus on the vision above him. The presence of his God was far more potent than any other time he had ever experienced. Large horns jutted from its enormous head, and spots covered its entire body. Romulus had never seen his God up close and so very personal. His presence had never evaded him, but a clear representation was only now visible.

Romulus wanted to pray, but his throat barely had enough room to allow breath to squeeze through to his lungs. Tears welled in his eyes as his heart seemed to grow too large for his chest. Rage, bitterness, and raw power filled every nerve in his body. The convulsions then seized, but the heat would not remove its suffocating claw.

"Kill them all!" the Aveston shouted.

Its voice was strong and clear. Romulus had no way of shrouding the intent. He pulled his eyes open and sat upright, stroking his neck. A fresh resolve overpowered Romulus. He rushed at the narrow passage, limping slightly from the cut on his shin.

The corners of Romulus' vision remained tainted a dull red. He longed to see Mia ripped apart and would stop at nothing until she was dead.

***

Valah enjoyed the attention he received from the woman he had chosen. Several times she had kissed his feet and rubbed his shoulders, all to save her lowly life. Threats weren't necessary, and he loved that.

He was about to undress himself when his door was shoved open.

"Sir, come quickly; it's the emperor. He has gone mad!" Hamid shouted.

The young blacksmith was acquainted with his master's irrational orders, but this was beyond himself. He recalled to Valah how Romulus had stumbled into the armoury grabbing at several swords, unable to choose one he liked. He barked orders to the men to be ready to ride out as soon as Romulus was mounted. "To battle!" he had cried as spittle flew in all directions.

Hamid was certain that he saw blood foam at the corners of his mouth. Romulus had no life in his eyes, and his voice was deeper than he remembered. It was as if the man was possessed by something far worse than anything he had ever seen.

Valah studied the boy. He was known for his bravery, but even now his face showed such terrific fear it made Valah extremely uneasy. He stood from the bed but said nothing. Hamid watched him as he donned his breastplate, dagger, and three swords in different scabbards. The man was ready to kill an entire troop of buffalo.

Valah stepped from his chamber into a hallway filled with chaos. He looked back at the young boy.

"Hamid, stay here. Watch her and do nothing until we return."

"Yes, sir." Hamid nodded.

Hundreds of soldiers rushed past Valah. Half of them were already dressed, and the others attempted to do so on their way out. It was the middle of the night, and Romulus had the mind to pursue after an entire afternoon of nothing. He had thought the emperor was crazy for not pursuing immediately, but Valah never objected his orders.

Romulus had been acting peculiarly all afternoon, and Valah assumed that their prized plunder was more than enough to satisfy the man, but he was wrong. Mia was still out there, and he was certain Romulus was about to pursue her until the very last breath vanished from his lungs.

Valah stepped from the tunnel into the courtyard, searching for his horse. The animals scattered all around the clearing. Soldiers fumbled with blades, armour, and even saddles as they attempted to ready their animals in the darkness.

The sky was covered in thick fog, and the moon had long ago vanished from sight. He walked amid the men, trying to prepare them with encouraging words, but most of them only looked at Valah with so much uncertainty that he feared for their lives in battle.

Valah was uncertain of their enemy's numbers and allowed nothing to chance. All the fighting men were already riding out of the gate in a rush. He spotted his groom holding onto a magnificent stallion. Valah ordered that the Achaean horse not be slaughtered but brought to him instead. The white stallion was fierce looking, and Valah wondered if he had made the right choice.

Without further thought, he mounted the animal, kicked hard in its side, and spun in a smooth circle towards the drawbridge. He gave a last glance at the keep and set out after his emperor.

28

Mist covered the entire valley. Valah was not accustomed to the thick fog that settled around them. The canopy above allowed for enough cover to keep fog from forming under its protective cap, but tonight the cold mist invaded every available open space. An eerie silence hung about the troupe. The soft winnow of horses and metal in motion was the only thing he could identify. Every man was on high alert, their swords ready for an assault.

The approaching wall was hidden from view. Valah himself ordered the capture of the Achaean horses and made sure that the valley exit would be impassable. He expected to see the pile shoved aside or trampled to escape the valley, but he could see no such indentation in the shape in front of him.

He raised his hand, and the entire regiment halted. Valah could sense his emperor's eyes following him, watching every calculated move. Valah was confident that his strategic plans would succeed without fault; every step was calculated to perfection.

Unlike the rest of the men residing in the keep, Valah always kept a clear objective. He was always on guard and always sharp. His men might have been frazzled by the sudden uproar of their emperor, but Valah expected his response. He did not revere the man but did follow him, and he would do so all the days of his life.

Valah remembered well when he first saw the man. He never did understand how Romulus' mind worked or how he came to conclusions the way he did, but Valah wanted to share the amount of power Romulus exuded. In order to appreciate such power, Valah had to serve like a slave to learn all he could, and one day he would become emperor and rule over his subjects. He promised to do so with more vigilance.

Valah dismounted the spectacular stallion and again marvelled at the creature. It was strong and bold and did not shudder in fear as many of his previous animals had. It followed his every command, and that reserved the respect Valah paid in return.

He stepped into the dense fog. The hairs on his neck stood on end when he saw the carnage of bodies. Numerous tracks could be seen. Valah had ordered the horses to be maimed but not slaughtered. The realisation that each horse had carefully been relieved of their pain was not a surprise.

The Achaean forces had come and released their own from a world of anguish. The thought made him shudder. If pursuit was set out as soon as the warriors fled from view, they would have been cornered and murdered as they paid tribute to their magnificent animals.

His horse stirred uncontrollably. It sensed its companions, and its natural instinct to protect was evident. Valah stepped closer to the animal and placed his palm against its quivering flesh.

"Shush," he comforted.

The animal seized its shaking and settled.

"Where are they, Valah?" Romulus thundered in the silence.

Romulus kept stroking the amulet he had found in Rosenduz' chamber; the object was similar to the covenant mark Bijan had embedded in his skin. He was certain the bargaining chip would come in handy.

"They didn't go this way, my liege," Valah answered.

"Then where do you suppose they could have gone? There is no other way out of this Godforsaken valley."

Valah was unsure how to respond. He knew that there was no other route. All the roads converged into one single fissure, broadening out into the Eurotas Valley below. He stopped to look in all directions but could see no other movement besides his own men.

"There is a way." A voice sounded from the rear.

"Come forward!" Valah commanded.

A frail old man of about sixty walked through the mass of horses. He was tall and lean. His frail hands were covered in battle scars and his face was strong. Blue eyes pierced from behind layers of wrinkles.

"My name is Aulerci." The man bowed low.

Valah faintly recognised the name. He had never seen him up close, but his reputation was well verbalised. He was descendent from the northern territories that Valah was not acquainted with. The man had fled from his own people in search of a better quality of life.

What he had found was far more glamorous than he had ever anticipated. Raised in a small village, Aulerci had never seen as extravagant battles as in Persia. When Romulus defected from Cambyses, word spread that a new stronger regime would be formed, and all who wanted to enjoy the riches of the land could follow him. Aulerci had never looked back. He had found his purpose, and like many of the men surrounding them, they lived a life that far outweighed that of their prior dreams.

"Please continue," Valah ushered.

"I have scouted the Parnonas Valley since our arrival, and I have found no routes leading out of the valley except for this one."

The soldiers started to laugh at his idiotic remark.

"However, there is one other route."

Valah listened intently and waited for the crowd to settle. "Continue."

Aulerci pointed to his left. "That way is a narrow path that leads to an average-sized clearing. The only way out from there is a vertical drop where a hidden waterfall makes its way into the valley below."

Valah squinted to get a better view, but all he saw were trees and fog.

"Are you certain you can lead us to this clearing?"

"Yes, sir. Though I do not suspect the army would have gone that way," he protested.

"And why is that?" Valah questioned.

"There is no escape, sire. If they had time, they would notice there was no way out except to leap into the unknown."

Valah pondered the thought for a moment, and he spotted ten graves upon closer inspection of their surroundings. If the Achaeans spent proper time tending to their fallen, they might still be in search of a way out.

"We will follow you into the cleft. Let's hope they are still inside," Valah instructed.

Aulerci ran to his stallion, mounted the animal, and urged the horse into a slight run up the hill to his left. Valah's was the next horse in line followed closely by Romulus and his personal guard.

The steep cliffs were smooth to the touch; not a single fissure broke the surface. Valah watched in amazement as the path twisted. The sky above was hardly visible, and steep cliffs disappeared in thick fog. Valah could see no farther than two feet in front of him. He followed Aulerci closely, so close in fact his horse shoved its head sideways to avoid the tail swatting at its eyes.

Claustrophobia threatened to sink in. When Valah was about to fall back, allowing space to breathe, the cliff face fell away on both sides. The rushing sound of water met him in the clearing. The sound was so overwhelming Valah nearly forgot to focus on the new surroundings.

The clearing was indeed of moderate size. He wondered if the entire regiment would be able to manage on the small allotment. To his surprise, the clearing was empty. The heavy fog lifted enough to see the entire field drop into an abysmal cliff.

Valah steered his horse to the water's edge. The river seemed to come from nowhere; he was certain it must be a spring boiling up from deep within. The water flowed with a surprising intensity and speed. The surge of water flowing over the edge into the deep dark pool of nothing below created a roar of its own. He longed to see the actual waterfall from the valley, for it was sure to be a magnificent sight.

Romulus spurred his horse to meet up with Valah.

"Where are they?" he asked urgently.

Valah sensed the tension in his voice.

"I haven't seen anything yet. The cliffs are clear, sir. There are no caves I can spot."

"Could they have jumped from the falls?"

"I doubt it, sir. The fall would kill them. And I can't see any rugged cliffs they could have climbed down on. They're smooth to the touch."

"Have you checked the water?" Romulus pointed.

Valah understood immediately. A perfect ploy that claimed many lives in their previous battle. Valah shouted orders, and several men wallowed into the water to test its depth. It was clear.

***

Elias sat upright when he heard the first horse approach. He motioned for the soldiers to fall into position. The clearing was far too great for thirty-two warriors to cover properly. Elias knew they would be far outnumbered. He said a quiet prayer as he waited.

***

269

The sun was bright, and Mia could see her warriors straining to camouflage themselves behind the sparse foliage. She had hoped that there would be another time to face her enemy, but Mia knew that Romulus would not rest until she was nailed to his wall, a gruesome trophy of sorts.

Mia controlled her breathing, not wanting Romulus to turn in her direction. She watched as several men surveyed the shallow spring and returned satisfied. It seemed impossible for the men not to have seen any of her warriors. There were no caves in which to hide, and the few crevices high up on the cliff face were hardly out of view. Three archers were ready—her only three.

Mia watched as hundreds of men spilled into the clearing. They filled the entire field, allowing truly little space for any kind of movement. The group was standing in a circular formation, protecting its emperor sitting securely amid more than 200 men.

***

Elias had estimated their number right—217 men. He shook his head in confirmation. Elias was about to move closer when something extraordinary happened.

Romulus and his army were standing ready, looking for Mia and her army but straining to see plainly. Elias moved closer to a soldier standing beside his horse. He walked up close. The man did not see him; he was looking right through him as if he wasn't there. Elias stepped back, shaking his head in disbelief.

***

The stallion beneath Romulus started to stomp its hooves. The animal was acting very strangely, as if it heard something terrifying. All the horses started to shove around. Steam was blown out in long streaks as their collective temperature rose. The

270

fog clung to the clearing, and all Romulus could see clearly was Valah beside him.

Romulus turned to seek answers, but Valah was as shocked as he was. The white stallion Valah had taken from the Achaeans was the only animal at ease. All was calm and serene except for the animals. They started to protest their restraints.

On the outskirts, a rider was thrown from his horse as the animal reared in protest. Several horses followed suit, shoving their riders from their backs. Chaos burst at the seams. Men lost their horses as the animals took to the narrow canyon, running back the way they came.

One soldier ran after his horse, screaming. The ranks broke free as the first blade was heard. It was unsheathed and hundreds followed. A sudden scream echoed through the clearing.

"Help!" someone shouted.

Romulus responded as soon as he heard the shouting.

"Attack them! No one survives! Annihilate them all!" Spittle flew from his mouth as he withdrew his blade.

He reared his horse and ran ahead as the circle burst. Men started to fight the enemy on all sides. Romulus was overwhelmed with their speed and agility. It seemed as if Mia was able to infiltrate the entire formation without being seen. Hundreds of enemies attacked men everywhere. He then gave a loud guttural shriek as his horse suddenly threw him to the ground.

Romulus swerved his sword in a high arch and started to sever limbs from his enemy. These warriors were strong and without mercy—as one woman attacked his right flank and fell, another thundered with clubs from his left. Romulus was covered from head to toe with blood, but he kept fighting as hard as he could. He couldn't see who he was connecting with, but every muscle in his body raged with hatred and disgust. His enemy would not see the day; he would be crowned victor and his triumph would be known all over the world. No man would dare to cross him again.

The sight before Mia made her cringe. The regiment was attacking itself—the men turned on each other. The chaos that ensued made her heart stop. To witness the slaughter in the clearing broke her heart.

She had difficulty understanding what happened. The sun shone brightly, and the sky seemed to have been wiped clean with fresh morning rain, yet her adversary was shrouded in a darkness she could not see. She was suddenly reminded of a scripture written long ago by the prophet Zechariah.

"On that day I will strike every horse with panic and its rider with madness," declares the Lord. "I will keep careful watch over Judah, but I will blind the horses of the nations."

Yahweh was fighting on their behalf. He promised Mia that He would never forsake her, and Mia understood that God was not a man who could tell a lie; His word is true. The sight was marvellous and terrifying at the same time. She had never witnessed anything like it in her entire life.

***

Mia's soldiers gathered beside her, all struck by the scene before them. No one moved, afraid that the onslaught would turn to them. Countless men fell by the sword, bashed with clubs and punctured with daggers. Danelle was certain that the grass had more than its share of blood this very day. Eugo whispered softly into her ear.

"The battle is the Lord's," he chuckled.

Danelle looked above her but still saw nothing; the army that Eugo so lavishly described was nowhere in sight. She looked back at Mia and saw in time the command to spread between the fighting men. Fear gripped hold of her heart. She had never faced an enemy, not to mention men twice her size.

Eugo gave her a slight nudge towards the eastern side of the clearing. He had promised to stay by her side if it was possible. All around her, men turned to strike their opponents only to strike the man behind them.

The regiment encircled the battle. Danelle saw the mayhem swallow her friends. Eugo had disappeared in the mess, but she heard his voice call out to her. It was surreal. Danelle believed what she saw could only happen in dreams. Soldiers fought with such intensity it was impossible not to stare. A pathway cleared before her, and she was allowed to enter the forbidden battle.

***

It seemed like an eternity until the sky cleared, suddenly exposing Mia and her regiment among fallen bodies. Valah gasped when he saw her. She was standing ten feet away from Romulus, and his back was turned towards the woman he hated more than life itself.

Valah had long ago jumped from his horse to battle on the field. Around him were about fifteen bodies, and he studied the fallen in a single sweep. In a ten-foot circle surrounding him lay none but his own men. The revelation was astounding. Valah could not explain how more than two thirds of his army had fallen by their own swords. The few armed Achaeans were untouched, their armour glistening in the bright light and their bodies uncontaminated by the blood and gore that darkened the field.

"Romulus!" he shouted.

***

The emperor turned towards Valah in time to see the blow coming his way. Romulus ducked as a blade narrowly missed his

273

ear. A stunning vision stood before him. She rushed at him, grabbed the amulet around his neck, and disappeared just as fast. No one would rush an opponent only to steal a trinket. She must have been the woman Rosenduz had so desperately wanted to have as his own.

Romulus recounted their meeting, but it was of no importance to him at the time. He spun around to see his men fallen all around him; not more than a third of his army remained. The battle had momentarily frozen. As if in slow motion, men searched the clearing for meaning but found none. The Achaean army gave one loud shout in unison.

"For Yahweh!"

The sound thundered above the waterfall and echoed off of the sheer cliffs surrounding the clearing. Romulus shouted in response, and the battle ensued. Women and soldiers collided. Blades chimed and blood flowed.

***

Mia spotted an opening in the crowd. Battling soldiers perfectly framed Romulus, and Ariana rushed at him and ripped her amulet from his neck. Mia had expressively asked her not to engage in battle with her sworn enemy. Any blood that would flow from the fight would be laced with revenge and in turn would choke the very life from her. Reverting to purity after such action was impossible.

Mia broke through the last remaining protective flank around Romulus and rushed towards him. Their eyes met for a moment before Mia was shoved hard on her chest. She flung backwards, falling on her side as her breath wrenched from her lungs.

Mia rolled onto her left side, barely missing the boot coming down on her. She instinctively bit the man in his inner thigh. He kicked her away, sending blood sprawling all over her face and upper body. Mia spat the piece of meat from her mouth, nearly vomiting into the dirt.

She steadied herself and pulled both her blades free from their scabbards. The man ran towards her, raising his battle axe high in the air. The weapon came down hard on a tree stump beside her. He had misjudged her speed, and Mia could see his resolve faint. She rushed at him in fluid motion, severing the arm still locked on retrieving his axe.

***

Valah stumbled backwards, holding the stump gushing blood in his other arm. The princess had taken his arm in one turn. Astounded, he froze. He could hear Romulus scream in his direction, but it all became incredibly quiet. Mia then rushed at him, pushing him down to the ground. She ripped a piece of linen from her garment and pressed hard on the wound.

Valah couldn't understand her actions. She yelled to a young girl to come and help. Valah saw Daelia like he had never seen her before. She was fully clothed in an intricate leather copy of the Achaean armour; she was radiant. She said something to Mia, but he no longer heard anything. His world went black.

***

Romulus stared in bewilderment as Mia severed Valah's arm but spared his life. Fear gripped his heart for the first time. Most of his men had fallen but himself, and many surrendered and laid their lives down. Romulus counted only thirty-two soldiers from Achaos. His mind was at a standstill.

Aulerci rushed from behind Romulus. Seven of his personal guard surrounded him. Romulus was certain that these men were more than capable of protecting his life.

Mia watched the small group of men surrounding Romulus. With a quick flip of her wrist, she indicated her next move. Elias, Ariana, Eugo, and Danelle all rushed the group at the same time. Elias attacked two men at once while Eugo slipped in between the group to scatter them father away. Danelle was quick on Eugo's heels and assisted wherever she could, adrenaline keeping her mind in complete control.

Aulerci stormed at Mia as she approached. She ducked beneath his swing but came up short at the end of his fist. Her head spun with intense pain as her jaw cracked. She felt a tooth jumble around in her mouth, and she pulled it free from its cradle before spitting blood to the ground.

Mia was ready for the next assault, and she dashed with full intensity into the frail man. Aulerci stumbled backwards but kept steady on his feet. He grabbed her hand and pried her sword from her grasp, but Mia twisted around the man and pulled his dagger free from his belt.

Mia pulled back with enough force to pry her hold from the man. He was reaching for his dagger when her small fist connected with his neck. Her hand twisted and embedded the blade deep into his throat, slicing through his jugular vein, spinal column, and ending by the hair of his neck. He fell backwards, still in protest from her swing, and hit the earth with such force that his head severed from his body. Mia landed in a perfect arch on her feet, eyes focused on Romulus.

Romulus stared back at Mia as shock filled his eyes. Mia straightened her back and walked towards Romulus. All his men had finally fallen or relinquished to fight another day. He was about to surrender, but the hatred he harboured in his heart was far too great.

Romulus rushed at her, screaming at the top of his lungs. Mia swerved to her left, but Romulus anticipated the move. He stumbled into her, throwing them both to the ground. He heard a faint squeal as he pulled her hair and a bundle of frayed strands came free in his hands. Mia twisted beneath his weight, trying to shove the man from her. Romulus kept pushing down, but his strength eventually failed him.

Mia was stronger than he ever remembered. She kicked hard, shoving the last bit of weight from her. They rumbled for another few rounds before she found her niche. She shoved hard on his stomach, forcing the wind from his lungs. Romulus gasped, clutching at the small hands compressing his throat.

She relented, stepping back. Romulus was about to strike when he felt the cold steel against his neck. He breathed heavily as Mia hunched beside him, her blade cutting the top layer of his skin. She motioned to the girl who had taken the amulet from his neck to remove her left wrist covering.

***

Mia did not let her gaze shift from Romulus for a single heartbeat. Ariana shoved her arm in front of his face and whispered into his ear.

"You may have taken my husband, but you can never take our covenant."

"I have already taken all you had; a mere marking can never console you from the loss you will never recover!" he retorted.

"You are wrong," Ariana interjected. "It is in Yaweh that we are set free. Your God will flee at the mere mention of His name."

***

Romulus twisted underneath Mia's blade and pried free from her grip. The dagger cut deeper, allowing a thin line of blood to gush stronger. Romulus was about to charge when an unnatural scream erupted from his throat as black bile spilled out from his stomach through his mouth, burning his insides. A strong force threw him down prostrate where Mia was still crouching. His body convulsed, and Romulus could feel the power he so desperately needed leave his body.

His eyes cleared, and the red rims of his vision dissipated as he understood what had happened. The Aveston had left his body, screaming in fear under the presence of Yahweh. The presence was so strong, yet Romulus still resisted.

Fear filled his heart, and he felt lost.

***

Romulus lay at Mia's feet, unmoving. She lifted his face from the ground with her sword, and he rose to all fours and looked at her. His eyes were a dull light brown, and he seemed momentarily confused.

"Please kill me ..." Romulus pleaded, watching Mia closely.

"Your life is not mine to take," Mia explained in a soft, gentle voice.

Romulus looked at her. The surety with which she spoke made him quiver.

"Amyntas of Athens will decide your fate."

Romulus' expression shattered. "No, Amyntas has no mercy; his hatred for me is insatiable. Mia, please! Spare me from Amyntas, I beg of you! I beg of you!" he pleaded in anguish as they dragged him away.

EPILOGUE

Mia threw the dagger to the ground as they dragged Romulus away. Belarus' blade had fulfilled its duty. She retrieved her stained sword from the mulch, returning it to its cradle, and turned towards the water's edge tainted with the blood lost on this fateful day. She fell to her knees and dropped her head to her chest.

The rumbling water subsided as she breathed out strained breaths. Blood trickled off her forearm as she relinquished her strength, dropping her hand to the ground. Her shoulders hung limp, and blood pooled in her open palm, spilling on the ground and moistening the earth. A soft thundering of drums started to echo off the walls as feet stamped the ground. A voice rang out in the distance, and a victory call was announced.

Mia screamed at the top of her lungs in reply, throwing her hands in the air. Thirty-one young soldiers raised their hands behind her to their unseen God. Mia rose to her feet as the thumping grew louder with each phrase of the Anthem. Looking back at her army, she was once again encouraged.

Frail yet unbroken, the women stood in submission to their leader and their God. Tear-streaked, blood-splattered faces revealed smiles of victory. Mia retrieved her sword from its scabbard and raised it to the sky, shimmering bright red in the noonday sun.

"To Almighty God: Victory!" Mia's voice rippled along the cliffs, recoiling back to the waterfall in a beautiful echo.

Ariana bowed beside Mia and clutched Belarus' amulet close to her heart. Tears stained her dirty cheek. Shouts of approval rang in her ears and all she could muster was a shallow "thank you". Ariana hugged Mia in a strong embrace as both women surrendered to their God.

***

Danelle watched in amazement as the sky turned a dark red. Sunset was far from creeping closer, and she was puzzled and spun around to see a sight she only imagined in her wildest dreams. All around the clearing stood thousands upon thousands of warriors clothed in bronze.

Their armour was more intricate than hers, with the name of Yahweh written in burnished bronze on golden breastplates. Large swords hung sheathed in golden scabbards at their sides. Their hands were raised in the same manner as all the women beside her.

The Lord's army praised together with the saints in a thunderous chorus. The sky lit up from the mighty horde as their hearts rejoiced in the victory belonging to God, for His glory and name that is above every other name.

Danelle marvelled at the sight, and her eye caught Eugo's. She couldn't believe she was seeing the army, just as he promised she would. Eugo dipped his head, smiled at her, and continued to worship the only true God, Yahweh.

ABOUT THE AUTHOR

Magdalena Brynard was born and raised on the plains of southern Africa, where storytelling has always played a pivotal part in her life. Since her childhood, her free time was spent in the creativity department of the school, studying history and Shakespeare.

After completing her bachelor's degree in Drama and Film, her pursuits were set on the West End, and she portrayed various characters on the London stage. Her love for history and story-telling then led her to The Writer's Bureau in Manchester, where she completed a comprehensive writing course, and a new stage was set.

Magdalena has written several children's stories, including *Milo en Rocco* and *Die Avonture van Blou,* and often entertains her children with tales of adventure and intrigue. Her first novella, *Nkosazana Africa – Hope in Transit,* was published on Amazon KDP in 2019.

In collaboration with KREST Publishers, her dream of becoming an author has been realised.

She lives with her husband and three children in Pretoria.